BEYOND EDEN

A SWEET, REDEMPTION ROMANCE

TINA NEWCOMB

DEDICATION

To my husband, Rick. Without your support and hard work this book would still be a dream,

Love you to the moon and back.

CONTENTS

CHAPTER 1

Misty Garrett grabbed her distended belly with both hands and hissed, air whistling through her clenched teeth. The rock hardness of her stomach sent a chill through her, even as perspiration wet her hairline and upper lip. The bone deep ache that had plagued the small of her back all morning crept around her sides and dug in with claws extended. She sucked in a ragged breath and exhaled on a groan.

Just as suddenly as it struck, the pain eased leaving her limp as wilted lettuce.

She eased back in her father's recliner and wiped the sheen of sweat from her forehead with the tail of her husband's flannel shirt.

Her due date was still two weeks away, so she couldn't be in labor.

At her last appointment, Dr. Jessica Thompson had assured Misty and her worrywart husband that everything was right on schedule.

"I've heard most first babies come late," Misty's husband said.

The doctor looked up from between Misty's knees and smiled at Beam. "Most first babies do come late, but every birth is different."

"So we should stay close to Seattle just in case."

"Well, don't feel like you can't go places, but I wouldn't recommend traveling very far."

Her doctor had yammered on and on about what they should do if… Make certain they had… She even mentioned something about false contractions. By that time, Misty's eyes had glazed over. Even the Energizer Bunny would be yawning after a few minutes of Dr. Thompson's monotone. If Beam were here, he'd repeat the doctor's monologue verbatim. Her husband's rapt attention, note taking, and quoting from pregnancy books was equivalent to living inside the Discovery Channel.

Misty rubbed two hands over her belly. All was still, so she picked up the carton of Ben & Jerry's Cherry Garcia she'd dropped on the side table. The ice cream was now soft enough to dig out the chocolate chunks and sweet pieces of cherry. She scooped a bite into her mouth and turned her attention back to the exciting drama unfolding on the *Real Housewives* of somewhere. The major mischief-maker was on the verge of being discovered and… "Awwhhh!"

Viselike tentacles of agony seized, doubling Misty forward, squeezing until she thought she might implode. She struggled for air, desperate to remember what to do, but her only clear thought was, *if Beam were a gloating man, this would be his moment to shine.* When she'd insisted on coming to Eden Falls, he'd argued she was too close to her due date, the weather in January was unpredictable, being two and a half hours away from Seattle and her doctor, who said to stay close to home, was irresponsible. She'd ignored his protests and come anyway.

When the pain eased, Misty heaved herself from the chair

and waddled toward the kitchen where her cell phone was charging. She dropped the ice cream carton into the sink with one hand, and held her stomach up with the other. This baby was not coming out until Beam got her back to Seattle. He'd gotten her into this condition, and he would witness every throe of agony she was forced to suffer.

She gasped as warm liquid flooded down her legs. Bending over, she tried to see the puddle now soaking her socks. At least she'd made it to the tiled kitchen. *Sorry Dad.*

She grabbed her phone, and a new panic struck. Who could she call? Her dad's truck driver called in sick this morning, so he had to make a large lumber delivery himself. He'd be without cell coverage most of the day. Beam would take over an hour to get here in the Cessna, and that was only if he wasn't already chauffeuring a group of gawking tourists out to see Seattle from the air. Then the flight back would be another hour. She needed someone now. Stella was in a classroom surrounded by screaming second-graders, and Jillian would be at the gym, which left only one option.

She gripped the countertop for support when another pain ripped through her middle. More of Beam's words ran through her head, *"We've got to attend prenatal classes, Misty. We need to know what to expect."*

"What's the point?" she'd argued. "The doctor promised drugs, and I intend to get them, so there's no reason to sit on the floor of the clinic learning to breathe with a bunch of strangers."

Except now there is.

How did the women in movies do it? In through the mouth and out through the nose or was it short quick breaths? The pain slowly subsided before she could decide which method to try. Next contraction, she'd use them all.

She scrolled through her contact list until she reached the name of her go-to friend of twenty-two years, the one she'd refused to talk to since New Year's Eve. She hit the call button and put the phone to her ear.

After an eternity, she heard, "Good morning. Pretty Posies."

The happy voice made her eyelid twitch. "Put Alex on the phone."

"Misty?"

"Tatum. Get Alex!"

"Okaaay."

Misty wondered, for at least the zillionth time, why Alex had hired someone as incompetent as Tatum Ellis. After waiting an eternity, she decided to hang up and call back. Just as she pulled the phone from her ear, she heard, "Hello, Misty."

"I'm in labor and Beam's not here. You have to drive me to Seattle."

"Where are you?" The cautious tone Alex answered the phone with had been replaced by her no-nonsense business one.

"My dad's."

"How far apart are your contractions?"

"I don't know." Misty glanced at the puddle on the floor. "My water just broke."

"I'll be right there."

Misty disconnected the call and wrapped both hands under her stomach, which felt like it had dropped to her knees. She hated when her husband was right. She should have listened to him—not that she'd admit that aloud.

Walking up the stairs was a slow process, but she finally made it to her childhood bedroom. Longing tugged at her heart. Childbirth was a mother-daughter moment she wouldn't get to share with the woman who'd walked away over twenty years earlier.

Frills and girly ruffles still adorned the bedroom her mom

decorated when Misty was five. A nearly threadbare pink and white gingham comforter covered the white canopy bed. The doll her mother bought for Misty's sixth birthday held a place of honor near the headboard, propped into a sitting position by delicate eyelet pillows. Misty's pink ballerina jewelry box and a photo of her mom at the base of Eden Falls, her happy smile forever frozen in black and white, were side-by-side on the matching white dresser.

Misty hadn't changed a thing. One day her mother would return and be thrilled Misty had kept everything exactly the same.

She felt another pain building, and stumbled to the edge of the bed, gasping for breath from her already oxygen deprived lungs. One moment, she was afraid she might pass out, and the next, she wished she would. The last nine months, from peeing on a stick until now, had been a nightmare. One she couldn't awake from no matter how hard she pinched herself.

When the pain released its clenching grip, she pulled off her wet things and wiggled into dry panties and a pair of warm but extremely tight leggings. She had eaten her way through pregnancy. Each day introduced new cravings. She discovered unique and quite ingenious ways to add chocolate or maple syrup to almost anything. This baby had kicked, elbowed, and stretched her body into a blimp. Once she gave birth, a few visits to her in-laws' gym for some much-needed toning would get her back to her original size four. These excruciating pains marked the countdown. She *would* be back in a bikini by June, less than six months away.

She discarded the thought of calling Beam's parents as soon as it popped into her mind. Dawson and Glenda Garrett's enthusiasm about first-time grandparenthood was over the top when she *wasn't* in labor. Being happy all the time should be against the law, but happy ran through the

Garrett clan like blood through veins. And she'd married smack into the middle of them.

Stepping into the adjoining bathroom, she made the mistake of glancing in the mirror. Her unwashed hair pulled into a high ponytail highlighted her blotched, puffy face, which looked even worse than usual. She hadn't worn makeup in a week, trying to clear up a pimple outbreak on her forehead. Her black eyebrows had almost grown together in the middle since her last waxing, and the mole near her chin —which she'd always believed to be alluring—had a coarse black hair sprouting from the middle. She pulled open a drawer, but before she could grab tweezers to perform a quick extraction, another contraction shot through her middle, paralyzing her.

The doorbell chimed, yet she was helpless to do anything but grimace through a pain too intense to yell.

Please, please, let the door be unlocked.

She released a sigh of relief when she heard a male voice echo up the stairs. *Beam! But he wouldn't ring the bell. He has a key.*

"Misty?"

She released a groan and not from pain. JT Garrett. What was he doing here?

She sank to the toilet seat as his heavy footsteps hit the kitchen tile. "What the…?"

Great. He found the puddle I left.

Suddenly, the footsteps thudded up the stairs. "Misty? Where are you?"

He appeared, filling the bathroom doorway, taking up too much space, a talent the Garrett family seemed to possess. His dark hair and the shoulders of his police chief overcoat were covered in snow. "I hear my first cousin once removed is ready to make her appearance." His expression turned thoughtful. "Or is she my second—"

"Shut up."

"You okay?"

Misty wanted to smack the smile he was fighting from his face. "No, I'm not okay. I'm having a contraction."

He leaned against the doorframe and lifted a booted foot. "Yeah, I think I just stepped in one of those contractions."

She glared, trying her best to look fierce.

Losing the fight, he grinned. "It's good to see labor hasn't clouded your sunny disposition."

She was in too much pain for a witty comeback. "Where's Alex?"

"She's right behind me. She thought my SUV would be a more comfortable ride to Harrisville Regional than her dilapidated Jeep. Can you stand?"

"I'm not going to Harrisville Regional. My doctor is in Seattle."

He flashed an indulge-the-female glance as he slid his arm around her waist and helped her to her feet.

"Don't look at me like that. You're a cop. Turn on your lights and sirens, and get me to Seattle."

"How far apart are your contractions?"

She wrapped a hand under her belly and inhaled as deeply as possible. "I don't know."

The front door opened and slammed shut. "Misty?"

"We're upstairs," JT shouted.

Another set of footsteps pounded up the stairs and Alexis Blackwood careened around the corner, narrowly missing them in a head-on collision.

JT put his hand out to protect Misty's stomach. "Whoa."

"How we doing?" Alex asked breathlessly.

"Peachy keen. What took you so long?" Misty mumbled.

She and Alex had been best friends since kindergarten, but that had changed on New Year's Eve when Alex announced her engagement to bestselling author Colton McCreed.

"Aww, there's my sweet natured friend. I've missed you."

Misty scowled at the traitor.

Alex winked and ducked under her other arm. The brother-sister team got her halfway down the stairs before she sank to a riser, another contraction ripping through her. Alex rubbed her back and babbled instructions. JT gave her a hand to squeeze. After endless minutes, they finally reached the living room sofa.

"Where are your boots? It's snowing," Alex asked.

"In the bedroom."

Alex ran up the stairs. "Not your five-inch stilettos, Misty. Your sensible snow boots," she yelled, running back down. "Did you bring sensible boots with you?"

"Here they are," JT said carrying a pair into the living room along with Misty's coat.

Alex knelt in front of her and held out a boot. "Where are your socks?"

"I got them wet when my water broke."

"Oh, that reminds me." JT went into the kitchen.

Misty heard paper towels pulled from the roll and assumed Dudley Do Right was cleaning up the puddle she'd left. Alex made a third trip up the stairs. She ran down with clean socks in hand. "Is Beam on his way?"

"I haven't called him."

Alex performed her legendary—pursed-lip, squinted-eye —judgmental expression.

"When exactly would I have had time?"

"JT call Beam," Alex called to her brother.

JT returned to the living room, cell phone in hand. "I already did. He's on his way, but with the storm, he'll have to drive. Glenda and Dawson will meet us at the hospital."

"Call Beam back and tell him not to come here. I'm

having the baby in Sea—" Misty released a low moan and grabbed her stomach when the next contraction took her body hostage.

JT offered his hand again, and Alex massaged her lower back. "Keep your breathing rhythmical, Misty. Your in-breath should match your out-breath. I know it hurts, but try to relax. As soon as this one is over, we'll get you in the car."

"I'm not going to a backwoods hospital to have some country bumpkin deliver this baby," Misty hissed on an out breath. She glared at JT. "You have to get me to Seattle."

"You're going to deliver this baby on your dad's living room sofa if we don't get going," JT said. "Your contractions are less than five minutes apart."

Misty swung a fist that connected with JT's chest. "I don't care if the baby is half out of my body. I'm not going to Harrisville."

JT and Alex ignored her as they helped her down the front steps to the SUV. She hefted her rear end into the backseat, and Alex followed. JT shut their door and ran around to the driver's side.

Misty massaged her belly and tried to relax the tight muscles. No one had warned her how bad this would hurt. She knew it wasn't going to be a walk in the park, but there were supposed to be drugs involved. She'd been promised drugs.

She glanced through the front windshield when JT turned left instead of right as they exited her dad's neighborhood. "This isn't the way to Seattle, JT."

"Misty, it takes two and a half hours to get to Seattle on a good day. It's snowing, the roads are slippery, and your contractions are less than five minutes apart. I'm taking you to Harrisville, which is only fifteen minutes away. You can argue with the hospital staff about an ambulance ride to Seattle."

"I hate you."

He caught her eye in the rearview mirror. "You'd hate me even more if we had to deliver this baby on the side of the road."

She imagined JT pulling over and her baring her assets for the passing cars with Tweedledee and Tweedledumb as her delivery team. She turned her glare on Alex who winked. "I hate you, too."

"It's wonderful to see my good natured friend back to her old self. I was afraid labor might dampen your happy spirits." Alex echoed her brother's earlier sentiments, sealing it with the same Garrett grin.

The whole situation enraged Misty even as an unladylike snort of hysteria escaped. She was in labor, her ex-boyfriend was driving her through a snowstorm to a hospital in the sticks, while her ex-best friend sat beside her, and the baby's father was stuck in Seattle. This was the perfect setup for a comedy.

Or a horror flick.

~

*B*eam Garrett finally made it out of the city, headed east. The rain was coming down in sheets, but traffic was moving. The snowstorm had settled in over the Cascades and the wind gusts predicted by the National Weather Service made taking the Cessna to Eden Falls impossible.

He blew out a frustrated breath as he turned on his blinker to pass a slow moving truck. Misty was the most exasperating woman alive. He'd begged, argued, and even resorted to bribery trying to keep her from going to her dad's this close to her due date. As usual, she refused to listen to reason. When she lived in Eden Falls, she couldn't wait to leave the small town. Now that she lived in Seattle, she wanted to go home every week.

He was sure a lot of that had to do with feelings of missing out. She was afraid her friends were out having fun without her. Misty liked to go out every night, but pregnancy had slowed her down, and she wasn't used to a sedentary life.

Luckily, the rain kept him grounded today. Not many tourists were interested in flying when visibility was so low. He was in the office when JT called. He'd raced home to get the diaper bag he'd put together for the baby and the suitcase he'd packed for Misty, because she'd refused to pack one for herself. He put both in the truck. Concerned he didn't have enough for the baby, he ran back in for a second diaper bag that he stuffed with more diapers, blankets, warm sleepers, and a soft little lamb that rattled. Not sure how long they'd be in Eden Falls, he added some things of his own to a duffle bag.

Beam hadn't been around an infant since Alex gave birth to her son. Charlie was six now. Misty had refused to go to any prenatal or parenting classes, so he felt completely unprepared for this monumental, life-changing event. He'd read books and searched the internet, but still felt far from being prepared to actually hold and care for his daughter.

Daughter. A peaceful feeling of awe settled over him. By the end of the day, he would be a father.

The windshield wipers beat furiously as the heavy rain changed to a wet snow. I-90 was clear now, but for how long? And what would SH-97 be like when he got there? The Washington State Patrol closed that road when conditions got too bad.

His cell phone played a familiar tune, and he pressed the accept call button on his truck console. "Hey, Mom."

"Hi, honey. JT said you're on your way."

"I've been on the road for about thirty minutes."

"Your dad and I are at the hospital. Misty arrived safely thanks to JT and Alex. JT said she put up a fight. She wanted him to take her to Seattle, but her contractions are too close together. Alex is in the room with her now."

Beam could only imagine how that fifteen-minute ride had gone for his two cousins. "Have you seen Misty yet?"

"No, but Alex came out to tell us she'll deliver quickly."

"Is the baby okay? Coming early?"

"According to Alex, the doctor said the baby's heartbeat is strong. There are no signs of distress. She's just impatient to arrive."

Amazing how those few words eased the tight cords along his neck and shoulders, yet caused his heart to plummet. He would miss his baby girl coming into the world. He'd miss her first moments of life, her first breath, her first cry. After the anxious months of anticipation, he was going to miss his daughter's birth, because his wife was stubborn and selfish. He swallowed his disappointment. "Will you keep me updated, Mom?"

"Of course. Drive careful. And don't worry. Misty will be fine."

Misty would be anything but fine. Still, he assured his mom he would be careful. Soon, another being would be dependent on him. He'd drive this route more cautiously than he'd ever driven it before.

"Hold on a minute, honey. Your dad wants to talk to you."

"Hey, Beam. Where are you?" His father's deep voice was crystal clear. That would change the closer he got to home. Reception could be spotty along SH-97.

"I'm still two hours out."

"How are the roads?"

"The rain is just changing over to snow, so they're not bad, yet. How are they there?"

"They're becoming snow covered. JT just checked with

Highway Patrol. They said 97 is still clear. The plows are ready to roll."

"Good. I'll be there as soon as I can, but from the sounds of it, I won't make it in time for the birth. Is Misty's dad there?"

"He had a lumber delivery near South Fork and isn't answering his cell. JT sent Mac Johnson out to locate him."

"Will you let Misty know I'm on my way?"

"We will, son. Drive safely though. Misty is in good hands."

Misty might be in good hands, but she was probably causing more trouble right now than the hospital staff could handle.

Beam eased around another eighteen-wheeler and fought to see through the splatter that hit his windshield.

Missing his daughter's birth would be something he would always regret. He'd looked forward to this day since Misty told him she was pregnant. With the first ultrasound image in his breast pocket, he bought his daughter her first stuffed animal. He painted her room, and put her crib together. He shopped around until he found a rocking chair that fit his bulk, just so he could rock his daughter to sleep.

If Misty weren't so pigheaded, they'd be together right now. He'd be holding her hand in anticipation of their daughter's arrival. Instead, he had two hours to accept that somehow this situation would end up his fault.

He also had two hours to reconsider their future.

CHAPTER 2

Clenching the sheet in both hands, Misty screamed, "Get this baby out. Get it out. Get it out!" She didn't care if everyone in the hospital heard. She'd never been in this much pain in her life. How did people endure having more than one kid?

"You're doing great, Misty. Your baby girl is almost here." The nurse sitting between her legs repeated the words she'd been saying after every contraction. "Have you picked out a name, yet?" she added this time.

"No." Misty was aware of her snarky tone, but didn't care. She collapsed onto the pillows when the contraction subsided. Perspiration covered her forehead and irritated her scalp. The acrid smell of sweat mingling with antiseptic hung in the air around her. Her legs, which hadn't been shaved in weeks, probably looked like they belonged to a pregnant gorilla. Her matted, greasy hair was a tangled, disgusting mess. She wanted to laugh at the nurse whose job was to sit between someone's raised knees, and cry at the injustice at the same time.

The universe was decidedly against her, spinning madly in the wrong direction, and she couldn't make it stop. She was always in control, but someone else had jerked the wheel from her hands. If only she could find a way to jump from this crazy ride. She'd lost her sense of normalcy, and was afraid she would never see it again.

She wanted more than ice chips to ease her burning throat and medication to ease the excruciating pain. She wanted life to go back to the way it had been nine months earlier. She wanted a warm beach and a cabana boy delivering umbrella drinks. Most of all, she wanted this baby out and this day over.

The door opened and the doctor on call walked in. She wasn't a toothless country bumpkin, but a woman beautiful enough to be a model. "How are things progressing in here?" she asked in her sweet I-just-got-out-of-med-school voice.

Misty wanted to throw a full bedpan at her. "My doctor in Seattle said I wouldn't feel any pain. Why can't you give me something?"

The doctor revealed extremely white teeth that gleamed under the fluorescent lights. Misty tried to run her parched tongue over her own teeth. Had she remembered to brush them this morning?

"I'm sorry, Misty. By the time you arrived, you were too far along. The good news is you're so far along the baby will be here any minute." The doctor moved to the foot of the bed and leaned over the nurse's shoulder. "Hmm," she said as if she were leisurely scanning a selection of baked goods in a pastry shop.

The nurse stood and came to Misty's side. The doctor placed a mask over her nose and mouth and took the seat between Misty's knees. Probing fingers went to work before the doctor's eyes met hers. "Your husband isn't going to make it in time for this delivery. Is there anyone else in the waiting area you'd like to invite in to be with you?"

Misty looked up at the smiling face above her. The universe raised its head and an evil "Bawhahaha," echoed through the room. Alex had been with her since they'd arrived. If not her, then who? She didn't want Beam's mom this up close and personal, which meant she had no other choice. Under no circumstance would she admit that Alex had been comforting in her obnoxiously nurturing, goody-two-shoes way.

She narrowed her eyes. "Anyone but her."

"She's kidding. She really loves me." Alex set a cool washcloth on Misty's forehead that felt heavenly. "She's just ornery because she's used to getting her own way, but today the baby's in charge. We've been BFFs since kindergarten and became family when she married my cousin."

"A *BFF* doesn't stab you in the back by stealing your boyfriend," Misty hissed through clenched teeth as a contraction began to build.

Alex slid an arm behind Misty's back and helped her sit forward. "Trying to steal a boyfriend is a move I learned from you in high school, but we both know I didn't steal Colton."

"Colton as in Colton McCreed, the author?" the nurse asked as she supported Misty's right leg.

Misty glared at the Pollyanna nurse whose wide-eyed stare was directed at Alex.

"You're Mayor Blackwood. I should have recognized you from the *People* magazine article. Did Colton really come back after four months and propose with a single camellia blossom?" The nurse glanced at the doctor. "In the language of flowers that means 'my destiny is in your hands'. Isn't that romantic?"

Misty's "Are you kidding me?" was ignored.

"The language of flowers?" the doctor asked.

"Each flower means something different, right?" the nurse asked Alex. "That's how they communicated in old times."

"Feelings couldn't be openly expressed in Victorian society, so gifts of flowers or plants were arranged to send a coded message to the recipient," Alex explained.

"Cool," the doctor said, like she was passing the time at a hamburger joint.

"Hello, I'm having a baby."

The doctor looked at Misty, her smile oozing phony sympathy. "Everything is moving along nicely." Her glance moved to Alex. "I've read one of Colton McCreed's books."

"One? I've read all of his books. My favorite is the one about the college kids who wreck their boat on that island. I can't remember the name of it…" the Pollyanna nurse continued as if Misty wasn't contorted into a position no human should assume. She was writhing in pain, and they were discussing books. She wanted to reach out and slap all three of them.

"The article in *People* said Colton's next book is based in Eden Falls," the nurse said. "Do you know when it's coming out?"

"Sometime in the spring." Alex dabbed Misty's forehead with the washcloth.

"It's time to push, Misty," the doctor said. "Take a deep breath and release it slowly to the count of ten. BFF, will you count it out for her? This little girl is ready to come into the world."

Misty took a breath, but released it in one whoosh when pain tightened her stomach hard as a rock. A low guttural moan more animal than human filled the room. If she hadn't heard it herself, she would never believe she was capable of producing such a sound. The pain was worse than anything Misty had ever experienced and something she would *never* go through, again. Her body was being ripped in two. "Get this baby out nooowww!"

"There's the baby's head. Look at all that black hair," Alex said.

As the contraction subsided, Misty fell back onto the pillow and sucked air into her lungs.

Alex took Misty's hand. "Give me your fingers."

"No."

"You'll be able to feel the—"

"Shut up, Alex. I don't want to feel anything." Misty squeezed her eyes shut so tight there were bursts of color behind her lids. She was so tired she just wanted to sleep. Her nights for the last four months had been spent trying to roll from one side to the other in an effort to get comfortable, which only lasted as long as her squashed flat, pea-sized bladder held out. When this was over, she planned to sleep for a week straight. She turned her head and was shocked to see the hands on the industrial sized clock had only moved forward forty minutes since she'd entered this room.

The universe's chuckle grew to a robust laugh.

A man entered the room and introduced himself as a pediatrician. Misty forgot his name within seconds. Beam had already picked out a pediatrician in Seattle. Every time he saw someone pushing a stroller, he rushed over to ask for recommendations. While she'd been so miserable the last four months, Beam had been getting all his little ducks in a row.

Two women followed the pediatrician through the door. One pushed a table holding a scale. The other maneuvered a bassinet in behind her.

If the cool cloth Alex kept dabbing at her forehead didn't feel so exquisite, Misty would have shoved her hand away.

She was tired of Alex hovering, tired of her encouraging words. Being around her ex-friend for very long was exhausting.

She felt another contraction building and shook her head. "I can't do this anymore. I don't want to do this."

"Hang onto my hand, Misty. You're almost through. A couple more pushes and your beautiful daughter will be here," Alex said. "Can we move the mirror a little so Misty can see?"

Misty imagined her fingers closing around Alex's throat. "I told you, I don't want to see."

"Big push, Misty. Here she comes. Hello, baby girl. Welcome to the world," the doctor said, her tone turning butter-soft.

"Oh, Misty." Alex actually sobbed.

Misty caught a quick glimpse of what looked like a wet black kitten, and conflicting emotions hit her hard. Her first impulse was to reach out for the baby, but she turned her head.

She wanted to be like her mother, free to come and go as she pleased. Unlike her friends, she hadn't been born with maternal instincts. And that fact didn't bother her. Feelings of devotion and tenderness were beyond her comprehension and she didn't care. All she cared about, all she really wanted was to open her own salon. She wanted to be the boss, and make enough money she could travel wherever she wanted. She wouldn't let a child interrupt those plans when they were finally within reach.

"I can't do this," she mumbled, before her eyes slammed shut in an effort to erase the image from her mind. Yet, it lingered…tufts of inky black hair, the same color as hers. A tiny being in need of a mother, a role she couldn't fill. Would the baby have her blue eyes, or mossy green ones like Beam?

She opened her eyes when she heard a sniffle. Alex wiped

tears from her cheeks. "What are you crying about? I'm the one in pain."

Unexpectedly—but not really, because it was Alex—she leaned forward and hugged Misty tight. "She's a miracle. Your daughter is a beautiful miracle coming into the world."

"Misty," the doctor said. "One more big push and you'll have your daughter in your arms."

"I'm too tired." Misty wanted to sleep, to cry, to scream, but the next contraction bent her forward. A groan worked its way up her throat, and a new sheen of sweat broke out across her forehead. She took one quick breath and pushed, then fell back with a sigh as the room erupted in sounds and movement. She was aware of the wet kitten mewing somewhere in the background, causing her heart to heave in her chest. Again, she stomped the tender emotions down.

"Here's your daughter, Misty," the doctor said.

Without thinking, she opened her eyes. Besides black hair, the baby had an angel's face. Misty turned her head as tears stung her eyes. She tried to swallow around the thickness in her throat. "I can't hold her. I'm too tired."

Alex took the baby from the doctor and gathered her close. "Hello, sweetheart. Oh, my goodness, you are gorgeous. Your daddy is going to be so proud of you."

Misty closed her eyes at the sight. She heard snatches of conversation—the doctor said she needed two stitches, the pediatrician spewed numbers. Her eyes fluttered open when she felt a dip in the mattress. Alex sat beside her, sans baby, and laid a hand on her arm.

"Beam will be proud of you too, Misty. Despite the pain, which I'm sorry you had to endure, you did a good job. Luckily, it was a quick delivery."

"Shows what you know. If I were lucky, I would have been in labor longer, so I could have drugs," she mumbled.

She closed her eyes, shutting out Alex, and everyone else in the room. Finally, she was able to drift into sweet nothingness.

~

*B*eam strode through the hospital doors, stopping at the information desk long enough to get directions to Misty's room. On the seemingly endless drive, he'd called Tatum at Pretty Posies and ordered two-dozen pink roses to be delivered. Tatum informed him pink roses stood for grace in the language of flowers. He didn't understand any of that stuff his grandmother had passed along to Alex, but Alex had explained it all to Misty, who took the interpretations literally. He tended to keep things simple. Pink for their baby girl and roses because Misty liked them. Hopefully, grace would be well received.

When he pushed into the hospital room, his eyes immediately fell on his mom sitting in a rocker with a tiny pink bundle in her arms. Even from a distance, he could see her finger stroking a shock of silky black hair.

His dad, off to the side in another chair, audibly sighed with relief. "I'm glad you're here safe and sound. The weatherman is saying this storm is a doozy. How were the roads?"

"Bad," Beam said, unable to tear his gaze from the fuzzy down. Three steps and he was next to his mom's side, where he beheld a tiny face so beautiful it stole his breath away. His daughter's skin was flawless. Her tiny button nose and rosebud mouth adorable. He squatted down and ran a giant finger over the black cap of flyaway hair, just like his mom had been doing. At his touch, her tiny mouth started working. The sight filled his eyes with tears and a laugh erupted at the same time. The contradictory emotions that swamped him were so overwhelming he wasn't sure which to give in to first.

"She's a beauty, isn't she?" His dad's heavy hand fell on his shoulder. "She the first girl to be born into this family since Alex."

Beam had no words. Beautiful wasn't enough, not even close to adequate to describe his daughter. The fact that Misty carried this tiny being, a part of him, inside her for eight and a half months was simply beyond his understanding. The whole idea was too massive for him to comprehend; yet it was done every day by thousands of women. He was in awe. "I…" He cleared his throat. "I can't think of the right words to describe…"

"Perfect," his dad said. "She's perfect."

Beam glanced at his mom. "Is she okay? Is everything okay?"

The look on his mom's face was lustrous, her smile radiant. "Like your dad said, she's perfect. She was just anxious to get out of her tight accommodations." Glenda stood. "Take off your coat so you can sit and meet your daughter."

Beam did as he was told, and his mom laid the beauty in his arms.

"Be careful to support her head." She pulled a piece of paper from her jeans pocket. "I wrote all her information down for you. It will be on her birth certificate, but until it comes…"

He read the paper she held. Born on January 16 at 4:22 p.m. Beam glanced up at his mom. "Six pounds, two ounces. Is that good?"

She pulled the pink blanket loose, took a miniature fist, and laid it on Beam's thumb. "Six-two might be a touch below average, but nothing to worry about. The pediatrician said she's perfectly healthy."

Beam's dad moved in front of him, and took several

pictures, but Beam was too mesmerized to look up. His daughter's tiny hand made his thumb look gargantuan. Her almost transparent eyelids twitched and his throat closed up, again. When he heard a stirring on the bed, he composed himself enough to ask, "How's Misty?"

A look of worry passed between his mom and dad. In that split second, many words were said in their unspoken conversation.

"Alex and JT got her here too late to have an epidural. No fault of theirs," his mom was quick to add. "Misty told the doctor she'd been having low back pains since early this morning, so she must have been in labor without realizing it. She was in a lot of pain during the delivery. Luckily, this little one was in a hurry to be born. Misty was here less than an hour before giving birth." Her glance jumped to the bed. "She's been sleeping ever since."

"Was her dad here?"

"Mason was delivering a load of lumber this morning and hit a patch of slick road. The truck ended up in a ditch. Mason's okay, but he couldn't leave the load. He had to wait for another truck to get there and unload the lumber before a tow truck could pull him out. He's on his way."

Misty stirred again, and Dawson said, "We should go and give the three of you some time alone." He picked up his wife's coat and held it for her while she slipped her arms in.

His mom bent and kissed Beam's cheek, then the baby's head. "Alex stayed with Misty the whole time," she whispered close to his ear. "She helped with the delivery."

That nugget of information spoke volumes. "If you can think of some way I can thank her, let me know. Meanwhile, thank you both for staying. Thank you for everything."

"We'll see you tomorrow," Dawson said. Then they slipped quietly from the room.

Beam spent a few quiet minutes studying the perfection

that lay in his arms before Misty turned with a groan. She blinked, and their eyes met. As carefully as his big bulk could move, he stood and walked to the bed, trying not to jostle the pink bundle. It would take him some time to get used to handling something so tiny. He was even more careful not to jostle Misty's bed.

"Hey, baby, I'm so sorry I couldn't get here in time. How are you feeling?" He lowered his free hand to touch her face, but she turned away.

"Like I gave birth to an elephant."

"I don't think she's quite that big." He glanced down at their tiny daughter and smiled, feeling strangled by emotion once again. "She's gorgeous, Misty. More beautiful than I could have ever imagined."

Misty didn't answer.

He dialed his tone of voice to sympathetic. "Mom said you were in pain, but the labor was fast."

Misty rolled her eyes dramatically. "The word pain doesn't begin to describe the agony I was in."

"I'm sorry. I wish I'd been here." This time when he reached out, she allowed him to run a knuckle over her cheek. "Mom said Alex stayed with you."

Misty snorted. "Yeah, lucky me. By the way, grace?" She pointed to the vase of roses on the windowsill.

I'm a guy. I shouldn't have to explain this. "I ordered pink roses because the baby is a girl and so are you. You know I don't understand all that flower language stuff."

"Stop being condescending. I got enough of that from the brother-sister tag team."

"I'm not being condescending." *I just don't know how to make you happy.*

She pulled the covers up to her chin. "I'm starving. Can you see if they plan to feed me anytime soon?"

"Sure." He bent to lay the baby in her arms, but she

turned her body away. "Will you hold her while I check with a nurse?"

"Put her in the bassinet. I'm still really tired."

Beam stared at his wife for a moment. This was the reason his parents had exchanged the worried look. A nurse came through the door. Her lips were pressed together in an apprehensive smile as her glance darted from the bed to Beam.

"Hi, I'm Carol. You must be Mr. Garrett."

Beam shook her offered hand. "Hi, Carol. I'm Beam and this is my wife Misty."

"Misty and I have met," she said. She looked from him to the bed, then she smiled down at the baby. "Congratulations. You have a beautiful daughter."

He glanced down and was surprised to see two little eyes staring up at him. Another wave of emotion flooded him. "Thank you. She is pretty spectacular."

Carol touched the foot of the bed with the tips of her fingers. "Misty? Would you like to try breastfeeding, now that you've had a chance to rest?"

"I'm not breastfeeding."

Beam had read about the benefits of breastfeeding. He and Misty had never discussed the subject, but he'd hoped… "Misty, the baby will—"

"I said I'm not breastfeeding." She shot him a back-off look.

Her reply was loud enough to startle the baby, who fluttered the tiny fist Glenda had freed and released a tiny burst of mad. Beam couldn't help the laugh that escaped, loving the first sounds of his daughter, wishing he had a recorder to capture the moment. Then the mad became louder, and his smile died. He glanced at Carol.

"I'll get some formula, and we'll feed this sweet girl." Carol peeked at the tiny scrunched up face. "She might be tiny, but she comes with a powerful set of lungs. I'll be back in a minute."

"While you're out there, do you think you can get me something to eat? I'm starving,"

Misty hollered as the door closed.

The baby's fist waved wildly as her cries escalated in volume. Beam gently bounced her up and down the way he'd seen Alex do when Charlie was a baby. Alex and Charlie were his only reference on parenthood. The baby just became more red-faced and demanding. By the time Carol returned, Misty had a pillow over her head to block out the cries. And Beam was frantic. He'd paced, jiggled, and hummed, but nothing seemed to pacify the little being who was scarlet with fury.

Carol set a tray of food on Misty's bedside table and pushed it close. Then she pointed Beam to the rocker. "Have a seat."

She pulled a chair close to the rocker and handed him a tiny bottle.

"Touch the nipple to her lips."

Beam did as the nurse instructed and the open-mouthed baby turned her head back and forth frantically.

"She's rooting, which is normal. She'll latch onto the nipple and release it several times before instinct kicks in."

"It's right here, baby," Beam cooed softly, following the moving mouth with the nipple. As his daughter continued to search and reject, a drop of formula formed on the tip of the nipple, and dropped to her lips. She latched on, and Beam chuckled. "There you go, sweetheart."

He looked at Misty, and caught a moment of wonder on her face before she masked it with disinterest. He tried not to let it bother him. She'd been through a lot today. Instead, he watched the formula pool at the corner of the baby's mouth, while listening to the humming sounds coming from her throat when she swallowed.

Carol spent a long time with him, giving him tips on feeding, and discussing different formulas. She showed him how to rouse the baby, if she fell asleep before finishing a bottle.

He loved the way his daughter's eyes looked distant, yet intense as if wondering about this new world where she'd been so abruptly deposited. Her dark fringe of lashes made her skin appear translucent. The way her little lips puckered and worked even in sleep was adorable. He loved her fingernails, no bigger than the head of a pin, and the sweet dimple in her chin. He would be content to sit with her for days, just watching her become acquainted with life outside the home she'd grown used to.

He felt like a clumsy oaf, propping her tiny body in his lap and supporting her head with one hand while patting her back with the other. He liked her on his shoulder where, when they were very quiet, he could feel her flutter heartbeat next to his. He was proud of them both when a small burp escaped her milky lips, and then completely enthralled when she fell asleep cuddled into his chest. He didn't think he'd ever tire of gazing at her perfect face. She was a marvel, the ultimate miracle.

The clumsy oaf in him should have received a medal for feeding the baby, compared to the blundering, ham-fisted, klutz he was when changing his first diaper. Thankfully, Carol was patient and encouraging, making sure he felt comfortable with the process before leaving him to fend for himself. Her parting "Tomorrow we'll bathe her before she goes home" terrified him.

When the door shut, Misty pushed herself up in bed. "That nurse was flirting with you."

"What?"

"I said, *'Hi, I'm Carol'* was totally flirting with you."

He shook his head, not quite catching what Misty was talking about, because his daughter yawned, and it was the cutest thing he'd ever seen.

~

*M*ason Douglas pulled into the hospital parking lot at nine that night. He wasn't sure about visiting hours, or if visiting hours at hospitals still existed, but he had to take a peek at his new granddaughter. She would probably be his only grandchild, and he didn't want to miss her first day.

The squeak of his rubber-soled boots echoed through the silent corridor. As hard as he tried, it was impossible to walk quietly. He stopped at Misty's closed door. He didn't want to knock, for fear he'd wake her and the baby if they were asleep. He pushed the door open as quietly as possible and peered into the room. The only light glowed from the bathroom, where the door stood slightly ajar.

Misty seemed to be asleep. Beam, his six foot-five, two hundred and thirty pound son in-law was reclined in a chair. His enormous hand rested on a bassinet. Mason tiptoed around the foot of the bed. His granddaughter lay on her back in the bassinet, sleeping peacefully. She was as beautiful as Misty had been with her silky black hair and sweet angel face.

For a moment, he let himself feel sorry for the woman who'd left him and Misty twenty-two years earlier. Arleen was missing the first hours of her granddaughter's life. Such a sad loss.

"I heard you had a long day." Beam's voice was barely above a whisper.

Mason let his gaze move from the baby to Beam. "Not nearly as long as you. Congratulations."

Beam smiled. "Same to you, Grandpa."

A whimper came from the bassinet, and Mason looked down. "She's stunning. Reminds me of Misty the day she was born. She had the same fly-away black hair. Is she okay?"

"A pediatrician came in to check on her about an hour ago and said she's fine." After another whimper, Beam sat up and peered over the edge of the bassinet. "Yes, we're talking about you, baby girl."

"Have you named her?"

"No. Misty wasn't ready to talk about it earlier."

Mason glanced over his shoulder. "How is Misty?"

Beam didn't need to say a word. The evidence of Misty not taking to her daughter sat heavily between his brows. Misty seemed to lack the same maternal instinct that had been missing in her mother. Arleen had never wanted the baby she'd already been carrying when she met him. She wasn't far enough along to show, and Mason had pretended ignorance when the baby was born "prematurely". Really, the fact that Misty wasn't his had never bothered him. He loved her as his own from the first moment he saw the plump baby with her head full of hair. He tried to love Arleen enough to make her stay, but nothing he did was ever enough.

Mason studied the man he would have surmised the least likely choice for Misty. Beam was big and brawny, outdoorsy, and the complete opposite of any man Misty had ever dated. He'd known Beam since he was a kid. In high school, Beam had worked for him a couple of summers at the hardware store. In their youth, he and his brother Rowdy had been a little on the wild side, but Mason couldn't have ordered a better son-in-law. Beam was down to earth like his parents. He was honest and hardworking, and left no doubt in Mason's mind that Misty and his granddaughter would be well cared for.

He patted Beam on the shoulder. "I'm going to get out of

here and let you get some sleep. It may be the last you get for a while. Tell Misty I was here, and I'll be back tomorrow."

Beam stood and shook his hand, then pulled him in for a back-patting hug. "Thanks for coming, Mason."

Mason was a sentimental man, and the gesture touched his heart. He admired his granddaughter one last time and then smiled at Beam. "You do good work."

CHAPTER 3

Beam opened the front door wide and wanted to weep in gratitude. "Thanks for coming, Low-rider," he said, using the familiar nickname he and his brother had given their pint-sized cousin when she was about four.

Alex stepped inside and slipped her coat off, trading it for the screaming baby in his arms. After hanging her coat, Beam led her into his father-in-law's living room, where he sank down heavily on the sofa. His body quivered with exhaustion, as disjointed thoughts tumbled over each other, unable to find a place to settle.

Alex swayed gently from side to side, running her finger across the baby's forehead and over her cheek. Her squalling settled down to little squeaky hiccups. The quiet that settled over the house seemed louder than the baby's crying had just seconds before. Bending forward, Beam put his elbows on his knees and his head in his hands. They'd been home from the hospital for four days, and Misty had barely left her bed.

Alex sat next to him and rubbed her free hand over his back. The physical contact seeped through his flannel shirt, filling him with warmth, renewing his strength, and reinforcing his belief that there was still good in his little world. He turned his head sideways when he heard an insistent sucking. Alex had the baby lying along the seam of her legs, and she was working furiously on Alex's knuckle.

"Looks like she might be hungry."

He chuckled without humor. "She's always hungry."

"When did she last eat?"

Beam glanced bleary-eyed at his watch, trying to get the numbers to focus. "Two hours ago."

"Fix a bottle, then go take a nice hot shower and a very long nap."

A shower? And a nap? He almost wept for the second time since Alex's knock on the door. "That's too guilty a pleasure."

She ran a hand over his back, again. "I'm serious, Beam. You're dead on your feet. You won't be any good to this sweet little darling as tired as you are."

He fell back onto the sofa cushions and closed his burning eyes. "Alex, I didn't call so you would take over for me. I just couldn't get the baby to stop crying."

"You're so tired you're transferring your frustration to her. Go on. We'll be fine."

"What about Pretty Posies?" he asked, opening his eyes.

"Tatum is at the store. She knows where I am, and will call if something she can't handle comes up."

"Are you sure?"

"I wouldn't offer if I wasn't sure. I've wanted to get this doll in my arms since you got home from the hospital. I'm glad you thought to call me." She looked down at the baby, whose restlessness was making it known that a knuckle wasn't sufficient sustenance. "Where's Misty?"

Beam sucked in a breath and blew it out slowly. He wished clearing his lungs would release the pent up frustration he felt toward his wife. "In bed."

"Would you like me to have a word or two with the princess?"

"No. That will only make things worse."

"You're probably right, but still..." Alex wiggled her eyebrows up and down mischievously.

He was too tired to laugh, but he did indulge in a quick smile.

"Has your mom been here?"

"She stopped by yesterday. I told her everything was fine." He knew Alex would understand his reluctance to tell his mom about Misty's lack of concern.

"Has Misty talked to her doctor? This may be a very treatable case of postpartum depression."

He glanced out the front window. The weather hadn't improved since they left the hospital. Snow was still falling off and on, and was supposed to continue for the rest of the week. "I'm pretty sure postpartum depression isn't Misty's problem."

"Still, to be on the safe side, you should have her call her doctor."

"Yeah." He pushed to his feet and weaved into the kitchen to warm another bottle.

"Believe me, Beam, what you're going through is normal sleep deprivation," Alex said when he returned. "A shower and a nap will enable you to leap tall buildings, stop runaway trains, and take care of this demanding little soul."

Her words lightened his dark mood just a little. He knew his problem with Misty was big, but his baby daughter was his first concern. Alex was right. He needed sleep to care for her. "Thanks, Low-rider. And thanks for taking Misty to the hospital, then staying with her. I know she can be..."

"Difficult?" Alex offered. "You're welcome. Misty puts up a fierce front, but she's really just as vulnerable as the rest of us. She did well, considering she didn't get her way. I wouldn't have been happy delivering in another hospital with a doctor I wasn't familiar with either. Life is unpredictable and she didn't want to bend, but sweet cheeks here…" She smiled down at the baby. "You didn't give mommy much choice, did you?" She glanced at him. "Now that Misty has a baby, she'll discover she has to go with the flow more often than not."

Beam climbed the stairs, as Alex's words bounced around in his head. Misty wasn't a go-with-the-flow kind of person. He continued past the guest room he shared with the baby, and opened Misty's bedroom door. She sat on the bed, propped up by pillows, flipping through a fashion magazine with an open bag of potato chips lying next to her. The sight fueled the irritation flowing through him. "Your daughter has been crying for an hour, Misty."

"You don't think I know? Every time she cries my breasts leak like punctured milk jugs."

"You haven't picked her up once since we left the hospital." Misty had barely touched their daughter since her birth. He'd been learning the world of babies on his own. Changing diapers with his big fumbling hands, stumbling through bath time. He'd gotten up with her every time she made a sound, and touched her chest to make sure she was still breathing when she didn't.

"Who's here? I heard the doorbell."

"I called Alex when I couldn't get the baby to settle down."

"Greaaat. Alex to the rescue," Misty muttered. "She thinks all she has to do—"

He shut the door before Misty could finish her sentence, because he couldn't take her negativity right now. He stumbled back to the guest room, too tired to fight with her. Too tired to take the shower he knew he needed. He was too tired to know how to handle the situation he found himself in. He shut the door and fell across the bed, barely aware of his head hitting the mattress.

~

Misty tiptoed from her room, down the back stairs into the kitchen. She could hear Alex talking quietly to the baby. Her baby. Only the baby didn't feel like hers. If she wasn't still fifty-five pounds overweight, didn't have a sagging belly, and breasts the size of cantaloupes, she'd feel far-removed from the whole situation. Her life had turned upside down crazy in a matter of months, and she wasn't sure how to turn it back upright.

The universe winked.

She and Beam's relationship wasn't supposed to be permanent. She was between guys when she spotted him at his brother Rowdy's birthday party, which she'd crashed because Rowdy hated her. Beam was older by nine years, and had always held an elusive bad-boy reputation around town. He was a rough, longhaired, whisker faced enigma. He intrigued her enough that she made eye contact across the crowded room and held it until he came over. They'd ended up at her apartment.

After that night, he came knocking on her door every time he was in town. He surprised her by suggesting a more permanent relationship, a commitment she wasn't willing to give. Beam wasn't the kind of man she'd ever consider seriously. He was the in-between kind of guy. Even though his bad boy reputation had fascinated her, he wasn't the polished wealth she was searching for. She wanted a big house, beautiful clothes, and an enviable car—none of which Beam could provide. He was just for fun, nice to have around until the real thing showed up.

Then she discovered she was pregnant and freaked. There was no other word to describe the desperation she'd felt.

When Colton McCreed, *New York Times* bestselling author, flew into Eden Falls, researching small town life for his next novel, Misty saw a solution. She could have her big house and fancy clothes. All she had to do was convince Colton the baby was his. Her carefully orchestrated plans to escape Eden Falls turned topsy-turvy when Alex discovered the truth. She knew what she was doing was wrong, but she'd truly felt she had no other option. Colton could get her out of this backwater town. He could provide her with the type of life she deserved.

Misty grabbed a coat to cover the tunic she put on to conceal her bloated figure. While pregnant, she'd craved foods that had never been a big deal before. She wanted sweets followed by salt, and she wasn't picky about the sources. Before pregnancy, sugar had been take it or leave it. Now, she wanted cakes and cookies and brownies—all topped with frosting, glaze, or powdered sugar. She dreamed of cheesy macaroni or popcorn drenched in butter. She packed on the pounds as she ate her way through each long, uncomfortable day, until she looked like the Stay Puft Marsh-mallow Man.

The baby squawked in the next room, and Misty's chest tightened, making it hard to breathe.

"Aren't you a happy girl now that you're dry and fed?" Alex said.

The couple of times Misty held the tightly swaddled bundle in the hospital, she'd tried to remain disinterested. She pretended to be too tired to pay attention, while Beam learned to feed, bathe, and change the beautiful baby. She'd never been around a newborn in her life, except for Alex's son. She'd never had any desire to hold one. Stubbornly, she insisted—to herself—that desire hadn't changed. True, she had never experienced the maternal pull her friends talked about. But while pregnant, she'd been amazed by a tiny heel or elbow moving across her abdomen when the baby turned. Overwhelmed by tender feelings that tugged on her heartstrings when she least expected them, surprised by the emotions that invaded no matter how hard she fought against them.

She didn't know the first thing about domestic responsibilities. She didn't know how to cook, and hated to clean. She had failed as a wife, and she would fail as a mother. In a small town like this, where her mother's abandonment was remembered—and she was sure, still talked about—her own failure would be monumental.

Better to never try.

Before the baby was born, Beam had brought up several names for their daughter. Naming meant you were taking possession of, or claiming something as your own. Her dad told her years ago that her mother named her. That knowledge tied her to Arleen like nothing else. It meant there had been a bond at one time—a bond her mother had broken by leaving. Because she would one day leave too, she wouldn't break that bond with her own daughter if it was never made.

Alex, always one to run to the rescue, began singing, "Dream a Little Dream of Me". Good old reliable Alex, the one person in this town Misty felt inferior to. No matter what she did, Alex always came out ahead. She would never admit to jealousy, but it was there, just under her skin, like an irritating rash.

She was still angry over Alex's engagement to Colton McCreed. She'd denied any attraction to him, but every time Misty turned around, they'd been together. Then, as soon as Beam was revealed as the father of Misty's baby, Alex and Colton became inseparable.

Of course, Alex didn't want the big house and fancy

clothes. She was small time, small town born and bred, and didn't strive for anything bigger. The thing that really irked Misty was the fact Colton had come back to little Eden Falls for Alex, gave up everything for her. He sold his LA mansion to live in a tiny three-bedroom cottage in the middle of nowhere. He traded his Maserati for a Land Rover, exchanged cocktail parties for quiet dinners at home, tuxedos for jeans, glitz and glamour for fishing and a place on a bowling league, and caviar for nachos.

Colton picked Alex over her, and the whole town knew.

Misty opened the kitchen door and slipped out into the snowy afternoon.

~

Beam walked down the stairs two and a half hours later, carrying his duffle bag, the baby's portable bed, and two diaper bags. Alex lay on a blanket on the living room floor with the baby next to her. His father-in-law, perched on the edge of the sofa, turned to Beam. His eyes flickered over the things Beam set by the front door, and then moved back to the baby. Beam clapped Mason on the shoulder before joining Alex on the floor. He ran a big hand over his daughter's black hair as tiny sounds for attention escaped her rosebud mouth. The light of his life was content.

Alex's eyes caught his and he wondered what she was thinking. Possibly, what a mess he'd gotten himself into. At the moment, he couldn't disagree. He couldn't even plead innocent, because he'd known Misty long before they started dating.

Her face suddenly lit with a smile. "You're a lucky man, Beam. Your daughter is precious and has a very sweet disposition."

Just the positive sort of thing Alex always said at just the right moment.

"I know you're exhausted, but I promise it will get better."

He read the recommended books, asked the questions he believed to be important, and thought he knew what to expect. He was wrong. His exhaustion, coupled with his anxiety over Misty's unwillingness to help or even acknowledge their daughter, overwhelmed him. He knew she wouldn't move into motherhood joyfully, but he had expected her to feel something when she heard her daughter cry. Something more than complete indifference. He was wrong on that count, too.

"Thanks for coming, Alex. That nap revived me. I'm ready to meet any demands this little peanut asks of me."

Alex rubbed her index finger under the baby's chin. "Have you and Misty decided on a name?"

"Not yet." Beam glanced at Mason. "Do you have any suggestions?"

"Oh," Mason stammered with wide eyes, obviously surprised Beam would ask his opinion. "I'm not good at that sort of thing. Misty's mom got the name Misty from a 1970's psychological thriller starring Clint Eastwood. Arleen had a thing for Clint."

"What was your mother's name, Mr. Douglas?" Alex asked.

He wrinkled his nose. "Sophia."

"Sophia is a gorgeous name."

"No," Mason protested, and then settled his gaze on his granddaughter. "It's a little old-fashioned, don't you think?"

Beam got up on his elbow and looked down into the baby's face. Her blue eyes were locked on something over his left shoulder. "I think your cousin—"

"Honorary Auntie Alex," Alex corrected.

Beam smiled. "I think your honorary Auntie Alex is right. Sophia is a gorgeous name. What do you think? Do you like Sophia?"

The baby blinked in wonder, and then a tiny coo escaped her mouth. Beam laughed. "Sophia it is. Now for a middle name. Alice or Glenda are out. No offense to either my mom or yours," he said to Alex. "But neither work for me."

"How about Marie for Grandma Garrett?" Alex asked.

"Sophia Marie Garrett...I like it." He stared into his daughter's eyes. "You'll be named for two great grand-mothers."

"The name is as pretty as you are," Alex said to the baby before patting Beam's cheek. "I need to get home. Charlie went over to Tyson's after school, but he and Colton will be ready for dinner soon."

Alex glanced up at Mason. "I hope you don't mind. I found some ground beef in the freezer and threw a soup together. There should be enough for the three of you."

Mason pushed his glasses up his nose. "I'm pretty sure I won't mind that someone else cooked dinner tonight. Thank you, Alex."

Beam stood and pulled Alex to her feet. "Thanks for coming, Low-rider. I was so tired I wasn't thinking straight. I feel like a new man."

"You look like a new man," she said with a laugh. "Your daughter will be ready to eat again in about an hour. It was good to see you, Mr. Douglas. You sure have a darling grand-daughter."

"Thanks, Alex. And thanks for the soup. It smells delicious."

Beam walked Alex to the door where they stood quiet for a moment while she slipped into her coat. She put her hands in her pockets and looked up at him. "I'm sorry you're going through this, Beam."

His nod was more resignation than acknowledgment. "Any suggestions?"

Her glance moved to Mason who was absorbed in his granddaughter. "I wish I had one or two. I can try to talk to her."

Beam was torn, afraid talking would push Misty further away. In reality, how much more removed could she be? "Would you? For me?"

"Of course." She looked down at the things he'd set next to the door. "Are you going back to Seattle?"

He shook his head. "I took a couple weeks off work. I'm going over to Mom and Dad's for now."

"If you need anything, call me. I can usually sneak away from the shop when Tatum's there, or call my mom. She would be thrilled to help."

Beam watched his cousin get into her rusted out Jeep and drive away, before he returned to the living room. He lifted his daughter, cradling her on one arm.

"Where's Misty?" Mason asked.

"She was in bed." Her door was still closed when he came downstairs.

"Her car is gone."

If she left, Beam didn't know when. "I called Alex because So-phi-a…" he said slowly, allowing each syllable to roll off his tongue. The name fit his dark haired, blue-eyed beauty. The smile on Mason's face was a dead giveaway that he was touched by Beam's decision to use the name. "Sophia had been crying for over an hour, and I didn't know what to do to make her stop. Alex said I was probably transferring my frustration and exhaustion to her, which makes sense. As soon as Alex took her from me, she quieted. I was sent off to take a much appreciated nap."

Mason leaned forward, elbows on knees, fingers laced together. He raised sad eyes. "You don't have to explain to me why you called Alex. I know what it's like to raise a daughter alone. I relied on Alex's mom so much after Arleen left. Alice Garrett saved my hide on more occasions than I can count."

Beam ran a finger over Sophia's silky cheek, and she opened her little mouth and turned it in anticipation. "I'm going to stay at mom and dad's house until I can find a place to rent."

Mason's eyes widened at the news. "You're not going back to Seattle?"

Beam sank into a chair. "I can't do this alone. Here, I have family to help."

"What will you do?"

"I'll find a job in Eden Falls or Harrisville. With spring around the corner, Rance might need help at The Fly Shop. Rowdy can always use an extra hand at his place. Something will come up."

"What about your plane? Can't you fly tourists in and out of Eden Falls?"

Beam shook his head. "Not enough to make a living."

"You'll sell?"

"I'm not sure yet. With this little someone needing me around, I think I'll have to. It was a fun stint while it lasted, but babies have a way of changing your life." It felt odd discussing his life's plan with his father-in-law before anyone else, but, over the last few months, he'd grown close to Mason, and respected his opinion. "To tell you the truth, I don't think I'll mind being grounded."

"I can always use help at the lumber yard, Beam."

Beam stood and laid Sophia on the sofa next to her grandpa. He dug her fuzzy pink bunting from one of the diaper bags. "I don't want things to be uncomfortable between us if Misty and I…can't make our marriage work."

Mason frowned. "The only way things will be uncomfortable is if I can't see my granddaughter."

"That will never happen, Mason. You have my word." Beam dressed Sophia in her warm coat while Mason stroked her cheek. Her eyes fluttered closed.

"Have you discussed your plans with Misty?"

"Misty hasn't said a full sentence to me since we brought Sophia home." *She probably won't even know we're gone, except the quiet will keep her breasts from leaking.* Beam zipped the bunting. "Alex suggested Misty see her doctor for postpartum depression. See if you can talk to her."

Mason released a huff of air. "She isn't going to listen to anything I say."

"Probably not, but it won't hurt to mention it."

Mason picked up Sophia and stood, cuddling her close. "You don't believe this is postpartum depression any more than I do."

Beam shook his head as he shrugged into his coat. While Sophia stayed in the warm house with her grandpa, he loaded the truck with their things. By leaving Misty at her dad's, he was dumping his problem on Mason. But he couldn't coddle Misty the way she wanted, take care of Sophia, and look for a job at the same time. Back inside, he watched Mason kiss Sophia's forehead. The smell of soup permeated the house and made his stomach rumble, but he didn't want to take the time to eat.

"You're welcome to visit anytime, Mason."

Mason kissed Sophia's cheek before handing her to Beam. "I'll see you both soon. Let me know your plans."

Beam nodded. He turned to leave, but stopped on the porch. "I love your daughter, Mason. I'd hoped I could make her happy."

"I know, Beam."

"Tell Misty she can visit, too." Even as he said the words, he knew she wouldn't.

Mason smiled. "You take care of my granddaughter."

"That is something you'll never have to worry about."

~

Mason watched Beam's taillights until they disappeared in the distance. Hollowness settled over him, knowing things were about to change, and probably not in a good way. He took full responsibility for the situation and wished he had the power to make it right. Actually, he'd love to push some of the blame onto Arleen's shoulders, but knew she wouldn't care that her daughter was following in her footsteps. She'd been gone so long it wouldn't be fair, even if that blame were only in his mind. To place blame was easier than to accept it. The time for honesty was here. The time to admit his utter failure as a single parent, as a father, was long past due.

He walked to the carved mantel over the fireplace and stared at the long line of pictures accumulated over the years. Misty was in every one of them. Misty surrounded by friends. Misty at the beach, on the river, or with a birthday cake in front of her, candles glowing. The only picture that included him was from her high school graduation. Alice Garrett insisted they stand side by side. She'd sent the framed photo over with Alex. Today wasn't the first time the picture had filled him with sadness. He and Misty stood close together without touching, stiff as corpses. He'd tried to put his arm around her, tried to congratulate her, but she'd shrugged him away, as usual.

With the hardware store and lumberyard, he'd been able to provide Misty with every material thing she ever wanted.

What he couldn't give her was the one thing she wanted most —the love of her mother.

He'd tried to console the little girl who cried herself to sleep every night, even when his own grief carried him to the same place. Misty wouldn't be consoled. She also wouldn't give up on the belief that one day her mother would come back for her. He tried to shower Misty with all the love she felt she was missing after Arleen left. Misty not only pushed him away, but also blamed him for her mom's abandonment.

One more thing he could blame himself for. He should have tried harder to hug his rebellious daughter.

Arleen had been bigger than life when he met her. She was beautiful and funny. Vibrant. He couldn't believe his luck when she turned all that sunshine and warmth toward him. What he'd mistaken for love had turned out to be nothing more than hope that an older man—fourteen years older— with money, could rescue her from the dullness of working in a dingy diner for minimum wage, and be a father to her unborn baby.

What did he know? He was a naïve thirty-year-old with zero experience due to extreme shyness.

Arleen had grown up with abusive, alcoholic parents. Running away from home at a very young age, she survived the only way she knew how. None of that mattered to him. He loved her. After they were married, he discovered she was only sixteen, living with a stolen ID. When she started show- ing, he realized she must have been pregnant before they met. None of those things changed his feelings for her. Sadly, her feelings for him weren't the same.

Six and a half months after they married, a very healthy, full- term baby girl was born. He'd loved Misty on sight and never questioned Arleen about Misty's biological father. He realized now, maybe he should have. He had such big dreams for their life together, but Arleen's desires were bigger, and Eden Falls was too small to fulfill them. He never could keep up with all Arleen wanted. She left on Misty's sixth birthday, chasing after an illusive happiness she would never find. Always believing there was a pot of gold in another place with another person, rather than within herself, she would always be disappointed.

When she left without a word, she cleaned out their personal savings account. He got home that evening and found Misty sitting on the front step, clutching the doll Arleen bought on credit, tears running down her little cheeks. She was shaking from the cold and had soiled herself. He had no idea how long she'd been left sitting alone and was furious with Arleen, but let her go without a fight, because she left Misty with him.

Misty's sadness eventually morphed into anger, all directed at him. He didn't have the heart to tell her that her mother had probably never intended to stay. Him saying as much wouldn't have mattered. In Misty's eyes, he hadn't done enough to keep her mother with them. He was a constant disappointment to his daughter.

~

*M*isty pulled up her father's long driveway after midnight, and noticed Beam's truck wasn't parked out front. The house was dark, except for the light over the stove, which cast a glow through the kitchen window.

She slipped through the back door and flipped off the light. How many times, through her middle and high school years, had she turned off the light and stolen up the front stairs, bypassing her father's bedroom, after curfew? She hadn't been caught often, because her dad worked a physical job and came home exhausted most nights. He wasn't aggressive with punishment anyway. She was usually sneaking in again the very next weekend.

After graduating from Evergreen Beauty College and securing a chair at Dahlia's Salon the Town Square, she moved into her own place. Her dad paid her first six months rent and bought several pieces of furniture to get her started. That had been a lifetime ago. The apartment was tiny. A one bedroom with awful green carpeting and a tangerine orange bathroom, but she'd loved the freedom it gave her. She no longer lived under her father's roof. Independent to come and go as she pleased, though independence hadn't changed her life as much as she'd anticipated. Alex was married to her Marine husband by then. Other high school friends, Stella, Jillian, and Carolyn were away at college. Only Jolie went to college locally, and she was already dating Nate.

She walked down the hall to the front stairway, so she wouldn't wake her dad. Even though she was grown and no longer abided by his rules—not that she did much of that before—old habits died hard.

"Misty."

She jumped and spun around with a hand on her pounding heart. Her dad sat in one of the wing-backed chairs by the front window. The moon, reflecting off the snow on the front lawn, eerily lit one side of his face. "You scared me half to death. What are you doing sitting in the dark?"

"What are you doing getting home after midnight?"

She laughed. "You're kidding, right? I'm twenty-seven years old. I can get home when I want."

"You just had a baby, Misty."

She came into the living room and collapsed onto the sofa. "Yeah, well, I had to get out. I feel like I've been cooped up since I got married." She glanced toward the stairs. The house was too quiet. "Where's Beam? His truck is gone."

"He and Sophia left."

A jolt of alarm forced her to sit forward. "Sophia? Who's Sophia?"

Her father shook his head. *"Your daughter."*

She frowned in confusion, her brain a little fuzzy from the couple of drinks she'd consumed. "The baby's name isn't Sophia."

"As of today, it is."

"No," she said, shaking her head. "Where did that name even come from?"

"Alex asked my mother's name. We all liked it, so *your daughter* became Sophia. Her middle name is Marie after Beam's grandmother."

Her dad's emphasis on the words *your daughter* was as irritating as the thought of Alex being involved in naming the baby. "Alex doesn't get to decide the baby's name."

Mason, whose elbows rested on the arms of his chair, put his fingertips together as if creating the steeple of a church. "When were you planning to name her? In fact, when do you plan to feed Sophia, change her diapers, or bathe her? When are you going to start acting like her mother?"

"I needed my sleep. I just gave birth."

"That's right, Misty. You just gave birth to a baby girl who needs you. You've done nothing to bond with her."

"I've been tired."

"Well, you can get plenty of sleep now. Beam and Sophia moved to his parent's house." Her dad pushed to his feet and headed for the stairs, but stopped at the bottom. "Alex mentioned something called postpartum depression. She told Beam maybe you should see a doctor."

"Alex can mind her own business. And the baby's name isn't Sophia!"

CHAPTER 4

Beam joined his parents at the kitchen table with a howling Sophia, and a warmed bottle. They hadn't asked any questions when he'd appeared on their doorstep the night before, a duffle and two diaper bags in one hand, a baby in the other. He knew they wouldn't, but he owed them an explanation. He'd taken the spare bedroom in the basement in hopes that Sophia's cries in the night wouldn't wake them. Luckily, she'd been on her best we-need-a-place-to-crash behavior and had fussed like a little lady, rather than a sailor.

The smell of cinnamon rolls filled the kitchen and made Beam's mouth water. His mom made the best county fair, blue ribbon, cinnamon rolls in town.

Beam settled back in his chair, appreciating the inherent comfort his parent's kitchen always brought him. A place he could grab a peanut butter sandwich before little league practice, a gulp of milk straight from the carton—*sorry mom*—after school, or an apple from the ever-present bowl of fruit that sat on the scarred table. How many nights had he and Rowdy spent at this table, fretting over spelling words, fractions, or each state's capital? The table had survived two major kitchen renovations that included new cupboards, granite countertops, tile floors, and shiny new appliances.

He wanted a metaphoric kitchen table—a stable home, surrounded by solid, loving people who could be counted on for his daughter. For Sophia.

She fell asleep halfway through her bottle, and he propped her on his shoulder. After a few gentle pats, she released a very unladylike burp. His father chuckled and his mom held out her hands. Glenda settled her granddaughter in her arms to feed her the last two ounces. Dawson pushed the sports section of the paper across the table to him. The morning felt like a thousand others spent just this way, except he'd been under eighteen, and a baby hadn't been present.

The oven timer buzzed. Beam pushed to his feet, and pulled the rolls from the oven. A bowl of frosting sat on the countertop, so he spread a thick layer over the tops, watching it melt down through the spirals of cinnamon. He sprinkled chopped nuts on top before bringing the whole pan to the table. After two trips back and forth for a carton of milk, forks, glasses, plates, and napkins, he finally sat.

He poured a glass of milk and took a healthy gulp, not sure why he felt so nervous. Neither of his parents had lifted a fork or said a word, but sat quiet. Waiting.

"I've been thinking about this for some time, even before Sophia's birth. Probably since the wedding." He set his glass down and leaned back. "I've decided I want her to grow up around family. I'm going to put my plane and house up for sale and—"

"Selling your plane?" His father's question overlapped his mother's, "You named her Sophia?"

Beam smiled. "She looks like a Sophia, don't you think?"

Glenda gazed at her sleeping granddaughter. "Actually, I think Sophia matches her perfectly. Where'd the name come from?"

"It was Mason's mother's name." He glanced between them. "Alex suggested Marie for her middle name, after Grandma Garrett."

Dawson's expression turned thoughtful. "I like that."

Glenda wiggled the bottle still in Sophia's mouth, and her sleeping granddaughter roused. "Hello, little Sophia Marie."

"Does this mean you'll live in Eden Falls?" his dad asked.

"Yes. Well, if I can find work. Rowdy is always complaining he's short handed at his place. Rance might be able to use me at The Fly Shop, once summer hits." The look that passed between his parents was encouraging.

Now, for the uncomfortable question. He hadn't lived under his parent's roof since he left for college, and it wouldn't be easy to do it again. "I was wondering if we could stay with you until I find a place. I'll check with Alex about her rental. Hopefully, it will be available after she and Colton get married next month. Do you know if she's found a renter?"

Dawson shook his head. "I haven't heard, but you can stay here as long as you need. There's plenty of room and we can find a place at the gym if—"

"No." Beam held up a hand. "I don't want to put anyone out of a job. I have enough in savings to get by for a while."

"What about Misty?" Glenda asked.

Beam glanced at the ceiling, wishing he could answer that question with any conviction. "I'm not sure about Misty. For now, she's staying with Mason."

A long, uneasy silence followed. Beam knew his parents were mulling over his situation, and wished he could reassure them. Glenda broke the silence first. "I thought you loved Seattle."

"I do, and I love flying. But…something bigger, bigger than me, something so much more important came into my life." He laughed at his own words. "I want to do what's best for Sophia, and I think Eden Falls is best. For now. Things may change down the road, but I really think this is where Sophia and I belong."

"We can all help," his mom said. "Your Aunt Alice told us she'd be happy to babysit any time you need her. We can take Sophia to the gym. Your dad and I can take turns staying with her in the office. Can't we Dawson?"

"Absolutely. Since we hired Jillian Saunders as assistant manager, we both have more time. We'll make this work."

Beam knew he'd have their support, but that didn't make him appreciate it any less. Their offers of help eased many of the doubts fluttering at the edges of his mind. He was beginning to think single fatherhood was going to be inevitable, and the idea overwhelmed him. He'd been lucky to have two loving, supportive parents—something he'd taken for granted. His thoughts shifted to his cousin's happy son, whose father had been killed in Iraq. Single parenthood wasn't the ideal situation, but Alex made it work and he could, too.

"I have to go to Seattle to pack things up and do some minor work on the house before I put it on the market."

Dawson sat back in his chair and drummed the table with both hands. "If Jillian can cover the gym, we'll all go. With the three of us working, we'll be able to accomplish much more than if you went alone."

Rowdy entered the kitchen through the back door. He stopped short when he saw them all sitting at the table. "Uh oh. What happened?"

"Perfect timing, Rowdy," Dawson said. "We're planning a trip to Seattle. Can you get someone to cover the bar for a couple of days?"

～

*M*isty rolled over and grabbed her cell phone from the nightstand, ready to blast whoever was calling this early on a Saturday morning. Alex's sunny smile lit her screen. Misty pushed the decline button. Before she could drop the phone back on the nightstand, it rang again. This time she accepted the call. "What do you want?"

"Open up. I'm at the front door."

Misty groaned. "Go away. It's too early."

"It's nine o'clock, and I'm not going anywhere, so you might as well open the door. And hurry up. I'm freezing."

"You're going to get a lot colder." Misty disconnected the call and pulled the covers over her head.

Just as she closed her eyes her phone rang again.

Misty swung her feet to the floor, and grumbled all the way down the stairs. She flung the front door open, and was greeted by Alex's "Good morning."

"It was good before you woke me up." Misty turned her back on Alex, walked into the living room, and fell back onto the sofa. "What do you want, Alex?"

Alex unzipped her parka but didn't take it off. "I want to talk."

"You couldn't wait until I was awake?"

Alex grinned. "You're awake."

Misty rolled her hand. The sooner Alex got talking, the sooner she'd leave.

Alex walked over to the fireplace and picked up the picture of Misty and her dad at high school graduation. She turned toward Misty. "Remember this day? We were so happy to be out of school for the summer. Sad we were all going in different directions, but excited to be moving on to the next phase of our lives. Maybe a little afraid…" She smiled. "Carolyn was terrified to be going off to culinary school in San Francisco. She'd never been out of the state of Washington.

Stella was headed to the University of Arizona, Jillian was off to the University of Utah, and you were—"

"I know where everyone went to college." Misty pretended to pick up a gun, put it to her head, and pull the trigger. "What's your point, Alex?"

"Life sure didn't turn out the way I thought it would."

Misty dropped her head to the back of the sofa.

Alex replaced the picture and picked up another—this one of her, Alex, Stella, Jillian, and Jolie posed at the foot of Eden Falls. "This was taken the day before I married Peyton. Only Carolyn couldn't make it back for my bachelorette party. I spent the day with four of my five besties at the falls, hiking and picnicking."

She sank onto the other end of the sofa. "I thought Peyton and I would be together forever, instead of two short years. We'd have half a dozen kids—not a son I'd raise on my own. I never thought I'd be a widow at twenty.

"I imagined I'd graduate from community college and work with my grandma in her shop. Instead, I inherited Pretty Posies due to a freak car accident that took both my grandparents away too soon. Life isn't always fair and very rarely turns out as we expect, Misty, but we have to make the most of what we're given."

"Oh, happy day. Words of wisdom from Little Miss Sunshine." Misty rolled her head to look at Alex. "Geeet tooo the poooint or gooo hooome."

Alex set the picture on the cushion between them. "I came to say I think you're making a mistake."

"Mistake about what?"

"Your husband and daughter."

"You don't know anything about the situation."

"Let me tell you what I know, and you can correct me if I'm wrong." She held up her index finger. "You made a choice to sleep with Beam, and got pregnant. You tried to pass Beam's baby off as Colton's, to trap him into marriage. That didn't work so you married Beam, but only because he told you he'd finance a salon for you after the baby was born. FYI—wrong reason to get married." She held up a finger every time she made a point.

"You've made some major choices in your life, but forgot choices come with consequences. Now, you need to step up and honor the commitments you've made."

Anger crept up Misty's back, twisting her stomach and tightening her chest. She sat forward and glared at Alex. "I didn't make any commitments."

"You made a commitment to Beam when you married him." Alex leaned toward her. "And to Sophia when you gave birth." Her voice softened, as did her eyes. "Beam loves you, Misty."

The anger vanished. Replaced by a longing so intense it hurt. Love. All she'd ever wanted, for as long as she could remember, was her mother's love.

"Crazy as this may sound, he needs you. Your baby girl needs you."

Yeah, well I needed my mother, too. Misty pushed to her feet and crossed the room before Alex saw the tears that blurred her vision. She knew Alex was right. Beam did love her, but she would fail him. She'd fail them both, because she didn't know how to love. She wasn't wife material. She didn't possess a motherly bone in her body, and there was nothing she could do about it.

Without looking at Alex, she headed up the stairs. "Go bore someone else with your lectures, Alex. I have a bed calling my name."

～

*B*eam bundled Sophia up for their short trip into town. She'd been fussy since breakfast, but as soon as he put her in the truck and started the engine, she settled down.

Eden Falls was built around the two-block town square with a one-way street running around the perimeter. Beam circled once before he found a parking space close to Pretty Posies. Alex had the place lit up against the dreary day, casting a golden glow through the windows.

He opened the back door of his crew cab and released Sophia's carrier from the car base. With her blue eyes zeroed in on him, he said, "Hey, beautiful. We're going to visit Auntie Alex, and hopefully secure a place to live. You need to be on your best behavior. A sweet smile just might seal the deal. How about it? Can you do that for daddy?"

Her tiny mouth formed a perfect O and his heart melted. "That's it, sweetheart. You've got the idea."

He threw a blanket over the carrier to keep the cold out, and headed into Alex's shop. The bell over the door tinkled merrily when they entered, and the warmth of familiarity wrapped itself around him. He'd spent many memorable hours here helping with large deliveries, moving the enormous armoires his grandmother used for display cases, and just hanging out. The shop brought back happy recollections of his youth. Alex hadn't changed the interior much since becoming proprietress. She'd kept the bones of the place the same. Touches of Grandma Garrett were visible with overlays of Alex.

His cousin and her fiancé, Colton McCreed, were behind the counter, lip-locked. Beam flew the author into Eden Falls eight months earlier, and would never—not in his wildest imagination—have matched the two of them together. They couldn't be more opposite. Their backgrounds were north and south, their dispositions, like adding grape jelly to a cheeseburger, but somehow they worked. Colton chided Alex about being a prude and she called him an arrogant city-dweller, as the love they shared radiated from both.

Colton arrived from LA as a self-indulgent, self-professed bachelor for life. Eden Falls had subtly whittled down his rough edges, and Alex had softened his impermeable skin. Before Colton knew what hit him, he was fishing, picnicking, and eventually falling in love.

Colton finished the book he'd come to write and moved back to Los Angeles. Four months later, he showed up at Pretty Posies to claim the woman and her six-year old son, who had wrapped themselves around his heart. He proposed, Alex accepted, and they announced their engagement that same night at a New Year's Eve party. The lovebirds wedding was set for February 14, as if owning the only flower shop in town didn't keep Alex busy enough on Valentine's Day.

She pulled away from Colton and smiled. "Oh, McCreed, look who came to visit."

Before Beam could set the carrier down, Alex had unbuckled and unzipped his daughter's head-to-toe bunting. She pulled Sophia free and cuddled her close. "Good morning, sweetheart. You look gorgeous in pink."

Colton glanced at the baby, and Beam wondered what was going through his mind. The murder mystery author had believed this baby was his for two weeks back in July. He was prepared to accept the responsibility of fatherhood, until Alex discovered Misty was trying to deceive him and Beam both.

"Wow." Colton chuckled. "Look at her hair. Do all babies have that much hair?"

"Charlie did," Beam and Alex said at the same time. Then they shared a laugh.

"Congratulations."

"Thanks," Beam replied, shaking Colton's offered hand.

Alex held Sophia up. "Look, McCreed, she has a little lamb on her bottom. Isn't it cute?"

"Adorable."

Alex's instant frown at his placating tone quickly turned to an impish grin. "Hold her."

He held up both hands. "Nooo. I don't know anything about holding babies."

"Oh, don't be ridiculous," Alex chided, giving him no choice by settling Sophia in his arms. "Just be sure to support her head."

Colton, stiff as a marble statue, reminded Beam of himself the first night he'd held his daughter. His panic was palpable. And amusing.

"Am I?"

"Are you what?" Alex asked her fiancé.

"Supporting her head?"

"Relax, honey. She won't break." Alex smiled at Colton's impatient anxiety. You're doing a fabulous job."

Colton lowered his tight shoulders, but his facial expression remained a grimace of tension.

Alex bent her nose to Sophia's head. "Oh, baby, you smell wonderful. Smell, Colton."

"I'm not smelling her, Alex."

Determination settled between Alex's brows. "Smell."

Colton gave his fiancée the stink eye before carefully lowering his nose to Sophia's hair, while making a concerted effort not to jostle her. Beam chuckled. His petite cousin had this famous author wrapped around her tiny finger.

Colton glared at Beam before he slowly backed to one of the stools at the counter and sat. His body still rigid, but he seemed content to stare at Sophia. "Her eyes are so blue and alert. I thought babies slept all the time."

"They do sleep a lot," Alex said, leaning over his arm. "Isn't she pretty?"

"Her nose is kind of flat."

Alex bumped Colton's shoulder with her own. "She just came from very cramped quarters."

Colton braced at the slight jarring. "Alex, don't do that."

"Relax, McCreed." Alex laughed. "So? What do you think? Holding a baby is kind of nice, isn't it?"

Colton's eyes narrowed. "Don't try to play me, Sunshine. I know what you're up to."

"Play you?" She feigned, adding an innocent lash flutter, and Beam laughed. Alex would be pregnant with a little McCreed before Colton knew what happened. He'd professed never to want a wife or kids, but Alex and Charlie had, quite innocently, changed his mind on both counts. With the help of Sophia, Alex would do it again. Colton was a goner.

Alex moved another stool from underneath the counter for Beam. "I talked to Misty this morning."

Beam's stomach lurched unpleasantly as he sat. "How'd that go?"

"About how you'd expect." Alex lifted a shoulder. "It ended with her telling me to mind my own business. Pointless on her part, because she knows I won't."

Beam knew how much Misty hated living in Eden Falls. Choosing to stay might mean the death of their marriage, but he felt it was the right decision for Sophia. "Thanks for trying."

Alex placed her hands on his forearms and squeezed. "Stay positive. It's only been a week since Sophia was born. Misty tried hard to hide her emotions, but I saw tears before she disappeared up the stairs."

"Misty doesn't cry."

Alex smiled as if she was sharing a delicious secret. "I know."

Beam stole a glance at his daughter, who'd closed her eyes. He wasn't ready to give up on Misty, but wasn't sure how to remain positive, either. His glimmer of hope was flickering. He raised his gaze to Alex. "I came by to see if you had plans for your rental after the wedding."

"No. I haven't had time to put an ad in the paper." Alex ran her finger over the top of Sophia's head. "Do you know someone who's interested?"

"Yeah, me."

Alex and Colton exchanged a glance, but Beam didn't wait for the questions. "I'm moving back to Eden Falls. I want to raise Sophia here."

"What about your job?" Alex asked.

"I'll find something around here."

"What about your plane?" Colton asked.

"I'm going to put her up for sale along with my house."

Another look passed between his cousin and her fiancé. "What does Misty have to say about all this?"

"She doesn't know."

He could read the doubt on Alex's face. She expected him to be in the fight of his life, when he did hear from Misty, and she didn't fight fair. "I'm not making a rash decision, Alex. I've been thinking about this for some time. If I could make a living around here flying, I'd keep the plane, but there won't be enough business."

"You love that plane."

"You're right, I do"—he lifted a shoulder—"but life has a way of changing your plans. I'll probably be a single father, and I'll be better at it with family around." There was another long uncomfortable pause, and for some reason, he needed to fill it. "Mom and Dad extended an invitation to stay with them, but I want a place of our own."

"The rental is yours for as long as you need it."

Colton grinned. "This sounds like a good reason for me to

move out of the rental and into your place ahead of time, Sunshine."

She pointed to the third finger on her left hand. "You'll move in with me and Charlie when I have a wedding band right here, McCreed."

Beam's chuckle mingled with a bit of jealousy at the relationship Alex and Colton shared. There had been no teasing or playfulness between him and Misty since before their wedding.

"We'll stay with Mom and Dad until then."

"When are you putting your house on the market?" Alex asked.

"Mom, Dad, Rowdy, and I are going to Seattle this coming weekend to do some minor work around the place, and—"

"If Colton and I can arrange it, would you like some extra hands?"

Beam felt the steam of frustration and worry slowly leaking from his body. He'd never taken his family for granted, but living away for so long, he'd forgotten the love and support they'd always shared. "I'll take all the help I can get. There isn't a lot to do, mostly painting and packing."

Alex leaned forward and gave him a tight hug. "I'm glad you're moving home. Charlie will be so excited to have a little cousin around."

As if sensing the tension in the air, Sophia opened her eyes and released a squawk. Her little face turned bright red right before a bubbling sound echoed through the quiet shop.

"Eww. What did this baby just do on my hand?"

The look of horror on Colton's face sent Alex into a fit of giggles.

Sophia's mouth quirked up on one side.

~

*L*ate Saturday morning, Misty went downstairs, and was met with silence. The cold weather had kept her indoors for several days, and the house was closing in on her. Her dad wouldn't be home for hours, and Beam hadn't called since he left almost a week earlier, which was unusual. He always called.

She wandered from the living room to the kitchen and back again. Near the fireplace, she picked up the picture Alice Garrett had snapped of her and her dad when she graduated high school. Her dad would turn fifty-eight this year, which made her mom forty-four. She told herself their age difference, along with small town life, was the reason Arleen Douglas ran away. Eden Falls' movie theatre only had one screen, and the shopping was at a minimum in this dull town. Concerts on the square and fall festivals wouldn't have been enough to keep her beautiful, spirited mom busy. Misty's stodgy, yawn inducing dad couldn't have been much entertainment.

Aloud, Misty blamed her dad and Eden Falls, but deep down she worried she was the real reason her mother left. Was her mom disappointed she was a girl rather than a boy? Even though her dad said different, maybe she'd been a horrid baby, who cried constantly, or demanded too much attention.

She couldn't remember much about her mother anymore. Arleen sitting at a small vanity in the master bedroom, smoothing floral scented lotion on her arms, or applying vivid red lipstick came to mind. She remembered her mother wearing a coral sundress with tiny flowers on the shoulders. She also remembered running fingers through her mom's long, black-as-night hair, but wondered if these were made up memories. Recollections she'd conjured to keep her mother close.

She did remember the last morning she spent with her mom. Her sixth birthday. She remembered the feel of her mother's hand holding hers tightly as they walked into Eden Falls Gift Shop. She remembered the back wall lined with what seemed to be hundreds of dolls.

"You can pick out any dolly you want," her mother said, squatting down so they were eye to eye.

Misty remembered the importance of the moment. The look in her mother's eye was sharp and steady. Even at six, Misty knew the right decision would make Arleen happy. Panic had bubbled in her stomach as she searched the wall for the perfect doll, the one that most resembled her mother— shiny black hair and big blue eyes.

Once they were back home, her mother sat her on the front porch steps and kissed her cheek. Misty clutched her doll close when she realized something very important was about to happen.

"Mommy has to go away. Be a good girl for your daddy. He loves you very much."

She remembered trembling as she watched her mother climb into their family car and drive away without a backward glance.

She was sitting in the same spot when her dad came home. The sky was dark, and the air cold. She remembered being so tired and hungry, and sad, because she knew something significant had happened, something she didn't understand. Had she made the wrong choice? Maybe she should have picked the doll in the yellow dress. Her mom liked yellow.

Over the years, she relived the moment over and over, remembering her mother's words, "He loves you very much." There had been no declaration of her mother's love. She hadn't given Misty a chance to say anything. Maybe if she'd started to cry, or told her mom not to go, she would still be with them.

Misty swiped at the tickle on her cheek, not realizing it was a tear until she saw her wet fingers.

She set the picture back on the mantel and wandered up the stairs to her bedroom. She studied the framed picture of her mom on the nightstand. Arleen was sitting on a boulder with the waterfall behind her, her smile so radiant. She must have been happy. There was no way she could be smiling so big and not be happy. The picture was taken before Misty was born. Why couldn't she have remained happy after she had a baby? Once she'd moved away and found the place that *would* make her happy, why hadn't she come back for her daughter?

If her mother had stayed in Eden Falls, Misty was certain her life would be different. Better. More fulfilling. Life in dreary Eden Falls wouldn't be so unbearable if her mother had stayed. She would be happy. She would be loved. She knew her father loved her in his own awkward way. But was there anything deeper, or richer than a mother's love?

She left her room and stopped in the doorway of the guestroom. Beam had cleaned it, down to stripping the sheets off the bed when he'd left. Her dad said Beam had gone to his parent's house. Hopefully, he was in Seattle by now, interviewing for a nanny.

Still, it wasn't like him not to call. He always called.

She'd have to go home eventually.

Alex was right. Her reason for marrying Beam was his promise to set her up in her own salon after the baby was born. During her pregnancy, while Beam was at work, she'd driven around Seattle searching for the perfect spot. She'd bruised her brain trying to come up with a witty name. Sadly, creativity was not her forte. She'd have to call Stella Adams for ideas.

As a second grade teacher, she possessed the imaginative mind in their circle of friends, always coming up with inventive idea's to keep her class of second grade monsters busy.

Misty walked back to her bedroom, suddenly desperate to get out of the house. After a quick shower and meticulous care with hair and make-up, she squeezed into her too-tight leggings and an oversized sweater to cover the muffin top spilling over. *Time for a new wardrobe.*

She drove into town and parked in front of the only clothing store within town limits. Excitement to be out of the house lifted her drooping spirits. New clothes would lift them even higher.

Misty tried on several pairs of jeans, went up a size, and tried on a few more. Even on the dressing room floor, sucking her stomach in until she almost passed out, she still couldn't get the zipper up. Her lifting spirits took a nosedive. Mrs. Whitney suggested she try a larger size, but Misty refused. She wouldn't go up a size just because the manufacturer screwed up.

She left the shop empty handed, and spoiling for a fight.

Pretty Posies was across the square, so she turned in that direction. Just crossing through town square had her out of breath, which only made her angrier. She pushed through the door.

Incompetent, Goth dressed Tatum was behind the counter. She glanced up—her mascara caked eyelashes looked like two caterpillars had taken up residence—and raised her eyebrows in a startled expression. "Misty, I thought you were in Seattle."

"Why would I be in Seattle?"

Tatum walked around the counter. She wore a black sweater with a neon green skull gracing the front, a black and white, skin-tight skirt that hit just above her knees, and combat boots. Purple hair completed the ensemble. *Smart choice in an employee, Alex.*

Still, Misty eyed Tatum's skinny waistline and flat stomach. Though she'd never admit it, she envied Tatum's ability to put such crazy clothes together to create a darling, yet, completely inappropriate outfit for work.

"I haven't had a chance to congratulate you. Sophia is really beautiful."

The comment surprised Misty. "When did you see her?"

"Beam came in with her a couple of days ago. I had just come to work, and Colton was holding Sophia when she filled her diaper. You should have seen the look on Colton's face. It was the funniest…"

Instead of listening to the punk rocker wannabe jabber on, Misty's thoughts flew to Colton. *He didn't want to get married when I told him I was pregnant. He didn't want kids, but he was holding the baby.* "Where's Alex?" Misty asked when Tatum stopped yammering long enough to take a breath.

Tatum frowned. "She and Colton went to Seattle with Beam."

What? "Why did they go with him?"

Tatum's face blanched, quite a feat since her complexion was already zombie white. "Um…they said…something about getting out of town for the weekend."

Lie. Misty narrowed her eyes, weighing her options before she turned toward the door. She stopped just short of opening it and cast Tatum a threatening glare. "For your information, the baby's name is *not* Sophia."

CHAPTER 5

Misty stomped into Get Fit. The girl at the desk tried to stop her, but she marched past to Jillian Saunders office. The door stood open and Jillian wasn't there. She turned, surveyed the gym, and spotted Jillian in a small room surrounded by windows teaching a yoga class. Great. She'd have to wait. The class probably ended on the hour, which was ten minutes from now, so she walked to the small snack bar and studied the menu on the blackboard.

"Can I help you?"

Misty lowered her gaze to the petite blonde behind the counter. Why didn't her in-laws hire people who needed to lose weight to work in their gym? Tiny employees like this girl only made a person feel worse about the weight they'd gained, while eating their way through a pregnancy. "Sure. What smoothie do you recommend?"

"For what?"

Misty frowned. "What do you mean for what?"

"Well, are you looking for more energy, or would you like one with ginger to help with digestion? Our strawberry-kiwi is high in fiber, and the blueberry-green tea is filled with antioxidants. We have—"

Misty held up her hand, tired by the girl's energy. "I'll take a Daily Sunrise without a shot of anything but sugar."

After the girl turned to make the smoothie, Misty slid onto a barstool and swiveled so she didn't have to watch people sweat. She'd never had to worry about her weight before. She ate when she was hungry, and exercised if a cute guy was involved. Digestion, fiber, or antioxidants had never played a part in her vocabulary. She wasn't even sure what an antioxidant was or what it helped. *Probably just one of the many health words that come and go, like a fad in fashion.*

Her stomach contracted with hunger as she waited on yet another incompetent employee. During pregnancy, she'd been ravenous all the time. And hunger seemed to trigger ornery. Good old, reliable Beam had been there to whip up a grilled cheese sandwich, or run to the store for a package of cookies. He'd weathered through her complaints, rubbed her back, and massaged her feet. She'd given him a hard time since their wedding day, and still he stayed like a faithful dog.

She'd thought once the baby came her hunger would diminish, but that wasn't the case. Her craving for sugar was out of control. She should have stopped at Patsy's Pastries before coming to see Jillian.

The girl set the smoothie in front of Misty. "Can I see your gym membership card?"

"I don't have one."

The girl took a step back, a muddled expression on her face. She glanced toward the entrance desk. "How did you get in?"

"My in-laws own this place. I don't need a membership card."

A sudden smile appeared. "Oh! You must be Beam's wife."

"You're very astute, especially since their other son isn't married." She felt a twinge of guilt at the look of hurt on the girl's face. She pushed it aside. *Buck up, cupcake. Life's tough.* Actually, a cupcake would taste pretty amazing right now. "Are Dawson and Glenda here?"

She received the same deer in the headlights look that Tatum had flashed. "They're in Seattle."

Everyone is in Seattle. What's going on in Seattle? Misty took a swig from her glass and grimaced. "Eww. This is terrible. Don't you guys use sugar?"

Before the girl could answer, the door to the windowed room opened. People poured out, followed by Jillian. Misty waved a dismissive hand. "Never mind."

She tried to hop from the stool, but her heel caught on a rung. She went down on all fours with an echoing *thud.* "Ouch!"

"Misty are you alright?" Jillian said, rushing forward.

"Do I look alright?" Misty pushed Jillian's helping hands away. "You should talk to Dawson about those stools."

When she was on her feet, her auburn-haired, model-thin friend embraced her. "I'm so sorry I haven't been over to see you since you gave birth. Congratulations, by the way. Sophia is beautiful."

"When did you see her?" Misty growled. Seemed the whole town had been invited to a viewing.

"Beam brought her in yesterday. She's just darling."

Why is Beam out running around in the cold with our daughter? Shouldn't she be at home where it's warm? "Yeah. Thanks."

"What are you doing here?"

Misty held her hands out. *Isn't it obvious?* "I'm here to get this weight off. How long will it take you?"

"Have you been released to exercise by your doctor?"

"I don't need to be released. I'm fine."

"You just had a baby, Misty. I can't help you with an exercise program until your doctor says it's okay for you to resume normal activities. I'll give you a diet plan that will be safe for a nursing mother until—"

"I'm not nursing."

Jillian's eyebrows rose. "The benefits—"

"I've heard all about the benefits. I'm not nursing."

"But—"

Misty held up a hand to stop the babbling. "If I get an okay from my doctor, can I get started on an exercise program Monday?"

Jillian shook her head. "You can try, but I doubt your doctor will agree until after your six-week checkup. You should start slowly, Misty. Take a daily walk by the river."

"I'm not going to lose fifty-five pounds by walking."

"You'd be surprised. Come into my office. I have copies of healthy diets—"

"I'm going to report you to Dawson and Glenda." Misty jammed her fists on her waist. "I not just anyone, Jillian. I'm their daughter-in-law."

Jillian shrugged. "I'm sorry, Misty. You had a baby less than a week ago, I can't—"

Misty turned and stormed out of the gym. She was so tired of nothing going her way. *Walking. No one loses weight by walking.*

The universe chuckled.

~

*B*eam sat at his parent's kitchen table going over finances, satisfied that things were coming together quickly. Eight of his family members were able to meet him in Seattle last weekend. They painted and packed while he met with a real estate agent. Alex's son entertained

Sophia, so the adults could get everything done. Since Alex's rental came furnished, everything, but the baby's furniture, went into a storage unit. He packed Misty's things separately and loaded her boxes into his truck, which he still had to drop off at Mason's house.

The realtor listed the house at a competitive price and was optimistic it would sell quickly, even at this time of year. Alex proved she was a whiz at staging. She'd arranged the items Beam left behind, making his barebones house look homey and appealing.

Beam had already received two calls on his Cessna. Selling that baby was going to be a heartbreaker. He could go back to flying someday in the future, but for now Sophia needed him grounded, which he didn't mind. In fact, he was pretty amazed by what he was willing to give up for his baby girl.

He felt guilty he hadn't talked to Misty before listing the house. Truth be told, he was tired of feeling guilty. He'd left Mason's two weeks earlier, and Misty had made no attempt to reach him. Not even a phone call to ask about Sophia. The house was his. Her name was nowhere on the paperwork. She hadn't made friends in Seattle, hadn't put down any roots, and had no job she was leaving behind. She brought nothing into their marriage, except boxes and boxes of clothes, and the few personal items he packed to bring back to Eden Falls. She left most of her things at her dad's as if the move to his home was temporary.

Hurt quickly replaced any feelings of guilt.

Life turning in a one-eighty didn't enlighten him on what to do regarding Misty. She'd been spotted out and about in a Harrisville bar, shopping for jeans at the Red Barn Clothing Store, talking with Jillian at Get Fit, in Renaldo's Italian Kitchen ordering pizza. Rumor was she already had another man, though no one had actually seen her with anyone. Life in Eden Falls would be dreary without spicy gossip ratcheting up the level of drama. He just wished his wife wasn't the one being talked about.

Guilt moved forefront, again. He shouldn't have pushed Misty into marriage. He also shouldn't have sweetened the pot to entice her further. Trap was a better word. He'd trapped her with the incentive of buying her a salon, once the baby was born.

He knew Misty wasn't in love, but had hoped, over time, she might learn to love him, to love their life together. *Wow. I sound so archaic. I was wrong to believe I could mold her to accept my way of thinking. I was wrong to settle for someone who didn't love me back.*

History had proven she was always the first to leave a relationship. He thought that might stem from her mother's abandonment—she left before she was left. So, he'd tried to provide stability and a sense of permanence. He wanted her to believe he was in this for the long haul, but nothing he did seemed to be enough.

Try as he might, he didn't understand how the mother of a two-week old baby wouldn't be anxious to know how she was.

His cell phone vibrated on the table where he sat. Sophia, asleep in her bassinet next to his chair, moved a leg. He laid one hand on her stomach and jiggled her slightly, while he connected the call from Mason with his other. "Hi, Mason."

"Beam, how are things going?"

"Pretty well."

"How's my granddaughter?"

Beam glanced into the bassinet. Sophia's big blue eyes were open and trained on him. He chuckled. "She's awake and will be wailing for a bottle in about sixty seconds."

"Then I'll come right to the point. I heard from your Uncle Denny that you put your Seattle house on the market and plan to move into Alex's rental after her and Colton's wedding."

He'd forgotten how fast news traveled through a small town. "All of the above is true."

"Do you have time to discuss a business proposition?"

"A business proposition?"

"I can be there in fifteen minutes." Mason paused a moment. "I'd love to see my granddaughter."

"Of course. Come on over."

*

*M*isty walked into Dahlia's Salon. She hadn't been back since her last day of work a week before her wedding. Dahlia Dallas and her two associates seemed cordial enough, but Misty knew the minute she left they'd laugh about her oversized body and tell everyone how much her looks had changed.

She had always been the beautiful girl, the one who turned the heads of men, no matter where she was, or whom she was with. She'd never felt uncomfortable in her own skin, or had any trouble finding appealing, alluring clothes to wear. But now, she got out of bed each morning and looked in the mirror, a stranger looked back—one with rolls of fat hanging over the top of her jeans and thighs that rubbed together with enough friction to start a fire. She wouldn't be in Dahlia's at all if she weren't desperate to feel better about her appearance, and Dahlia was the best hair colorist she knew—second only to her.

"I see you haven't filled my chair, yet," Misty said while Dahlia combed through her hair.

"Not yet."

Dahlia's chilly tone let Misty know she was still miffed about Misty leaving with no notice, but she'd had a wedding to plan. What did Dahlia expect? The girls should be thanking her. Being the most requested hair tech in the area, her leaving had to mean more clients for them. The sign over the door should have read Misty's Salon all these years. "No prospects?" she asked.

"Not yet," Dahlia repeated.

Misty looked down the line of chairs. Both Valerie and Lisa were working on previous clients of hers. "At least you didn't lose clients when I left."

The look Dahlia gave her in the mirror told her she was wrong, but what was she supposed to do about it? She certainly wasn't going to work for some small town place when Beam had promised her a salon of her own.

Misty shifted in the vinyl chair, trying to redistribute her weight. The extra pounds she carried made her feel like a stuffed sausage. She was tired of elastic waists and blousy tops. She'd expected the pounds to melt away once she'd delivered, but her appetite was still voracious and walking wasn't helping at all. Jillian had given her a menu plan that consisted of rabbit food, which was fine as long as she topped it with ham, cheese, olives, and plenty of ranch dressing.

To build her self-esteem, Jillian suggested buying a few outfits in larger sizes.

"My self-esteem isn't what needs rebuilding!"

"You can't expect results so quickly, Misty. It took nine months to put the weight on. It isn't going to come off overnight."

By the time Misty got out of Dahlia's, it was late after-noon. Heavy clouds hung low, threatening more snow. *Yahoo.* She pulled the coat that wouldn't zip, tighter around her middle as she stood looking around the dismal little town. Stella's car was in front of Pretty Posies. A talk with friends might cheer her. She stepped over a snow bank and crossed the square. The same cheerful little bell that had hung over the door for as long as Misty could remember announced her arrival. Tatum was behind the counter helping a customer. She smiled at Misty and thumbed over her shoulder toward the workroom.

When Misty entered, Stella and Alex looked up and then exchanged glances with each other. They may as well have announced through a bullhorn, "Hey! We were just talking about you."

"Hi, Misty," Alex said first, followed by Stella's, "Hey."

"What are you two doing?"

Alex held up a rose and inserted it into green floral foam. "Making centerpieces for the senior center's luncheon. Stella dropped by on her way home from school to help."

"Why don't you ever ask me to help? I can arrange flowers." Misty picked up a rose and jabbed it into the foam, breaking the stem.

Alex extricated the bloom from Misty's hand with a frown. "My clients like it when I deliver the stems with the flowers attached."

"Like any of those old bats are going to notice. Half of them can't see beyond their own noses."

Alex frowned. "You used to make a lot of money off the seniors you're calling old bats. You should watch your tongue. One day your comments will come back to haunt you."

Misty waved off Alex's comment. She wouldn't be cutting and curling any of those old biddies again. She plopped down on the stool next to Stella and then did a double take. Stella wore a blob of blue on the tip of her nose. "What happened to you?"

"One of the drawbacks of being a second grade teacher. I was marking papers and had an itch on my nose. I forgot I'd already taken the cap off the marker."

"So wash it off."

Stella performed her trademark eye roll. "What a brilliant idea. Why didn't I think of that?"

"She tried to, but it's permanent marker," peacekeeper Alex, quickly explained.

Misty picked up another rose and twirled it between her thumb and forefinger. "Want to have a girls' night out?"

Stella snorted. "From what I hear, you've been having a girls' night out ever since you had a baby."

"What's that supposed to mean?"

"It means exactly what I said. It's no secret you've been going out every night, while Beam stays at home with your newborn."

Misty stood, jutted out her ample chest, and glared down at Stella, going for intimidation. "Beam chooses to stay at home."

Stella, never one to back down, stood and took Misty on, nose to nose. "He doesn't have a choice. Someone has to be a responsible parent, and that person obviously isn't you."

Stella's sharp comment was an unexpected dart. Out of their group of friends, Misty thought Stella would be the one person to understand her situation. Alex always looked on the bright side—thought everything could be peaches and cream with a little work. But Stella lived in the real world. She, better than anyone, should know Misty had no maternal instincts and would fail miserably. There was no way she could care for an infant. She was barely able to heat a can of soup. Feeding and changing a baby, taking care of its needs was beyond her realm of ability. She had no desire to learn, and no reference to go by if she did.

"I thought you'd understand."

"Ladies," Alex said in a hushed tone. "I have customers out front. Could we keep this conversation between us?"

"I understand perfectly. You're unwilling to accept responsibility," Stella said a little more quietly.

"You don't know anything about the situation."

"I know what I can see with my own eyes," Stella said.

Hurt as she was by Stella, Misty wasn't ready to give up on the fight she had brewing inside. Misty could tell the battle with Stella was lost, so she jabbed a finger at Alex. "You don't get to name the baby."

Alex stopped what she was doing, and faced Misty. "I didn't name your baby, Misty. Beam said you two hadn't decided on a name. Your dad was there, so I asked him what his mother's name was. Beam liked Sophia and decided it fit your daughter. Besides, why would you be against a beautiful name that holds special meaning in your family?

"My grandma died before I was born, so the name doesn't mean anything to me. In fact, it sounds like a throwback from the 1960s. I was thinking Arleen after my mother." Even as she said it, she knew how ludicrous she sounded.

Stella laughed. Loud. "Arleen doesn't sound 1960s at all."

Misty turned on her heel, and stomped out of the shop. She'd changed her mind about a girls' night out. She'd obviously outgrown her childhood friends. She didn't need them anyway. She'd make new friends—friends who would understand her.

Except, she *did* need her friends. They'd been a part of her life since kindergarten. *Without them, I have no one.*

As she drove out of town, loneliness shrouded her like a heavy fog, engulfing her in a depression she'd never experienced before. How had she gotten here and how could she get out? She wanted her old life back, the one she was in command of, rather than the life that was commanding her.

*B*eam sat for a long time after his father-in-law left, contemplating how quickly the direction of life could change. The blink of an eye, a few heartbeats, a couple of words, and everything was different.

The offer Mason made was unbelievably generous, the timing perfect. His father-in-law said he was ready to slow down, had been contemplating retirement. He offered Beam a partnership in his hardware and lumber business. The store was the only one in Eden Falls, and the largest in the area. If Beam was interested, the partnership was his. If not, Mason would put the business up for sale a year from now.

He said he'd be willing to teach Beam the ropes, introduce him to distributors, and help him with the books. After that, he'd want to cut his hours to part-time. When Beam was ready, he could buy Mason out or bring in a partner. Beam knew the hardware and lumber store. He'd worked for Mason his junior and senior years of high school. He was already familiar with the setup of the stockrooms and a lot of the inventory. He had a business degree from Washington State University, but he'd found it more profitable to fly tourists around for someone else rather than start up his own business. He could finally put that degree to use.

If his Seattle home sold for his asking price, he would have the money he'd need to buy into the business. If the Cessna sold for what he expected, he'd have a nice reserve. Mason had done all right for himself for twenty years. He'd brought recent tax returns to show Beam the possibilities. The economy seemed to be improving, and new construction was springing up around the area.

He'd questioned Mason's motives, worried Misty played a part. Mason shook his head, sadness settling on his features. "No, my reasons are purely selfish. I've been toying with the idea of selling for a couple of years now, but my plans solidified when I heard you were staying. I'm not ready to throw the towel into the retirement pool just yet, but I do want to fish more. I want to spend time with my granddaughter. I want to travel. I can't remember the last time I visited my brother in South Dakota. This would keep you and Sophia close, and allow me some self-serving pleasures."

With Mason's offer, more pressure lifted from Beam's shoulders. Mason was willing to give him time for the plane and house to sell, so he'd just have to hope the market was as good as the real estate agent seemed to think.

A cry from the bassinet called for his attention. Beam peeked down at the little arms and legs beating a pattern only his daughter understood. Her plump bottom lip poked out in the most adorable way. He undid the leg snaps of her pants and made a face. "Oh, baby! How can something so cute smell so bad?"

One side of Sophia's mouth crooked up and turned his heart to mush.

He changed his daughter's diaper and held her close, breathing in the lavender powdery scent of soft. Sophia was the best thing to ever happen to him. If someone had told him a year ago he'd be standing in his parent's living room holding his daughter close, he would have laughed until his sides hurt. Now, he couldn't imagine being anywhere else. He opened her fists to examine each tiny finger, ran his enormous knuckles over her velvety cheek, and gave thanks for miracles.

In the kitchen, he put Sophia in the swing at the end of the table, propping her neck and head with blankets. With the oven warming, he pulled the chicken he'd been marinating from the fridge. As he placed the pieces in a shallow pan, his thoughts returned to Misty. After her mother left, she'd been farmed out to surrogate mothers, while her dad struggled with his new business. Would he be repeating history with Sophia?

That possibility was definitely something to think about and would require parental insight.

Misty was already echoing her mother's behavior. If she did pack up and leave them, how could he protect Sophia from the feelings of abandonment Misty still battled? He'd been excited by the prospect of becoming a partner in an already successful business. A job like that would mean he could stay in Eden Falls, make a good living, and keep Sophia close to family. But at what cost? He didn't see going back to flying tourists and placing Sophia in daycare any different. Alex had relied on her mother and in-laws rather than daycare for Charlie, and he was growing up a polite, well-adjusted boy.

As these questions swirled around his head, his parents came through the back door after their day at the gym. His mom took less than a minute to drop what she had in her hands and lift Sophia from the swing, cuddling her close.

"How was she today?"

"She smiled at me."

"Awww." His mother patted his arm.

"That's just gas," his dad said.

"Well, she had just filled a diaper."

His mom flapped at hand. "Everyone says a baby's smile is gas, but I think we have a smart girl here. She's already recognizing her daddy's voice."

Beam slid the pan of chicken in the oven. "I hope you don't mind that I invited Rowdy for dinner. I have some news, and need a family powwow."

Sophia drank a bottle, then fell asleep in her Uncle Rowdy's arms while Beam filled his family in on Mason's offer. The sight of his brother holding a baby was pretty mind-blowing, but most people who knew Beam would be just as surprised to see him carrying a baby around.

"I think buying into Mason's business is the perfect solution," Glenda said.

"I don't trust the offer, but only because I don't trust Misty," Rowdy said.

"Mason said Misty isn't involved in his decision."

"Misty has her nose in everything," Rowdy countered.

They discussed finances for a few minutes, then Beam voiced his concern about the impact it might have on Sophia. He went so far as to mention Misty and the uncertainty of their future together, which caused Rowdy to become even more skeptical.

"You need to buy Mason out now if you can afford it."

Beam lifted Sophia from Rowdy's arms when his voice startled her. He put her on his shoulder and rubbed her back. "He's not ready to retire yet, Rowdy."

"So work around that. Buy him out and keep him on as an employee."

"Mason is a good man," Dawson said. "He wouldn't do anything underhanded. He'd expect Beam to have an attorney look over the contract. That's just good business sense."

"He's a good man with a crazy daughter," Rowdy said under his breath, but loud enough for them all to hear.

Beam couldn't disagree. As much as he loved Misty, she did have some issues. He'd been so excited about the offer, he hadn't stopped to think what him accepting would mean to her. She wanted out of Eden Falls, and would hate that buying into the hardware store and lumberyard would keep them in town. Still, he had to think of what would be best for Sophia, because he wasn't sure Misty would ever come back.

He glanced at Rowdy. "I trust Mason. I've gotten to know him over the last few months, and he'd never do anything to hurt me or Sophia or Misty. He wants to be a part of Sophia's life. This would keep her close, but I don't think that's the only reason he's offering."

"The hardware store and lumberyard will be a good income, son," Dawson said. "Mason struggled to get that place up and running, and he's done a good job. Once the place was established, he became a very sharp businessman. He's trusted and well liked in this community, with residents and contractors alike. You won't have to put in the hours of work he did, so it shouldn't affect Sophia like it did Misty. She got a double whammy with her dad just buying the business and her mother leaving soon after."

Glenda stood to clear the table. "Speaking of Misty, what does she think about all of this?"

Beam shook his head. "I imagine Mason discussed it with her, but he didn't mention it."

"Have you even heard from her?" Rowdy asked.

"No." But he couldn't let her take all the blame. "I haven't called her either. The phone works both ways."

Rowdy pushed back from the table. "What mother doesn't want to have anything to do with her baby?"

"Don't judge, Rowdy," Glenda said. "We don't know what's going on with Misty. Maybe she just doesn't know how to take care of a baby."

Rowdy pointed at Beam. "You think Beam did? He hasn't been around an infant since Charlie was born six years ago."

"I know that," Glenda said patiently. "But Misty has other things going on, personal things you wouldn't understand, because you always had me and your dad."

Rowdy planted his hands on the table. "Misty has been using her mother leaving as her excuse for everything for as long as I can remember."

Dawson also pushed up from the table. "Not everyone is maternal. Maybe she's just scared. We have to give Misty the benefit of the doubt and hope she comes around."

"I'll bet most new parents are scared at first." Rowdy shook his head hard enough that his long hair tied at the nape of his neck flipped over one shoulder. "I haven't said anything, bro, because I love you and I'd do just about anything for you, but I just don't get what you see in that lunatic."

"Let it go, Rowdy," Beam said in a tone he knew his brother understood.

"They sure have a lot more books and resources now than they did when you two were born. Your mother and I had to wing it," Dawson said in an attempt to lighten the mood.

"The first seventy-two hours was trial and error for me. I'm sure Sophia and I will both be learning as we go along." Beam moved his now sleeping daughter to the crook of his arm. "I'm not going to push Misty. She might need a little time to come to terms with the idea of being a mother. She may never come around. Things have a way of working themselves out in the end. Whether Misty is a mother to Sophia or not, I'll be the best dad I can be. I'll make sure she never feels unloved or unwanted."

Beam knew Rowdy wasn't a fan of Misty's, but he wasn't sure how his parents felt. They allowed their sons to make their own mistakes, and only expressed their opinions when asked. They probably wished he'd chosen differently, but the heart doesn't always allow you to make the choice.

Rowdy stroked his niece's head. "So, what are you going to do?"

Beam spoke the only word that came to mind. "Wait."

CHAPTER 6

Misty decided it was time to drive to Seattle and check in with Beam. He'd moved out of her dad's house three weeks earlier, so he and the baby should be settled in at home by now. If she knew Beam, he'd have a routine in place and a nanny hired, so she could go about the business of leasing property and setting up her salon.

Still, she'd expected Beam to call and he hadn't, which was so unlike him. He always called.

She was sure he had been meticulous in picking a nanny. Misty just hoped the woman cleaned house, and was as sweet as Alice Garrett had been to her when she was little.

A dream she'd had a week ago still plagued her. She'd been holding the baby, running a finger over her cheek. The baby smiled sweetly. If possible she was more beautiful than the last time Misty had seen her. Suddenly, she was five or six and looked exactly like Misty had at that age. She whispered, "I love you, mommy." Then she squirmed to break free of Misty's grasp, even as Misty tightened her grip. Misty opened her mouth to speak, but the words stuck in her throat. She wanted to tell Sophia she was sorry, that she didn't know how to be a mother. She wanted to tell the innocent little girl not to hold onto dreams, because they never came true. She tried to hang on, but Sophia struggled until she got away. She ran straight into Beam's waiting arms. He'd hugged her close and turned an accusing glare on Misty. When Misty looked past him, the whole town stood behind him.

She woke with a start and tears on her face. For several nights after that, she was terrified to shut her eyes. When she did fall asleep, she awoke in a sweat.

Now, thoughts of the baby wove their way through her mind at all times of the day and night. No amount of pushing them back worked. Misty wondered how much she'd changed, if her black flyaway hair was longer now. She thought about the baby's tiny fingers, her dimpled knees, and her puckered lips when she was sleeping. Did she cry a lot? Did she smile? Was she fussy, or was she sweet natured?

The idea of seeing Sophia today had Misty's heart pounding with anxiety.

To keep her mind off Beam and the baby as she drove, she made a mental list of things she'd need to do first thing tomorrow. A reliable real estate agent was at the top of her list. The property for the salon had to be in an upscale area of Seattle—that point wasn't negotiable. She was impatient to know when she could expect the money from Beam. The real estate agent would have to know that amount before she could start looking.

She'd have to shop around for a reputable contractor for any needed renovations. Her dad could probably provide a few names. Best scenario would be to find a struggling salon or spa with an established clientele. She could mosey in and make an offer they'd be insane to refuse. That situation would be the ultimate.

Next on her list would be advertising for salon techs, manicurists, and estheticians, maybe a masseuse if space were sufficient. She'd hire an ad agency to come up with a catchy phrase or a fun jingle, something people would hear, remember, and sing along with.

She was so deep in thought, entering Seattle's city limits was a surprise. The light snow that had been falling in Eden Falls had turned to a cold, drizzling rain. She made a right turn onto their street and a left into the driveway, past a silver Lexus. She didn't know anyone who drove a Lexus. She pressed the button on the garage door opener. Nothing happened. She pressed it, again. *Great! Guess I'm getting wet.*

She slid from behind the wheel, leaving her suitcase in the trunk for Beam. At the front door she stopped. *What the heck?* There was some kind of box on the knob. She twisted the handle and the door opened.

Inside, she shed her coat and turned to drop it on the chair beside the door, but the chair was gone. In fact, the whole living room was set up differently. The sofa was against the wall and only one end table remained. The large picture of her and Beam next to their wedding cake that hung over the fireplace had been replaced by the mountain scene that used to be in the den. A small vase of fresh flowers sat on the coffee table, and her magazines were gone.

She walked down the short hall to the den. The pictures of Beam and his family were missing. Furniture had been moved around, and the corner that held Beam's desk was empty. The kitchen was spotless. Another vase of flowers sat on the kitchen table.

Then she heard a female's voice float down the stairs. A soft laugh followed. Anger clouded her vision and sent a tingle that started along her scalp zinging down her spine. *Oh, no, he better not have another woman in my house.*

She stomped up the stairs, fury leading the way. *Beam is going to be...* She came to an abrupt halt at the first bedroom. The baby's crib, dresser, and changing table were gone. The walls Beam had painted a soft pink were now cream.

"Hi!" said a friendly voice. A woman with short blonde hair and red-framed glasses leaned from the master bedroom doorway. "Can I help you?"

"You can tell me what you're doing in my house. Where is the baby's furniture?"

The woman's expression went from friendly to alarmed in a split second. She stepped into the hallway and shuffled through a stack of papers she held. "I'm so sorry. I was led to believe the owners had moved out."

"You were led wrong. I am the owner. And I never moved out." Misty moved forward, hands fisted at her sides. "Now, get out of my house."

"Of course. I am so sorry." The woman disappeared into the master bedroom, and Misty could hear her apologizing profusely to whoever was in there with her. She reappeared followed by a man and a woman. "I'm very sorry for the intrusion," said the first woman, completely red-faced, as the three filed past.

She waited until she heard the front door close before going into the master bedroom. The furniture was still there, but the closet was bare, the drawers in the dresser were empty. The master bath was completely cleaned out except for the towels hanging, decorator style, on the racks.

Have I fallen over the edge into insanity?

The universe waved.

Running down the stairs to the kitchen, she checked the pantry, pulled drawers open. Everything was gone.

She grabbed her purse from the counter and dug around in the depths for her cell. Before she could scroll to Beam's number, the phone rang. Beam was finally calling her.

"What is going on?" she shrieked when she connected the call. "There are strangers in our house. All my clothes are gone."

"I have all your things here in Eden Falls, Misty. I should have given the boxes to your dad when he was over the other day, but forgot."

"What are you talking about? Why are my clothes in boxes? And why are the boxes in Eden Falls?" She put a hand to her throat in an attempt to relieve the tightness that threatened to strangle.

"I put the house up for sale. Obviously, you didn't notice the sign."

"What do you mean you put the house up for sale?" She ran to the front window. Sure enough, there was a sign in the yard.

"I mean I put the house up for sale."

Confusion and panic fought to the forefront, waging war against the simmering fury. "Why would you do that? When were you going to tell me?"

"When you called."

The tingling from earlier moved down her arms into her fingers. "You were supposed to call me. You always call."

"I wasn't aware there were rules, Misty."

She sank onto the living room sofa. "Why did you put the house up for sale, Beam? Where are we going to live?"

"Sophia and I are moving into Alex's rental as soon as Colton moves out."

She jumped back to her feet. "What are you talking about? We live in Seattle."

"I'm moving back to Eden Falls. I think Sophia should be around—"

"Stop calling her that!" She stomped across the room and back again. She was sure everything would go back to normal as soon as she gave birth, but the nightmare she'd been living for the last nine months was growing worse. "I can't move back to Eden Falls, and even if I did, I'd never move into that cracker box Alex rents out."

"I said *Sophia and I* are moving into Alex's rental."

His words stunned her, like the sting of a bee zinging up her arm. Did he mean she wasn't included? Her jaw grew numb. Like her mother, her husband was abandoning her. "What about me? Where am I supposed to live?"

"That's up to you, Misty. I'll take your boxes to your dad's this afternoon. I should have done it earlier."

Alex and Colton were in Seattle, along with Dawson and Glenda. They all came with Beam to pack her house up and no one had told her. Who else had been here? Did everyone in Eden Falls know but her?

"Misty, the woman you just ran out of the house is a real estate agent. I told her I'd call her back. The clients she had in the house are very interested." He cleared his throat. "You'll have to leave, so they can come back inside."

She disconnected the call and threw her phone to the floor hard enough that it bounced in the beige carpet. Fury won the battle, surging through her, igniting every nerve ending. *Beam has lost his mind.*

The five-hour round trip, which turned into six because of the bad weather, was miserable. By the time Misty pulled into her dad's driveway, foul didn't begin to describe her mood. How could Beam do this to her? The whole situation was unthinkable. To sell their Seattle house made no sense. No matter how she replayed the scenario through her brain, she couldn't comprehend why he would do such a thing.

To top off his insanity, Beam said he was moving into Alex's rental. The place was tiny! And moving to Eden Falls would mean he'd have to fly into Seattle every morning for work. The only bright side of this whole mess, at least she could catch a ride into Seattle with him.

Why? Why? The question spun through her mind like an out of control tilt-a-whirl making her dizzy. She called him several times on her return trip to Eden Falls. The calls went straight to voicemail, which infuriated her further.

Alex lit up her phone twice on the drive back to Eden Falls, but Misty ignored the calls. She had no desire to discuss anything with Alex, until she'd straightened this mess out with Beam.

She slammed the backdoor closed as she entered the dark kitchen. Not even the light over the stove was on. A slight movement to her left startled her and she whipped around with a hand to her heart. "Stop lurking. This is the second time you've scared me half to death."

Her dad reached for the light switch and illuminated the room. "I'm sorry. I heard you pull up and came down to talk to you."

In her agitated state, her dad's calm voice was like fingernails on a chalkboard. She slashed her hand through the air. "Not tonight. I've had a rotten day. I drove all the way to Seattle, only to discover Beam put the house up for sale and didn't think that little tidbit of information was important enough to tell me." When her father didn't respond, she turned and studied his expression. "You knew about this?"

He pulled out a chair at the kitchen table. "Have a seat. We need to talk."

She eyed him suspiciously as she dropped into the chair. Her father, who was a somber human being, was acting even more so tonight. He pulled out another chair and sat across from her. "If you knew, why didn't you tell me?"

Mason leaned his forearms on the table. She studied him under the harsh lights. Gray strands wove their way through his curly dark hair. Surprisingly, the color was complementary, even as worn and tired as he looked. The wrinkles around his brown eyes and along his forehead seemed deeper. When had age started its slow march across his face without her noticing?

"If you lived with your husband, you'd know why Beam is selling the house."

She slammed a hand on the table. "He's the one who moved out."

Mason pressed his lips together in a tight line of tension, and Misty wondered for the first time in her life, what his yelling voice sounded like. In all her growing up years, she'd never heard him use it. Did he ever yell at work when a shipment wasn't delivered on time or the wrong parts were ordered? Somehow, she knew he didn't and suddenly, she wanted him to yell. She wanted to hear him vent his frustrations aloud.

"He left because you weren't acting like a wife or a mother," he said in his patient, fatherly tone instead.

"Well, gosh, I'm sorry. Having not had one, I'm not sure what a mother acts like."

"You've had plenty of good examples growing up to know what a mother acts like. Alice Garrett has treated you as if you were one of her own since you started kindergarten."

"Alice Garrett is Alex's mom—not mine. It's not fair of you to compare Alice to having a mother here at home."

"This conversation isn't about Alice Garrett or your mom. It's about you. You've done nothing to take care of Sophia. Beam is doing everything on his own, and he needs your help. Misty, your daughter needs you."

She slumped back in her chair. "Yeah, well, I needed a mother, too."

"It's time you moved past your mother's abandonment."

Her dad removed his glasses and rubbed the bridge of his nose between thumb and forefinger for a long moment. "I know her leaving was tragic. I know it hurt you deeply. I know you blame me, and maybe I am partly to blame, but—"

"Partly?" Even as she said it, she knew it wasn't fair to heap all the blame on her dad. Ever since having the baby, she was feeling more and more certain that her own birth was probably the cause of her mother's disappearance. The niggling thought wasn't something she could share with anyone. She was barely able to admit it to herself. The uncertain knowledge squeezed the empty cavern in her chest, the place where her heart should be located.

"It's time you stop using your mom's absence as an excuse for your bad behavior. The past is just that—the past. Let it go and move on."

Misty frowned. Telling her to forget her mother's abandonment was like telling her to close the book she'd been reading since she was six without finishing the last chapter. Her dad was asking the impossible.

"Your mom left a long time ago, and it broke your heart. Why would you do the same thing to Sophia? Don't you see you're repeating history? Sophia needs her mother."

"Her name is *not* Sophia."

Mason replaced his glasses. "We're not discussing the baby's name right now. We're—"

"I'm discussing it. No one asked me and I'm her mother. You can't just name my baby without discussing it with me!"

Mason sighed in resignation, and Misty wanted to pat her back in triumph. The universe had been moving against her for a long time now, but on this subject, she would get her way.

"Your daughter's name is Sophia. You weren't around to say differently, so Beam made the decision and had Sophia Marie Garrett put on her birth certificate. It's official."

Misty felt her small victory leak out and pool on the floor. Not to be defeated, she took a deep breath and straightened her back with renewed resolve. "I'll have it changed."

"No, you won't."

She opened her mouth to tell him exactly what she thought of his declaration, but he held up a hand.

"There's more you should know. I've offered Beam a partnership in the hardware store. It will give him a good living here in Eden Falls and he—"

She slammed both hands on the table. "What are you talking about? Beam has a job in Seattle, and I don't want to live in Eden Falls. He knows I hate it here!"

Mason reached out and took one of her hands, enveloping it in his. He never touched her. She made sure of it. At this moment though, his rough, callused hands felt oddly warm and comforting. As much as she wanted to pull away, if only to hurt him, she didn't.

"What is it you want, Misty?" His gaze searched her face as if he was looking deep inside, past her heart, into her soul. "Please, tell me what will make you happy, because I can't find it on my own. I've tried. Tell me what I can do to help you be happy."

Unexpectedly, her eyes filled with tears. She tried to blink them back to no avail. Crying was a weakness she didn't allow herself. Ever since having the baby, she felt on the verge of tears all the time. She summoned anger to cover the weakness. "I want my mother. If you hadn't run her off, my life would be completely different."

"Your mother chose to leave because—"

"Because she hated this small town." Misty pulled her hand from her father's grasp and swiped at the wet under her eyes. "She hated the lumberyard you bought. She hated the thought of owning a hardware store. She hated everything about Eden Falls. She was above this kind of life. She was vibrant and beautiful, and this place suffocated her."

Her dad blew out a breath, then he sat back in his chair. "Your mother lives in Sacramento, and has for years. Her last name is Honeywell."

"What?" She squinted through her tears. "You've known where my mom was all this time and didn't tell me?"

Defeat settled over her dad's face, moved into the cracks and crevices around his eyes and mouth. In that heartbeat of time, he looked ten years older. "That's the way she wanted it."

"The way she…" The words were too harsh to repeat. "Is she remarried?"

"No. After our divorce, she never remarried. Honeywell is her maiden name."

"Arleen Honeywell," Misty said reverently, looking down at the table. Her mom was Arleen Honeywell and she lived in Sacramento, California, a mere… "Why didn't she…?" Again, Misty stopped. She didn't want to know why her mother lived so close and yet had never been in touch or come to visit. Better to believe her mother never came back because of Mason and Eden Falls.

Mason got to his feet and pushed the chair under the table. He walked to the foot of the stairs, but turned back. His eyes filled with more determination than she'd ever seen "I'm done supporting you, Misty. You have three weeks to get a job. You can live here rent free for two months, then I'll expect three hundred dollars rent each month."

Misty stared at her father a moment before laughter bubbled up and over. This was all too much insanity to comprehend. Her dad was bringing Beam into the hardware and lumber store as a partner, had known all along where her mom was, and was expecting her to pay rent. "You've got to be kidding."

"I'm not kidding. It's past time you grew up. If you plan on living in this house, you will pay rent and contribute to the grocery bill."

After he disappeared up the stairs, she grabbed her keys and headed out the door.

CHAPTER 7

Misty woke mid-morning, dull headed and bleary eyed. She hadn't left her bed all day yesterday, mad at the world. After walking into Rowdy's two nights earlier and seeing all her so-called friends sitting around a table having a great time, and knowing she wasn't invited, had shoved her into a funk, and she couldn't seem to pull herself out. She'd been tempted to walk up and let them know what she thought, but the day's revelations had been too much. Between Beam selling their Seattle house, finding out her mother lived in Sacramento, and her dad's insanity about charging rent, her friends' betrayals were just the sprinkles on the ice cream sundae the universe was serving up. She'd walked right back out.

Her first impulse this morning was to stay in bed for life. Her second was to jump in the car and drive to Sacramento to find her mom. Her dad's words, "That's the way she wanted it," still felt very heavy on her shoulders and bruised her raw heart.

With so much information exploding like fireworks, shooting her thoughts in a million different directions, she needed someone calm to talk to, someone who could help her make sense of her life. Alex had always been her go-to person, but talking to her about any of this was impossible. After their conversation at Pretty Posies, she knew Stella wasn't going to help her. Jillian had never been that close of a friend, and Jolie was even less so. Her father was unsympathetic to her plight. As was Beam. She mentally ticked people off her list, and became more depressed. Was there no one who could help her?

Suddenly, she thought of Alice Garrett. Growing up, Alice had been like a second mom to her. She'd spent more time in the Garrett's kitchen than in her own. Alice would offer wise advice without judgment. She would also keep their conversation confidential.

After a quick shower, Misty shimmied into a pair of leggings and a long blousy top. Before her pregnancy, she never left the house unless dressed completely chic, her hair and make-up flawless. Lately, she was lucky to get a shower.

She drove to the Garrett house with her hair still wet, hoping Alice was home and, more importantly, alone. A cold front had dropped down from the north overnight and the temperature was barely double digit. *Cold enough to freeze my nostril hairs, but too cold to snow.*

She watched a puff of breath that seemed to freeze in place as she waited for someone to answer her knock on the back door. Alice was obviously busy, so she turned the knob and stepped inside. How many times had she and Alex raced for this door? She had the longer legs, but Alex was like the cartoon Roadrunner, always a step ahead. Same as life now. Alex always came out the winner.

The Garrett's kitchen still felt as welcoming as it had when she was a child. Alice was halfway across the room carrying something in her arms. When she spotted the tuft of black hair, Misty realized Alice was holding her baby.

"Misty," Alice said in surprise, but recovered quickly, a welcoming smile creasing her cheeks and crinkling the corners of her eyes. "Come in, honey. How are you?"

"I..." Misty's glance jumped from the baby, who was making cooing sounds, to Alice. Then back to the baby. To her daughter. Sophia.

Alice set a bottle on the table. "It's so cold out. Would you like a cup of hot cocoa? I have those mini-marshmallows you used to love."

Frozen in place, Misty was vaguely aware of the open door behind her, or the cold sweeping into the warm room, swirling around her legs like a mini tornado. "No, I needed... Uh, I was wondering if we could talk, but I see you're busy."

"No, hon, I'm never too busy for a talk." Alice held out her free hand. "Would you like to see Sophia this morning? She's all bathed and fed. We were just having a little conversation before naptime."

Misty couldn't stop her glance from bouncing back and forth between Alice and the baby. She had changed so much since Misty had last seen her. Her eyes were open and alert. And blue. Misty's knees began to tremble, and she couldn't seem to suck air into her lungs. She tipped her head toward the baby. "Why...?"

"Beam is running a few errands and didn't want Sophia out in this cold. Glenda and Dawson both had to be at the gym early." Alice wiggled her fingers. "Come in, honey. Let me put this cutie down and we'll go into the living room for a nice chat. I haven't seen you since the party on New Year's Eve."

"I...uh..." Misty's voice cracked and she cleared her throat. "I...I have to—" She turned and bolted through the door, not looking back when Alice called her name.

She jumped in her car and pulled out of the driveway without a backward glance. What had she been thinking?

Alice wouldn't understand. She'd side with Alex and Beam—they were family.

What she had to do was get her money from Beam and head back to Seattle. Beam couldn't sell the house out from under her. She was part owner. She had a marriage certificate to prove it. She'd move back in, get her money, and set up a salon in Seattle, just as she'd planned since their wedding. Or she could move to Sacramento. All she needed was the money Beam had promised.

She pulled over to the side of the road and swiped at the tears blurring her vision. Her phone vibrated and she pulled it from her purse. A missed call and voicemail from Alex. Had Alice already called her?

She scrolled to Beam's number.

$\sim$

*W*alking through Douglas Hardware and Lumber was surreal for Beam. He'd been here hundreds of times over the years. He'd always liked the orderliness, the tangy smell of steel, the sweet scent of wood. The layout of both the hardware store and the lumberyard were familiar to him and his father. He learned early in life, Garrett men didn't call a guy when something needed fixing. They read manuals, and researched, until they could fix it themselves. It wasn't often that between him, Dawson, Denny, JT, or Rowdy, they couldn't figure it out.

While he followed Mason and his dad down the isles, he took notes and asked questions. Mason said he was open to any suggestions Beam could offer. Not much had changed since Mason opened the doors almost thirty years earlier. Most people probably appreciated that. They could go right to the department and get what they needed without searching.

Still, a few items might sell better if placed in a new area of the store.

When they headed into the receiving area, Beam's phone vibrated in his pocket. He read the text under Misty's name.

We need to talk.

"I have to take this. It's Misty."

With a nod, Mason and Dawson continued into the back room.

Ok.

NOW!

They'd barely spoken since their daughter's birth, and this text didn't even ask how she was. It just demanded—as was Misty's style—which irritated him. What irritated him even further was that he cared enough to respond.

Now won't work. I'll meet you at your dad's in an hour.

One day, she'll have to accept the world doesn't revolve around her. He pocketed his phone and rejoined the other two men.

~

*M*isty paced the kitchen until she heard Beam's truck. Without success, she tried to calm her pounding heart. *I'm just eager to get my business up and running. This has nothing to do with seeing Beam.*

After he agreed to meet her, she'd taken the time apply make-up, fix her hair, and change her shirt. Still, she positioned herself behind the kitchen island so he wouldn't see the fat hanging over the waistband of her leggings.

His silhouette appeared through the curtain on the back door before he knocked. She hadn't thought of that. Since he'd moved out, he probably didn't feel it was his right to walk in. "Come in."

He rattled the knob. With a "phfttt" of frustration, Misty

realized the door was locked. She un-positioned herself, and pulled the door open.

Beam wore a Sherpa-lined, brown suede coat. His cheeks and chin were clean-shaven, his blond hair cut short, and he took her breath away. She hadn't really paid much attention to his appearance since their wedding. Now that she thought back, he'd exchanged his mountain man look for that of a respectable businessman…or father. His mossy green eyes connected with hers and her belly flip-flopped.

She wanted to exude an assertiveness she wasn't feeling. She used to carry herself with confidence, be so self-assured. Now, she was overweight and insecure.

"Hi," he said.

His lips induced memories of his kisses. He was a great kisser. He could… She squashed the sensations ricocheting through her system, hoping her face didn't reveal too much. Misty opened the door wider. "Come in," she said, attempting a cool monotone.

Beam stepped into the kitchen, his eyes moving over her body. And just like that, she felt feminine and desirable for the first time in months. She basked in the sensation.

He grinned as if he knew exactly what his glance had invoked.

"Let's talk in the living room."

"Okay," he said without hesitation. He shut the door, peeled off his coat, and hung it by the back door. The movement mixed his cold outdoor scent, and the cologne he wore, which awakened a thrum low in her belly. She put a hand to her stomach to squelch the sensation. *There will be no thrumming today.*

"You look good," he said as he followed her down the short hallway.

Liar. Was he trying to seduce her into forgetfulness? *Not going to happen, Bub.* Still, she should have let him lead the way, so he wasn't looking at the wide load she was carrying.

She sat in a wingback chair and tried to pull her feet up under her, but the extra weight wouldn't allow it, so she put her feet back on the floor.

He sat on the sofa and hung an arm over the back like a big open invitation. *Come sit by me, baby.* He was trying to seduce her! Well, even if she was inclined—which she wasn't —it was too soon after the baby. Besides, she reminded herself with a shake of her head, this was strictly a business meeting. *Take command of the situation. You are in control.* She swallowed. "We need to talk."

His smile was filled with smug Garrett self-assurance. "That's why I'm here, Misty. What would you like to talk about?"

She started to pull her feet up again, remembered she couldn't, and shifted in her chair. The best way to broach the subject was to just spit it out. "You promised, once the baby was born, you'd give me money to open my own salon."

"You're right, I did."

That was easy. Satisfaction produced a smug smile.

"But there were stipulations."

She lost her smile. He had put stipulations on everything before their wedding day, but she couldn't remember the ones concerning the salon. "What stipulations?"

He crossed an ankle over the opposite knee. "I said I would set you up in your own salon once the baby was born, but only if we stayed married."

"So." She fluttered a hand. "We're still married."

"And living together," he said, emphasizing each word.

She shrugged. "So, we'll live together."

"As husband and wife."

She slapped her hands down on the arms of the chair. "You're being ridiculous."

"I think I'm being reasonable. I'm not going to sleep in a separate room from my wife."

"But you know I don't love you. Why would you want to live like that?"

His confident expression slipped when her hurtful words hit their mark. He stood. "I don't. I'll have Owen Danielson draw up divorce papers."

She jumped up and chased after him as he walked down the hall toward the kitchen. "You owe me a salon."

He pulled his coat from the hook by the door and slipped it on. His masculine scent assaulted her again. "I don't owe you anything, Misty. The pre-nup you had me sign before our wedding says so. What's yours is yours and what's mine is mine."

At her insistence, Beam signed the pre-nup she'd had her dad's attorney draw up to prevent him from getting his hands on her inheritance. Total waste, since her dad was selling half of her inheritance to him anyway.

His eyes lingered on her face a moment before moving down her body. "It was good to see you, baby. Take care of yourself."

He left the door standing wide open as he jogged down the back steps and across the driveway to his truck, no doubt hoping she'd come running after him. He'd be waiting a long time before that happened. She slammed the door with such force the window cracked.

Fabulous.

What was she supposed to do now? Going back to Dahlia's with her tail between her legs wasn't an option. She'd laughed her way out of that place, promising she'd only be back to have her own hair and nails done.

She stalked back into the living room and watched Beam back into the circular drive. As he shifted into first, he didn't even glance at the house to see if she was watching.

~

A week later, Misty stared at the attorney in front of her, certain he was speaking a foreign language. She heard the words coming from his mouth, but what he was saying had to be wrong.

Leonard Royce was supposed to be a genius in a court-room. She'd made an appointment with him because his name floated around Dahlia's Salon, where her clients talked as freely as if she were a bartender. Anyone who mentioned his name said, Leonard was the man to have on your side if you wanted to win. And this was a battle she had to win. She'd gathered all the necessary paperwork and faxed it ahead of their meeting in his Seattle office. She'd barely sat down, when he started speaking nonsensical gibberish.

"I'm afraid you can't fight this, Mrs. Garrett. This prenuptial agreement was drawn up, signed, and dated accu-rately. There is nothing I can do for you."

"You don't understand. There has to be a mistake some-where in that agreement, a loophole." She shifted forward in the exact type of luxurious leather chair she planned to buy for her salon's office. "In the movies, there are always loopholes."

Mr. Royce rested his hands on her pile of papers. His fingernails were buffed to a polished sheen. Misty had never seen a mature man—or any man for that matter—with such shiny nails. He was tall and thin with thick silver hair, and held himself in a way that emitted wealth. Even the black-framed glasses perched on his nose looked expensive. Breathing the same air would cost her hundreds. "Unfortu-nately, Mrs. Garrett, this is real life."

"You need to read it again. Please," she said with hope her plea might somehow change the situation.

"There are no loopholes." His smile was indulgent, as

though he was dealing with a child too dim to understand his words, which was exactly how she felt at the moment. "Frankly, I'm confused as to why you're looking for any. You said your father's attorney at your request drew up this document. Have you discovered some undisclosed treasure your husband is hiding from you?"

Was he insinuating she was some money grubbing floozy? This was Beam Garrett they were talking about. So no, there was no hidden treasure. She bit back an angry retort that would get her nowhere. "Before our wedding, my fiancé promised to finance a salon for me, and now he's backed out of that agreement. I just want what is rightfully mine. He promised."

Mr. Royce tapped the papers sitting in front of him with an index finger. "I didn't see that agreement in the papers you faxed over. Did you bring it with you?"

"It was a verbal agreement."

"A verbal agreement isn't binding in court. Your husband's attorney would call it hearsay, because there is no proof. A game of he-said, she-said." He picked up an errant pen and placed it in a leather tray next to the blotter on his desktop. "Did someone witness the agreement between you and your husband?"

"No."

"Nothing was documented," Mr. Royce stated rather than asked.

"I told you it was a verbal agreement. He promised he would give me the money. I expected him to follow through, and he hasn't."

He held out his hands, palms up. She had her answer.

After leaving the attorney's office, $450 poorer, she headed to the nearest department store. Alex's wedding was five days away and she had nothing to wear. As she searched the racks, a cobalt blue lace dress immediately caught her attention. It would enhance the blue of her eyes and the style would hide her overweight flaws. She took a size ten into the dressing room, sent a salesclerk back for a twelve, and finally got a fourteen zipped up.

At the register, the salesclerk ran her credit card, and then glanced up with hooded eyes. "I'm sorry, but your card was declined."

Misty shook her head. "That's impossible. Try again."

The girl pushed a button and slid the card through the machine. They both waited in silence until the machine beeped. The girl bit her lip. "I'm sorry."

Misty pulled another card from her wallet. A moment later, the girl was shaking her head. "You've got to be kidding me. Something must be wrong with your machine."

Another clerk stepped over. "Is there a problem?"

"Yes. Incompetent help."

The second woman looked at the first who held up the credit card. "It's been declined." The second clerk swiped the card, and they waited. A beep sounded and she said, "I'm sorry, but it has been declined."

Misty stormed to her car while shooting a text to Beam.

What's wrong with my credit cards?

His response took forever.

If you mean my credit cards, I closed those accounts.

Why?????

Because they were MY cards.

She threw her phone to the floor of the car and pounded the steering wheel with both fists. *Why didn't you add a clause about the salon in the pre-nup? Because Beam rushed me. It's his fault that I'm in this mess. I was under the stress of planning a quick wedding and he took advantage.*

Misty's goal had been to outshine any wedding ever held in Eden Falls. She wanted a buffet spread that would be discussed for weeks after the event. She wanted people talking about how gorgeous the flowers were. "No, I didn't use Alex. Pretty Posies isn't the only florist in the area." The band was flown in from Seattle, and a five-tiered wedding cake was designed specifically for her. She wore a custom made dress that had cost her dad thousands.

At the time, the pre-nup was a distant second on her list of concerns. She wanted something drawn up and signed before she walked down the aisle. She wanted the assurance Beam would get nothing of hers when their marriage ended.

Joke was on her. Because of her dad, Beam would get everything.

Beam and her dad had to be working together to drive her insane. But they wouldn't win. She would not break. Leaning her head back on the seat, she tried to clear her mind. *Stay calm and think.*

When she finally got home, her dad was sitting at the kitchen table, a plate of spaghetti in front of him. The smile he offered was as weak as he was. If he were strong, he would have gone to any lengths necessary to find his wife and bring her home. No. What he should have done—what they should have done—was follow Arleen to Sacramento. If she'd been so unhappy here, they should have found a place where they could all be happy together.

Just the sight of him churned her stomach in disgust.

She fought the urge to stomp up the stairs. As bad as she wanted to be away from him, she wanted answers worse. She pulled out a chair and sat down heavily. "Why did you sell out to Beam?"

Mason pulled his glasses from his nose, folded them, and set them near his elbow. Then he pushed his plate back, and cleared his throat. She wanted to slam her hands on the table to get his attention. She wanted to reach out and slap him for all the hurt he'd caused her.

Finally, he raised his eyes to meet hers. "It's a partnership,

Misty. I didn't sell out to him. Beam wants to stay in Eden Falls. He wants to give Sophia a chance to grow up near family. I thought it would be a good investment for him, and a good solution for me."

She frowned. "A solution for you?"

Mason rested his hands on the table. "I've been thinking of retiring for a couple of years. By the time Beam learns the business and gets the place organized the way he wants, I'll be ready. That will give him time to get the money to buy the business, or find another partner to buy me out. I'm not in any hurry, but I am ready to work fewer hours and travel a bit. Enjoy time with my granddaughter."

She leaned forward. "But why Beam?"

"Why not Beam? If he wasn't interested, I'd be selling to a stranger next spring. Why not keep the business in the family?"

"Because he's using all his money to buy this business. He promised to set me up in my own salon after the baby was born, and he's not keeping his promise."

Mason tapped his fingertips together. "I'm sure there's more to the story."

Her poisonous anger resurfaced. "You think I'm lying?"

"No." His gaze held hers for a long moment. "I think you're not telling the whole truth."

"So you trust Beam over your own daughter?"

"That's not what I said, Misty."

"It's what you implied."

"You're twisting my words to fuel your anger."

She stood and slammed the chair into the table, knocking Mason's glass of milk over, before stomping up the stairs to her room.

~

*M*ason heard Misty leave the house an hour later, and decided to do the same. Driving was something he enjoyed and did often, once Misty moved into her own place. He took back roads, listening to Reba McEntire and George Strait, trying to unwind and make sense of life. The air felt balmy after the bitter freeze that had gripped the area finally moved east.

About thirty miles out of town, he pulled over at a lookout, and watched the Columbia River moving under the moonlight. This had been his fishing spot before he got married. He'd brought Arleen here with him a couple of times, but nature wasn't her thing. Spending money had been her thing. And lying. Lying had definitely been her thing.

He'd been so ignorant back then, and so astonished that a beautiful woman like Arleen would be interested in someone like him. Only, she wasn't interested, or a woman—just a girl who'd been forced to grow up too quickly. She compensated by looking for a man who could provide her with a better life than she could make on her own, working in a greasy spoon.

He often wondered what would have become of Misty if he hadn't come along. Would she have ended up in foster care, a ward of the state? Arleen was barely able to take care of herself. She proved, by leaving, that she had no interest in being a mother.

He was probably wrong to tell Misty where Arleen was. And that it was Arleen's decision to keep Misty in the dark, but it was time Misty accepted facts. Living with hopes and dreams was fine until they overtook reality.

Arleen left them long before she actually got in the car and drove away. The only time he ever heard from her was when she was desperate for money. The times she did call, she never asked how he or Misty were doing, and he never offered the information. If she knew how the lumberyard and the number of contractors he supplied had grown, or how well he'd invested, she would be calling much more often. In fact, she'd probably show up on his doorstep, which would only hurt Misty so much more, because Arleen wouldn't stay. She'd just bleed them both financially and mentally dry, and leave again.

He got out and leaned against the hood of his car. The night was clear and the sky filled with a million stars. Loneliness settled over him like an old friend. He'd tried to date over the years, but it never worked out. His concerns over Misty's insecurities were too heightened after her mom's abandonment. He knew his daughter well enough to know the trouble she would cause if he became serious with another woman. She would feel he was defiling her mother's memory. Misty wouldn't have shared their home, the place she believed her mother would come back to, with anyone else.

He was as guilty as Misty in allowing her to use her mother's leaving as an excuse for her bad behavior. He'd let so much slide to counterbalance a sad little girl's disappointments. Now Misty, Beam, and Sophia were suffering for his mistakes, and he didn't know if it was possible to fix the situation. He stood there in the cold for a long time, working things out in his mind, and wishing he had someone he could talk to.

CHAPTER 8

Beam arrived at Alex and Colton's wedding with a sleeping beauty in his arms. He hoped she stay that way through the ceremony but wasn't optimistic. She looked adorable in a dress the same color as her blue eyes. A blue and white elastic headband was his attempt at keeping her feathery black hair at bay.

At four weeks old, she'd developed quite a personality, displaying a feisty attitude when she was hungry or wanted attention. Kind of like her mother.

Rowdy shouldered his way through the crowd congregating in the foyer of the church and held out his hands. The action amused Beam. Tiny Sophia had intimidated her big, rowdy uncle at first. Now, he just tucked her into the crook of his arm like a football.

"She's asleep."

Rowdy frowned and wiggled his fingers. "I'll carry her quietly. Do you have any idea what a chick magnet this little cricket is?"

Beam raised an eyebrow as he shifted Sophia into his

brother's arms, trying not to jostle her. "You're using my daughter to pick up women?"

"Absolutely," Rowdy replied with his crooked grin. He straightened her dress, and then strolled into the middle of a group of females who immediately surrounded him.

The sight was comical enough that Beam laughed.

Colton came through a side door with his hand on the shoulder of Alex's son. Both were dressed in gray tuxedos.

"Look at me, Uncle Beam!" the enthusiastic six-year old exclaimed.

Beam squatted down to eyelevel. "You are going to make the *best* best man ever. You look handsome, Charlie."

"I know. Colton looks kinda good, too."

Beam looked up from the boy's perspective. "I'm not sure I'd go so far as to say this city dweller looks as good as you, but he does look *kinda* good." Of course, he was lying. Colton McCreed was born to wear fancy clothes and looked right at home in his tuxedo.

"You nervous?" Beam asked as he stood to shake Colton's hand.

"Surprisingly, no. For a day I never thought I'd be participating in, marrying Alex feels very right. I'm more worried about my mom and dad creating a scene."

"What's a wedding without some drama? And drama between your famous actress mom and equally famous screenwriter father will be front-page fodder for every tabloid in the country. What a way to commemorate the occasion."

Colton laughed. "I don't think Alex would want her wedding to be front-page fodder."

"Oh, I don't know. Somehow, I think Alex might get a kick out of a little drama. She's pretty cool about rolling with the punches." Beam winked at Charlie as the kid rushed off to pose for a picture.

"Hey, I heard through the Eden Falls gossip grapevine—

and by that I mean Rita Reynolds down at the post office—you're buying the lumberyard from Misty's dad," Colton said.

"Not buying. He's offered me a partnership, but nothing's official yet."

"Well, I think that's great. I know the Garrett clan would love for you to stay in town. Not sure they felt that way before Sophia came along, though."

Before Beam could reply, a man clapped Colton on the shoulder. "So Eve finally roped and tied you."

Colton laughed and pulled the guy in for a man hug. "I wish. Roped and tied might be kind of fun."

"You mean she wasn't tempted by your forbidden fruit?" The man's booming laugh echoed through the foyer, causing people to turn in their direction. "You were a goner the minute you set eyes on that little pixie. I'm surprised it took you so long to realize it."

Beam understood little pixie, but Eve? He looked at Colton for an explanation.

"Beam, this guy trying desperately to look debonair, is Jorge Reis, my business manager," Colton said by way of introduction. "The first time he came to Eden Falls, he said I'd found the Garden of Eden and Alex was Eve herself."

Jorge held out his hand while looking Beam up and down. "They sure grow them big around here."

"Beam is Alex's cousin, and the pilot who flew me into Eden Falls the first time."

Jorge glanced at Colton. "You said the pilot looked like a mountain man capable of skinning a grizzly."

"Capable of skinning a grizzly?" Beam chuckled.

"Hey, if the shoe fits. At the time, you had a beard down to your chest and hair to your shoulders. You've become civilized since then."

Beam felt a hand circle his arm and turned, expecting his

mom. Instead, Misty cozied up. The last time they'd talked hadn't exactly ended on friendly terms, but she was pressing against his arm as if they hadn't been separated for almost a month.

"Hello, Colton," she purred in pure seductress. "And it's John, isn't it?"

Before Beam could correct her, Jorge conjured a winning smile and said, "Martha, it's nice to see you again."

Misty's eyes narrowed and Beam realized she'd intended to embarrass Jorge, but he'd turned the tables. That didn't happen often. But why was she trying to embarrass him in the first place? Obviously, they'd already met and something had transpired between them.

"It's Misty." Her voice was sharp as ice.

"Right." Jorge snapped his fingers, his enlightened act apparent.

Misty glanced up at Beam. "Let's go inside and find a seat, honey."

He was surprised she planned to sit with him, but suspicion was on surprise's heel. Was her cuddling up the result of him cutting off her funds?

Rowdy picked that moment to return Sophia.

"She woke up and started to fuss. I don't do fussy females." He glanced at Misty and a wicked grin appeared. "Would Mommy like to hold her daughter?"

Misty glared, and Jorge looked confused. Yeah, something had definitely occurred between the two of them. Beam opened the diaper bag. "Hold her a minute while I get a bottle."

"I'll hold the little peanut," Colton said, taking Sophia from Rowdy. He gave the baby a stern look. "No pooping or spitting up on my tux, or Auntie Alex will be furious with both of us."

Sophia's lips quirked.

Open-mouthed Jorge yanked his cell phone free from an inner pocket. "I have to get a picture of this, because no one will ever believe me without proof." To Colton he said, "I knew this town had changed you, but you're holding a baby. In a church. Absolutely unbelievable."

Beam laughed as Colton posed with Sophia. By the time he'd produced a bottle from the depths of the diaper bag, Misty had disappeared.

~

Misty was aware of the whispers that followed her down the aisle of the chapel. She scooted in next to her dad, and jutted out her chin. Let the residents of Eden Falls judge. She didn't care. They were all nobodies in her book anyway.

The wedding was supposed to be an intimate affair with just family and close friends, but the place was packed. And hot. She was glad she'd found a sleeveless dress, though shopping at the consignment store in Harrisville had been a complete embarrassment. She'd never bought anything secondhand in her life.

Colton's movie star mother, Corinna, arrived with two of Colton's half-siblings. Both notable because they'd followed in their mother's acting footsteps. They took seats in the front pew. Colton's famous screenwriter father entered with his much younger wife and their toddler son. Corrina sent a scorching glance in their direction, and Misty smiled. A fiery family brawl would be worth the trouble of coming, and put a nice crimp in Alex's fairytale wedding.

The music started, and Charlie came down the aisle escorting a tall female.

"Isn't that Carolyn West?" Mason said.

Misty did a double take of the gorgeous redhead, who

used to be one of their girlhood five. She'd left Eden Falls for culinary school right after graduation. Model tall and thin, but shapely, Carolyn was a far cry from the gangly Pippi Long-stockings she'd been all through school.

Stella and Alex had befriended the girl with her orange braided hair and a face covered in freckles when she moved to Eden Falls in the third grade. Misty had never really connected with her. They got along okay, but didn't spend time together unless Stella or Alex was involved. She did remember feeling a slight kinship with Carolyn, when her mom and dad were killed in a car accident. She, like Misty, was now motherless. Misty thought the accident might connect them in a way the other girls wouldn't understand, but it hadn't. Instead, Carolyn became more introverted and shy than before.

Since she wasn't speaking to Alex, she didn't know any of the wedding details, but was glad to see Carolyn rather than Stella acting as Alex's maid of honor. She felt conspic-uous enough sitting next to her dad. She didn't want to be singled out as the only friend among the spectators as she had been at Jolie's wedding. Not that she and Jolie were great friends, but it had been embarrassing not to be included, and she hadn't spoken to Jolie since.

Alex appeared at the door of the chapel, and a collective "Ohhh" echoed through the room.

In Misty's opinion, Alex's pale gray wedding dress with its simple square neckline and three quarter length sheer sleeves, though pretty, was far too understated for the tabloid paparazzi waiting outside. She was marrying a *New York Times* bestselling author and should have dressed the part. The darker gray sash around her tiny waist was a perfect match to Colton and Charlie's tuxedos—way too icky sweet for her taste.

Most guests would assume the bouquet of flowers Alex

carried had been picked for their colors, but Misty knew differently. Alex's grandmother had taught her the Victorian age language of flowers, and Misty was sure a lot of thought had gone into every blossom. The red rose meant love and passion, the white Casablanca lily stood for celebration, and the purple heliotrope, devotion. She would have picked the fern for sincerity, and the camellia blossoms stood for you hold my destiny in your hands. Colton had given Alex a single camellia blossom when he proposed—another ick of sweetness. Misty had never taken Colton for a sentimental fool, but the camellia blossom had sealed the deal for Alex.

Misty glanced around at the sparsely decorated church. She would have added yards of tulle and roses to the simple pine boughs at the end of each pew. Alex probably felt she had to go understated because this was her second wedding, but she should have taken the photographers outside into consideration.

A tinge of resentment ran through Misty as she witnessed the love line between Colton and Alex—so taut it could have been plucked like a guitar string—while she walked down the aisle on her dad's arm. *Why couldn't he have looked at me like that just once?* Not that she would have returned the sentiment. She'd never loved Colton. He'd just been a glimmer of hope at the end of her very dark tunnel, a ticket out of this small town, the hope for a life more glamorous.

Preacher Joshua Brenner performed the short and sticky sweet ceremony, where the bride and groom vowed their eternal love for each other. Colton slid the wedding ring on Alex's finger, and then he lifted her hand to his lips. *Ickity ick ick.*

Misty glanced down at her own ring. Rowdy had been only too happy to inform her that his brother had gone to a lot of trouble and expense to meet her specifications. She'd been very particular, and Beam had actually picked a beautiful ring. Sadly, instead of the symbol of love it should represent, it felt more like a chain of bondage. She glanced across the aisle where her husband sat with his family.

Their eyes met.

He winked.

She looked away.

Since there wasn't a venue large enough in Eden Falls to accommodate Colton's town-wide reception invitation, he'd booked the largest hotel ballroom in nearby Harrisville. The only decorations were potted pine trees lining the walls, which filled the ballroom with the fresh scent of forest. Hundreds of flickering white lights were strung across the high ceiling, making the room glow as if lit by a sky full of stars. A simple pillar candle centered in evergreen boughs adorned the tables. Though pretty, in a winter wonderland sort of way, the setting was much too simple to please Misty's tastes.

Misty scanned the seating cards at each table, prepared to move whomever she had to for her own convenience. Luckily, it wasn't necessary. Stella was seated beside her. Across the table were Maude and Ed Stapleton, the owners of Pages bookstore.

Carolyn West took the last vacant seat at their table, and the conversation turned to her. Misty only half listened while she watched people file in and take their seats. The bride and groom sat at a large table up front with both their families.

"How are you, Misty?"

Misty glanced at Carolyn. "Having the time of my life. Why are you here?"

The deer-in-the-headlights look that came over Carolyn's face was predictable. She'd always been socially dysfunctional. "I came for Alex's wedding."

Stella produced her signature eye roll. "What do you think she's doing here? Why would you ask such a dumb question?"

"Dumb? Really? She hasn't been to Eden Falls in how many years, and suddenly she shows up." Misty raised an eyebrow. "While I'm asking dumb questions, here's one for you, Stella. Where's your so called boyfriend?"

"My boyfriend's name is *Len*, and he couldn't make it."

"On Valentine's Day, *Len* couldn't make it? Doesn't that seem a bit odd to you?" Stella was dumb as a rock to believe the excuses that guy handed her. They hadn't been dating long, but still, it was Valentine's Day for cripes sake! *Open your eyes girlfriend.* "You better have police chief Dudley Do-Right run a background check on *Len*. He's probably a drug dealer with major mafia connections."

"Len is not a drug dealer."

Misty didn't believe Len had anything to do with drugs either, but relished the edge of doubt Stella now wore around her eyes. She wouldn't be the only unhappy person here tonight.

"Here's a question for you, Misty. How come you're not sitting with your husband and daughter?"

Misty shot Stella her best eat-rotten-eggs glare before she leaned back to allow a cute guy in white tails to place a salad in front of her. She'd had enough mudslinging with Stella for the evening. She couldn't care less if Len turned out to be a drug dealer, an undercover agent, or a swimsuit model. Hot or not, the guy broke dates all the time, and Misty wouldn't put up with it.

She leaned forward to see Carolyn unfold her napkin. "Aren't you a chef at some fancy San Francisco restaurant?"

"Yes." Carolyn smoothed the napkin over her lap. "I work at Le Tour."

Misty was too busy poking her fork into one of the succulent bacon-wrapped scallops that accompanied the salad for follow-up questions. She didn't really care where Carolyn worked.

"I saw your daughter before the wedding, Misty. She's beautiful," Carolyn said.

"Mmm hmm," Misty mumbled around a mouthful of greens. The dressing was a cilantro-lime concoction and delicious. She glanced back at Carolyn. "You should have left the length of your hair alone. Your neck is too long for that cut."

Carolyn's fingers went to the carefree curls and tugged at the ends.

"Misty!" Stella snapped.

"I love that cut on you, Carolyn, and the color is beautiful," Maude Stapleton said, coming to the rescue.

From one redhead to another. Only yours comes from a box, Maude. Misty took another bite of salad, tuning out the conversation that continued around her. The next course was a moist chicken breast with some sort of lemon sauce. Misty had planned to pick at the food but everything tasted so good, and she'd starved herself for two days to get into this second-hand dress.

As dinner progressed and toasts were made—more ick—Misty finished every morsel on her plate. A sad little country band that played regularly at Rowdy's took the low stage on the far wall and began to tune up. At their signal, Colton led Alex to the middle of the room and twirled her once before encircling her in his arms. A surge of jealousy raged through Misty, like a freight train barreling toward a broken down car on the tracks. The force hit her so hard it physically hurt. That Alex was so blissfully happy was completely unfair. Everything always fell into place so perfectly for her. She was served from a silver platter with a gold lining.

Misty glanced around. Every eye was on the candy-corn sweet couple. She turned her back to the scene.

The next song, Alex danced with her father, and Colton with his mother. After that, couples moved onto the floor. Rowdy asked Stella to dance, which Misty took as a pity invitation, since her precious Len couldn't be bothered on Valentine's Day. She was surprised the longhaired bar and grill owner knew how to dance, but he moved Stella across the floor with confidence. She pictured him tuning in the sound system and practicing alone, after the bar and grill closed for the night. At least that thought made her smile.

Misty saw Colton's step or half brother head for the bar, and she decided to do the same. She recognized him from a popular daytime soap opera. A conversation with him might just liven up this boring reception.

Colton's arrogant business manager twirled Alex dramatically and then winked at Misty as if they were friends. On his first visit to Eden Falls, he'd brushed her off like a fleck of lint. If he lived here, he wouldn't have gotten away with that unscathed.

She reached the bar only to discover Colton's sibling had grabbed a drink and moved off in another direction. But a much bigger fish was heading straight for her. Colton's silver-haired father zeroed in on her like a torpedo. She wished she was twenty—okay fifty—pounds lighter, but knew her dress showed her curvaceous figure to perfection. She struck a pose with a hip against the bar and her chest out, only to have Mr. McCreed bypass her for alcohol. No wonder, with that screaming kid he'd been fighting since he and his wife had entered the reception.

Misty noticed JT and Carolyn at the opposite end of the bar. The timid bunny shifted from foot to foot nervously. She reached up to brush her feathery hair away from her face, and the sparkle of a narrow gold wedding band caught Misty's attention. She vaguely remembered Alex mentioning a quick courthouse wedding, and Misty had assumed Carolyn was pregnant. Obviously that hadn't been the case. She was sure Alex had filled them all in on the details, but Misty hadn't cared enough to pay attention.

Misty lied when she said Carolyn's haircut didn't suit her. In truth, it emphasized the high cheekbones on her porcelain skin. Even though Carolyn was socially awkward, she was beautiful. Pippi Longstocking transformed. She now had the body of a Victoria's Secret model, and Misty's resentment raised its ugly head for the second time that night.

Rowdy swung past with Stella, both laughing. There was definitely a story behind Len being AWOL on Valentine's Day. Misty would love to be the one to discover the dirt, if only to bring Stella down a notch. She better not turn her sights on Rowdy Garrett just because he'd asked her to dance a couple of times. He went through women like he went through beer. Only the beer probably meant more to him. He and his cousin, JT, were the biggest players in Eden Falls.

Alex and Colton danced past, and Misty turned from the sight. She'd had just about all the happily ever after she could stomach for one night.

~

Sophia was being passed between his parents and Grandpa Mason, so Beam was content to sit and watch couples dance past. He chuckled to himself, when he thought she was probably due a diaper change. Compared to a year earlier, his situation had changed drastically. He'd still be in the same place, still celebrating at Alex and Colton's reception. But he'd gone from scoping out the single women, and collecting phone numbers, to making sure his daughter was dry and fed.

He searched the room for his previous cohorts.

JT was busy talking to Carolyn West, who Beam hadn't

seen in years. She looked so different. He wouldn't have recognized her if his mom hadn't pointed her out when she came down the aisle on Charlie's arm.

He glanced around until he spotted his brother. Rowdy was paying a lot of attention to Stella Adams tonight. All through school, he, Rowdy, and JT, in fact most of the guys from high school, had steered a wide berth around the local girls. Too many wagging jaws in this little town. When things went south, and they always did when you were a randy teenager, the truth got twisted to suit the teller, and hard feelings resulted. Dating girls who lived outside of Eden Falls led to fewer complications.

"Has anyone ever told you what a handsome man you are?"

Beam turned to Alex. "No, and that statement coming from my cousin isn't all that comforting."

She flashed her sunlight smile, her green eyes twinkling with happiness. "I bet if I took a poll, half of the women in this ballroom would vote you as the most handsome man here."

"Either marriage has already messed with your mind, or you want something."

She took his hand. "I want to dance."

He allowed her to pull him up from his chair. "You didn't have to lie to get me to dance."

"I'm not lying, Beam. You look extremely handsome tonight."

Alex wouldn't say it if she didn't mean it. He twirled her onto the dance floor. "Thank you. You make a beautiful bride."

"Thank you." Her smile turned serene. "It feels strange, being married, again. After Peyton was killed, I thought I'd spend the rest of my life alone, but here I am, married for the second time. *And* to the most unlikely man alive."

"You're right about that," Beam said with a laugh. "I would have bet money on anyone other than Colton, but"—he grew serious—"I predict, you two, three counting Charlie, are going to be very happy together."

"I predict you're going to be right."

Beam glanced around for Misty as they swayed to the music.

"I wished the same for you. I'm sorry things aren't working out as smoothly as you'd hoped."

"I wasn't delusional enough to think marriage to Misty would be smooth sailing. She may come around, she may not." He spotted Misty talking to Jorge Reis. "I detected some tension between Misty and Colton's business manager earlier. Do you know what happened?"

To him amazement, Alex laughed. "Nothing. Misty ran into me, Colton, and Jorge having lunch at Renaldo's the first time Jorge came to town. She tried to horn in, and Jorge told her we were having a business lunch before dismissing her. She didn't take the dismissal well."

"I don't imagine so."

"You have nothing to worry about on that front. Jorge wasn't interested, and neither was Misty. She just didn't like that she was left out."

Alex let out a squeal when her husband came up behind her, swept her off her feet, and into his arms. "I think it's time for us to bid our guests *arrivederci* and begin honeymooning, Mrs. McCreed."

"Head to the microphone, and lets do our bidding, Mr. McCreed." She waved to Beam over Colton's shoulder. "Love you, cuz. Thank you for coming."

"Love you back. Don't do anything I wouldn't do."

～

ason clapped when Colton carried his bride to the stage. Alex looked radiant, just as she should. She deserved this happiness, and so did little Charlie. He was sitting between Alex's parents, cheering along with everyone else.

Mason thought back to his own courthouse wedding. Arleen hadn't been very joyous. Misty hadn't been happy at her wedding, either. She'd been more concerned about out-doing her friends, than feeling any happiness. Those memories made him sad, and he didn't want to be sad tonight. He hooted along with the rest of the guests when Alex thanked them for coming to their celebration. He cheered even louder when Colton announced the party was to continue, but as for he and Alex—the honeymoon was commencing. Immediately. He carried Alex from the ballroom with a grin on his face.

"It's nice to see Alex happy, isn't it?"

The voice so close to his ear startled Mason. He took a step back from vivacious Patsy Yarberry, Eden Falls' blonde bombshell, and proprietress of Patsy's Pastries. When she raised her brows at his abrupt movement, he felt heat rise up his neck. His shirt collar suddenly felt way too tight. "Yes. Yes, it is nice to see her so happy. I didn't think so at first, but Colton is a good man."

"Oh, I loved Colton on sight," she said, exhibiting a wicked, red-lipped grin against pearly whites. "I could see how you might not like him—thinking he'd impregnated your daughter—but hey, all's well that ends well. Right?"

He chuckled at her blunt remarks, but she hit the nail on the head with one swing. After Misty announced to the town that she was pregnant and Colton was the daddy, Colton had come to see him. Mason wasn't happy with the situation, but Colton said he'd take full responsibility for Misty and the baby. In the end, Misty had told the truth. Colton wasn't the daddy, and Misty married Beam. Mason and Colton weren't the best of buddies, but they'd come out on friendly terms.

Mason didn't know Patsy well, but everyone knew her reputation. She wore clothes to raise eyebrows, spoke without a filter, and gave Misty a run for her money in being the most gossiped about person in Eden Falls. She'd been married so many times he'd lost count—not that he'd been trying to keep track. His path didn't cross Patsy's very often.

"I meant that as a compliment. You got a good one."

He glanced at her in question. "A good one?"

"Son-in-law."

"Oh." He smiled as he pushed his glasses up his nose. "Yes. I have a very good son-in-law."

She tipped her head, her eyes drifting to where Sophia lay sleeping in her Grandma Garrett's arms. "You also have a beautiful granddaughter."

"Thank you. I sure think so." He watched Beam lift Sophia and cuddle her close, and wished he had a camera. He wanted to capture every beautiful moment between daddy and daughter.

"Colton said the celebration should continue." She lifted a shoulder. "Would you like to dance?"

The unexpected invitation stunned him. "Oh, no. I mean…I'm not much of a dancer. Two left feet." His ears felt extremely hot. "But thank you for asking."

She studied him a moment as if assessing the damage she'd inflicted by embarrassing him, then flashed an amused smile. "It was good to see you, Mason."

"You, too, Patsy."

She did a little finger wave and strolled away.

CHAPTER 9

When Misty woke up to the alarm, she went back and forth on whether to meet up with her friends or not. Stella had caught her arm just as she was leaving Alex's reception, and told her she, Jolie, Jillian, and Carolyn were meeting at Noelle's Café for breakfast before Carolyn left for San Francisco. She'd laughed off the invitation. Her friendship with Stella was strained and the other three weren't worth waking up early for. Then she pictured them around a table at Noelle's, laughing, having fun, and possibly discussing her. She decided it would be in her best interest to meet them. Besides, it had been a long time since she'd felt included.

She was the last to arrive and expected Stella to jump all over her for it, but the four women were so engrossed in discussing the wedding they barely acknowledged her arrival.

Stella ordered fruit and yogurt. Jolie decided on a bowl of cereal with strawberries, Jillian, an egg-white omelet with vegetables, and Carolyn ordered whole-wheat toast and oatmeal. Misty glanced around the table with contempt before ordering the ham and egg breakfast with a side of hash browns. She added a bagel that she slathered with cream cheese.

She had to give them credit. Not one of them made a comment. In their shoes, she wouldn't have kept her mouth shut.

As they ate, the discussion was still centered on the wedding. They oohed and aahed over the romantic tone of it, and laughed at how much Colton had changed. Carolyn hadn't met him before last night, so she didn't know he'd come to town a sworn member of the Forever-A-Bachelor Club.

"I wasn't impressed with the sparse decorations. It was Valentine's Day and everything was done up in pine boughs and gray like they were celebrating Christmas." Misty added more ketchup to her hash browns. "And what was with the gray dress?"

"She wore white for Peyton. I thought the gray was beautiful," Jillian said.

"I loved the understated," Jolie added.

"The hearts and cupids thing for Valentine's Day is so cliché. The subtle glow from the lighted pine trees was gorgeous," Stella said. "They donated all those trees to the forest service."

Of course they did. Miss Goody Two-Shoes and Sir Galahad will become invincible now—the golden couple of Eden Falls—riding through town, doing good unto others. Ick!

The conversation turned to Carolyn. When asked about her job, she morphed from caterpillar to fluttering butterfly. She loved her job, and Misty felt that tormenting shroud of jealousy as Carolyn talked about living in a big city. The butterfly lost a wing when Misty asked why her husband hadn't come to the wedding with her. Carolyn gave a vague answer about some big account he was working on at the office.

Misty was an expert at knowing when to push and when to tune out meaningless babble. She learned early on, while working at Dahlia's Salon, which conversations were worth listening to and which ones didn't deserve her attention. Something was fishy with Carolyn and the husband she didn't want to discuss, but Misty decided she'd rather eat than pursue. Who cared? Carolyn lived in California.

A gaggle of firefighters walked in and took the table next to theirs. She noticed Jillian sit up a little straighter. Misty studied the firemen, wondering which one had caught Jillian's attention. Brandt Smith glanced her way and nodded. She turned away without returning an acknowledgement. When he first moved to town, Misty had been interested. She'd approached and he'd turned her down in front of a group of men. She couldn't let that go, so she'd spread a few rumors around Dahlia's Salon.

She pointed at Jillian with a forkful of hash browns. "Who're you dating?"

Jillian glanced at the table of firemen, then looked down at her plate as her cheeks turned pink. She'd always been a blusher.

"I've been too busy at work to date much."

"Yeah? Why are you so busy?"

Jillian pushed a few vegetables around her plate with her fork. "Glenda and Dawson are buying that vacant building next to the gym to expand."

Misty frowned. "I didn't know that."

"You would if you were living with your husband," Stella said under her breath, but loud enough for everyone at the table to hear.

Misty glared across the table as she shoved the last bite of bagel into her mouth. She'd had about as much fun as she could stand for one morning, and had put up with all she could take from Stella. She stood, fished around the bottom of her purse, and set a few bills on the table. "This has been real entertaining, but I've got places to be. Tell Gertie she's only getting ten percent because she didn't refill my orange juice."

*M*isty sat on her bed later that night, going over her dwindling finances. Her checking account was down to three digits and her savings account had seen better days.

Her dad had knocked on her door earlier to remind her she was running out of time to find a job and was only a couple of months away from paying rent. What was he going to do, put her out on the street? Still, there was something very final in his words. He used a tone of authority, which she'd never heard. Something that told her he was serious this time.

She turned out her light, and spent an hour tossing and turning, thinking of her mother only a few hours away in Sacramento—so close, yet so far. If she'd known a year ago, even two, would she have searched Arleen out?

What was stopping her now?

She threw back the covers and crept down to her father's office. He never locked doors or drawers, so she started rifling through his desk. Then she moved over to the file cabinet. When she opened the bottom drawer, she discovered what she was searching for. In the very back was a thick folder with Arleen Honeywell printed at the top. She pulled it free and set it on her dad's desk. Her parent's divorce decree sat on top. Next, an envelope with a Sacramento, California, address, held copies of checks, with varying amounts from two hundred dollars all the way to a thousand. All signed by Mason.

Why was her dad sending her mom money? The amounts were erratic, so it wasn't alimony payments. The dates also varied, the last one sent three months earlier. She glanced through the divorce papers. There was no mention of payments, so why the checks? Unless… Could her dad be bribing her mom to stay away from Misty? Nothing else made sense. The thought infuriated her and sickened her stomach at the same time. Her dad had been paying Arleen to stay away from her own daughter all these years.

The next morning, after her father left for work, she packed her car and set off for Sacramento. She'd never traveled beyond Seattle alone. Her trip began as a wonderful adventure. Her nomadic spirit bubbled to the surface, reaching for the freedom she had always longed for. The open road spread before her with endless possibilities. Instead of exhaust, she'd leave a trail of sparkling wanderlust in her wake.

She soon discovered, after four hours of her own company, the open road wasn't all that wonderful. In Portland, Oregon, she pulled over at a roadside hotel, another thing she'd never done alone—stay in a hotel.

As tired as she was, anticipation kept her awake for hours. Tomorrow she would see her mother. She pushed all her fears of rejection to the side. She'd finally have all the answers to her questions. Her dreams would be fulfilled when her mother explained what had kept her away.

Everything would fall into place. Life would make sense again, and complete happiness would follow.

CHAPTER 10

Mason stood at Misty's open bedroom door. Everything was the same, yet different. He knew she was gone, even though there was no note and no visible evidence in her room. The open file cabinet drawer in his office told him all he needed to know. She'd found her mother's address and had gone searching for…whatever it was she was searching for.

Like her mother, Misty was never content with what she had, always looking for something bigger, better, and brighter. She craved glitz, but didn't want to work for it. She expected someone to come along and hand it to her, but only if it was all wrapped up with a pretty bow. She didn't understand peace and contentment could only be found within oneself. Outside happiness was fleeting.

His heart hurt for his daughter. When she came back—if she came back—she would be hurt and more broken than when she left. Her mother would strip her bare, leave her flailing in mid-air without a net to catch her. Arleen was an expert at leaving you feeling hollow and insignificant. She didn't care who she hurt as long as she got what she wanted.

He'd wait a few days before telling Beam. Highly unlikely, but there was always the possibility Misty would have a change of heart and come home, or that Arleen would send her packing before bleeding her dry. Though, that was also highly unlikely.

~

This can't be right.

Misty checked the address written on a scrap of paper in her hand with that of the run-down house, while all her fairy tale dreams unraveled before her eyes. This had to be a mistake. Her dad must have been sending money to the wrong address all these years.

Arleen lived in a big beautiful home, with a manicured lawn tended by a gardener. Roses bloomed year around in the solarium, and there was an indoor pool, and possibly a poodle named Chanel. Her mother would answer the door wearing a dress and heels, and wouldn't look a day over thirty. She would throw her arms around Misty's neck. Between hugs and kisses, her mom would say how horrible Mason had been to keep them apart all these years.

That was how Misty had imagined her mom's life.

The house in front of her was a tiny hovel in need of paint. Ten years ago. Instead of the luxury car she expected, a rusted vehicle that might have been blue…or possibly green…at some point in its pathetically long life, sat in the driveway.

No one would leave a nice home in picturesque Eden Falls to live here. No one would leave her husband and daughter for this, unless they were frantic to escape. Or insane.

Her mother was supposed to have life's answers. She was supposed to guide Misty in the right direction, give her valuable insight, because that's what mothers did. They tell you you're beautiful and talented and can do anything you set your mind to. They sacrifice, encourage, and love unconditionally.

Misty had anticipated this day for over twenty years. This was supposed to be the moment that altered her life, corrected injustices, and presented solutions. This was supposed to be *her* day.

This house tainted everything she'd set her heart on.

Misty sat in her car a long time, staring through the drizzly gloom of the day. *My mom left a comfortable home, a husband, and daughter who loved her for this.* The realization was too mind boggling to wrap her head around. She had looked forward to a mother-daughter relationship like Alex and Alice Garrett shared. Now she was here and couldn't find the courage to get out of the car. Fear of what she'd find behind that tacky front door kept her sitting in the cold.

Willing her fingers to pull the door handle, she forced her body to climb out, glad, at least, for a break in the rain that had been relentless on the drive from Portland to just outside of Sacramento. Walking down the crumbling driveway, careful to step over puddles, she took note of the peeling paint, lopsided shutters, and ratty yard. The curtains at the windows were drawn and everything was quiet, except for a furiously barking dog next door. She eyed the chain-link fence running between this house and the neighbors, hoping it continued to hold its prisoner at bay.

On the front stoop, the stench from a coffee can filled with rain-drenched cigarette butts and ashes reached her nose. A sudden memory materialized…her mother sitting at the open kitchen window, blowing smoke through the screen. She shook a finger at Misty. "Now, don't you go telling your daddy you saw me with this thing."

She'd forgotten her mom smoked when her dad wasn't around.

Her first timid knock on the front door went unanswered. The second knock carried more force. She heard, "Coming. Don't get your panties in a wad," before the door was yanked open.

Even after twenty-one years, Misty recognized the woman standing in front of her, but just barely.

"If you're sellin' somethin', you're wastin' your time."

Misty's heart sank below crashing waves, leaving her struggling for breath. Her own mother didn't have a clue who she was. She opened her mouth but no words came out.

"Well?"

"Mom…" Her shaking voice sounded small and pathetic. "Hi."

The woman squinted through a halo of cigarette smoke that she waved away with a hand, before recognition sharpened her frown and deepened the lines around her lips. "Misty?"

"It's me." Misty cringed at her hopefulness. *Please recognize me.*

Her mother's gaze dropped from Misty's face to her feet, and slowly raked back up. She sucked on the cigarette stuck between her fingers and expelled a cloud of smoke before she moved aside. "You better come in. You're letting all my heat out."

Misty stepped inside. The door shut behind her with the hollowness of a prison cell.

She took a moment to scan the dark room before her. The threadbare, sagging sofa sat against the front wall. Two mismatched chairs, stained so badly, she wasn't sure of their original color—not that it would matter in this gloomy setting —sat at odd angles as if they were dragged there and forgotten. What once must have been white walls were a dingy gray-brown, darkened in the corners from cigarette smoke. Tattered magazines, overflowing ashtrays, and moisture rings covered a rickety coffee table. The only hanging picture was a stormy beach scene, as gray and depressing as the room it hung in.

"Whaddya doin' here?"

The question, delivered sharply, felt like the flick of a fingernail to her cheek. Misty took a step back. "Dad told me you were here, and I wanted… I wanted to see you. I didn't know you lived so close. Well, thirteen hours on the road isn't exactly close, but…" She let her words die away as hurt seeped into her like blood into a dry bandage. Her mom had only been thirteen hours from Eden Falls, and had never come back for her.

Tobacco-stained teeth sank into her mother's bottom lip before she turned and left the room. Misty followed like a puppy struggling for attention, but she came up short at the threshold of the kitchen. Cabinet doors hung loose on exposed hinges, their white paint marred and filthy with grease and dirty fingerprints. The pink Formica countertops were worn and stained. A small table sat in the corner with two chairs pushed underneath. Misty's gaze zeroed in on a bowl of dusty, plastic fruit sitting on a stiff gray doily in the center of the table. The sight clogged her throat with tears.

"Want some coffee?"

Coffee? Coffee is the last thing I want. She nodded. "Please."

Arleen stuck the cigarette in one side of her mouth. "You might as well have a seat," she said through the other side

Misty pulled out one of the wobbly chairs tucked under the table and sat. It immediately tipped to the right, causing her to grab the edge of the sticky table, almost overturning a full ashtray. She watched her mom heat a cup of water in a tiny microwave, and then add a teaspoon of instant coffee.

She shuffled to the table and set the mug and a spoon in front of Misty.

"Cream and sugar?"

Misty looked down at the coffee with a slimy film floating on top. "Please."

Arleen set a carton of milk that was well past the expiration date, and a grimy bowl of sugar on the table. She pulled out the chair opposite Misty and sat. "You're heavier than I would have expected."

Misty flinched at the cruel comment. She hadn't seen her mother since she was six years old, and that was the first thing that came to mind? Not, "You're beautiful" or "You remind me of myself at your age". How did one respond to a comment like that?

Her hurtful remarks to Carolyn West at the wedding reception tumbled through her mind. *What are you doing here? You should have left the length of your hair alone. Your neck is too long for that cut.* She hadn't seen Carolyn in years, and those were the first comments out of her mouth. *Like mother, like daughter.* Suddenly, she wished she could retract those spiteful words and tell Carolyn the truth. Her haircut was darling, and showed off her high cheekbones to perfection.

Her mom sat back in her chair and lit another cigarette from the butt of the one still smoldering. She hadn't aged well. Misty knew her mom was fourteen years younger than Mason, but she looked at least ten years older than him. She was painfully thin with hollows in her cheeks. From her years at Dahlia's salon, she knew her mom's dye job came from a cheap box, and the outdated haircut aged her even more. Her foundation was too dark, and her blush, too garish. Glittery blue eye shadow, that made Misty think Vegas showgirl, had settled into the creases of her eyelids.

For the first time since stepping through the door, Misty

realized her mother was wearing a pink waitress uniform, complete with peeling nametag and stained white apron. The mother she'd fantasized about for years—the one who hadn't come back to Eden Falls to collect her daughter because of her high-powered corporate job—waited tables.

"Want to take off your coat?"

Misty shrugged her arms free of her coat, and felt vulnerably naked. She folded it in half and set it on her lap.

"Tell me about yourself." Arleen rolled her hand, her wrist so skinny it looked like it might snap off. "Whaddya do for a living?"

Misty glanced at her mother's hair, again. "I'm a hair technician."

"That a fancy way of saying you're a hairdresser?"

Misty winced at the implied insult coming from the woman wearing a waitress uniform. She was proud of her accomplishments as the most requested hair tech in the area. She knew color better than anyone at Dahlia's, and kept up on hair trends. "More politically correct."

Arleen rolled her eyes before pointing with the tip of her cigarette. "That's some major bling you got there on your finger. Is it real?"

Misty looked down at her two-carat diamond ring in its platinum setting with double bands of diamonds surrounding it. Misty remembered the night she told Alex she didn't want to marry Beam because they would always be poor. Yet, here she was wearing a ring that probably cost more than her mother made in two years. She raised her eyes to meet Arleen's hard stare.

"It's a simple yes or no question."

"Yes, it's real."

Ash fell from the tip of her cigarette onto the table, and her mom swept it to the floor with the side of her hand. "That looks like an engagement ring along with a wedding band. Where's the husband?"

"In Eden Falls." Misty swallowed, not sure if she should bring up Eden Falls, but her mom had asked. "Do you remember Glenda and Dawson Garrett?"

Her mother smiled for the first time, revealing her stained teeth. "I definitely remember Dawson *and* his brother Denny. Now they were some mighty fine lookin' men."

Not sure why, but it bothered Misty to hear her mom refer to her father-in-law that way. "I married Glenda and Dawson's oldest son, Beam—Everett."

Arleen sat back and crossed skinny arms over her middle. "How long have you been married?"

"Since July."

Arleen squinted through the smoke rising between them. "I think that kid was our paperboy. Industrious little bugger. Always there right on time to collect for the month." She sucked deeply on the end of her cigarette, tipped her chin, and blew a stream of smoke toward the ceiling. The way she cocked her mouth was disgusting. Misty smoked occasionally in social situations, and wondered if she looked as vile when she exhaled. If so, it would be the perfect reason to quit, which would make Beam happy. He hated to kiss her after she'd been smoking.

She shook her head to rid the thoughts. None of that mattered anymore. She was here. With her mom.

"Didn't Dawson have two boys?"

Her mother's voice brought her back to the dingy kitchen. She nodded. "Rowdy—Jefferson is their youngest."

"What's your husband do?" Arleen reached out and flicked ash into the overflowing ashtray.

"Beam used to—"

Arleen's penciled eyebrows puckered. "Why do you keep callin' him Beam?"

Misty smiled. "It's a nickname he got when he was small. His little league football coach said he blocked like an I-beam, and the nickname stuck. I've always known him as Beam, and his brother as Rowdy."

A leering smile appeared. "Is your husband as good lookin' as his daddy?"

Misty supposed Dawson and Denny Garrett were handsome for their age. Rowdy and Beam both looked like their dad. Thinking of Beam's mossy green eyes, his muscular shoulders, and broad chest invoked a silly sense of pride. Something she'd never felt before where Beam was concerned. "Yes, Beam's handsome in a Grizzly Adam's kind of way."

Though, not anymore. He's lost most of his rough edges since our wedding.

"What did you say he does for a living?"

"He used to fly tourists around the state, but he's selling his plane and—"

"He owns a plane?" Arleen asked leaning forward, eyes wide.

"Yes. He, Rowdy, JT, and Alex—do you remember my friend Alex?"

"She was that tiny thing with spooky eyes."

Spooky eyes. Misty had never thought of the Garrett green eyes that way, but they were a peculiar color. "All the Garrett's have those green eyes, except for Alex's brother, JT. Even *good lookin'* Dawson and Denny."

"That's right…" Smoke curled from Arleen's nostrils. "Only the color looked good on the men. It looked spooky on that little girl. So, back to the plane." She rolled her hand as if it was Misty who kept interrupting the conversation.

"All four of the Garrett kids inherited money from their grandparents. Beam bought a plane with his, and Rowdy bought a vacant building on Main and turned it into a bar and grill. It's the place to go on weekends."

"What'd the girl with the spooky eyes get?"

"She inherited her grandmother's flower shop, and her brother got his grandparent's house up on Mountain Ridge Ro—"

"Oh, yeah. Yeah," her mother broke in again. "I remember that flower shop. There on the square, right? Pretty Pansies… Petunias… Something like that."

"Pretty Posies."

Her mother's mouth turned down in a look of distaste. "The grandmother had those spooky eyes, too, but I loved going in that shop. If you looked in all the crooks and crannies you could always discover something fun and crazy in there. Does that girl run it the same way?"

Misty had never thought of Pretty Posies that way. To her, it was always just one more thing that landed on Alex's silver platter. Her mother was right though. The shop was unique and fun to explore.

"Why's your husband selling his plane?"

Misty wrinkled her nose against the stinging bite of smoke, as her mother lit another cigarette. Arleen's questions had the conversation bouncing back and forth like a ping-pong ball.

"He worked out of Seattle and"—she decided to leave Sophia out of the picture for now—"missed being close to family. He's going to buy into the lumberyard and hardware store."

"Your dad's place?"

Misty nodded.

"That place should be your inheritance. That stingy old man of yours should be leaving it to you, like that girl's grandmother left her the flower shop." A hacking cough brought their conversation to a halt for a moment. Her mom gasped for breath as she slapped the table. "Or at least the money from the sale should be yours," she wheezed out a moment later.

Misty hadn't thought of that. Her mom was right. Though she'd never wanted anything to do with the hardware and lumber store, the money should be hers.

Arleen leaned back in her chair, again. "How much is Mason selling it for?"

"He's not selling, Beam is going to be a—"

Arleen rolled her hand in impatience. "How much?"

Misty shook her head. "I don't know."

"You don't know how much your own husband is putting up to buy that place? Probably too much." Her mom tamped out her cigarette, pushed up from the table, and opened the outdated fridge. She glanced at Misty absently. "You want a Coke?"

Misty looked down at the coffee she hadn't touched. "Yes, please."

Her mother set a Coke in front of Misty, and then pulled the tab on her own can. "You know, I should get some of the money from the sale of that place. We were still married when he bought that junkyard."

But you left him. You left both of us.

Arleen snickered. "That's what I always called it—the junkyard. It used to make your dad so mad."

Dad doesn't get mad.

Her mom leaned a hip against the counter and crossed her arms over her middle. "So what're your plans?"

"My plans?"

"Yeah, where are you stayin'?"

Misty's stomach tightened uncomfortably. "I was…I hoped to stay here…with you." She shrugged. "For a while."

An instant frown brought her mom's penciled-on eyebrows together. "With me?" The frown turned speculative.

"Well, I guess you could stay for a couple of nights. But if you stay longer, you're gonna have to help with rent and stuff. I'm not gonna support you." Speculative was replaced by a tarnished smile. "It might be kind of a gas having you as a roommate. What about your husband?"

Misty took a sip of Coke, trying to think of a quick answer that would sound believable. "He won't mind if I stay awhile—to get to know my mom."

"Yeah, about that. You should call me Arleen." She set her Coke can on the counter. "I only have the one bed, but I work nights, so you can sleep in it. At least until we figure somethin' out. There's an extra house key in the bottom of that bowl of fruit."

My mother wants me to call her Arleen.

Her mom grabbed a coat from a hook by the back door, and slipped it on. Pulling a tube of lipstick and compact from the pocket, she stretched her lips over her teeth and applied a brash shade of fuchsia. She smacked her lips together and chuckled. "Roommates. That's a hoot."

She wants me to call her Arleen.

"See ya in the mornin'. Oh, and keep it down tomorrow. I sleep 'til about three."

All Misty had time to do was nod before her mom disappeared through the back door. The engine of the old clunker in the driveway turned over a handful of times before catching. She heard the grinding of gears, and the screeching of a fan belt as the car was backed from the driveway. Then all was silent.

My own mother wants me to call her Arleen.

Misty sat for a long time, not sure what to do next. She hadn't really thought past the initial open-armed greeting and tears she'd expected. She finally rose and returned to the living room to look around more closely. The space was sparsely furnished, no knick-knacks or memorabilia to distinguish it as Arleen's. A small flat screen sat on a table opposite the sofa. Her mom didn't have any photos or plants. No throw pillows to soften the hard edges. The tattered drapes hung from a curtain rod that looked as if it might fall from the wall with the slightest tug. A lone lamp sat on a cardboard box next to the sofa. The plastic lampshade, so cracked with age, would probably disintegrate at a touch.

Opposite the kitchen was a door leading down a short hall. The first room was a small bedroom, with an end table and lamp under a filthy window and a few boxes in the closet. Graffiti of wailing faces covered one wall. Misty imagined her own face there among the mournful. She stepped closer and studied the depressing work of art, brash colors against a black backdrop. Who was the artist and where was he or she now?

The bathroom, next door, held a tiny vanity and badly chipped porcelain tub. A medicine cabinet hung at a crooked angle, threatening to fall off the wall completely. The grimy linoleum floor was cracked and peeling back in places. Disgusting wasn't strong enough a word to describe the toilet.

The room at the end of the hall was her mom's.

She wants me to call her Arleen.

The unmade bed had no headboard, and bedding hung to the floor in filthy disarray. A floor lamp and another overflowing ashtray were situated close by. The only other furniture was a single chest of drawers. Dirty clothes—or clean, who could tell?—lay in a heap near the closet.

She slowly turned in a circle, searching. Arleen didn't have one single picture of the baby she'd given birth to twenty-seven years earlier. Her existence wasn't even acknowledged in her mother's house.

She slowly sank to the floor and wrapped her arms around her middle, imagining the gesture as the hug she'd hoped for from her mom. Never, in her wildest dreams, had she imagined meeting her mom under these conditions. As hard as she tried, she couldn't make sense of the beautiful mother of her memories living like this.

Misty glanced at the bed. She wasn't a clean freak, but knew she couldn't sleep on those filthy sheets. Pulling herself up, she walked back into the kitchen, and gingerly removed the grease covered plastic fruit in search of the extra key. Once found, she slipped her coat on and stepped outside. The dog next door barked wildly, and Misty eyed the fence, again.

She had every intention of staying for as long as her mother allowed. With that in mind, she drove to a Walmart she'd passed on her way into town. She bought a single inflatable mattress, a set of sheets, and a blanket. Then she added towels and a package of hangers.

Tomorrow she'd leave a message on her dad's home phone. All she'd say was she'd made it to Sacramento safely. *Let his imagination run wild with that news.*

She parked in front of the dismal little house, and tried to picture what her new life would be like. *My own mother wants me to call her Arleen.*

CHAPTER 11

Beam said goodbye to Jolie and walked down the steps of the only attorney's office in town. Owen Danielson had reviewed the sales contract for the hardware store and found everything in order. Mason was in the black, and had been every year but the first, since purchasing the business. Professionally, Owen thought it would be a good move for Beam. Personally, he agreed with Beam's dad, the hardware store and lumberyard would provide a good living for Beam and Sophia.

Beam glanced up at the threatening clouds overhead. Rain was in the forecast. He hoped it held off until after his drive to Seattle to sign the papers on his plane and house. He was pretty ecstatic that his plane sold for the asking price, and a bidding war between two interested parties jacked the sale of his house up several thousand over the listed price. Both transactions gave him the money needed to buy into the partnership with a nice reserve. He wished he could thank his grandma and grandpa Garrett for the generous inheritance they left. He, his brother, and his two cousins had no idea they'd been added to the will. The amount each of them inherited added to the shock of losing two people so prominent in their lives.

He'd left his truck on Main Street and, as he turned the corner, he bumped into Jillian. She released an "Eek!" as he grabbed her arm to steady her.

"I'm sorry," she said with a laugh. "I wasn't watching where I was going."

Beam held up his free hand. "My fault. I cut the corner short. How are you?"

"Good. You?"

He rubbed the back of his neck. "Tired, loving fatherhood, looking forward to when Sophia sleeps through the night. Not necessarily in that order."

"I bet the loving fatherhood is first."

"You're right. That is number one."

She smiled, but he saw the compassion in her expression. "I'm sorry you're going through this alone."

"Not alone. My parents are lifesavers. I don't know what I'd do without them."

"Your parents are pretty spectacular people. They sure have been fantastic to me."

Jillian managed the gym his parents owned, and they talked often of how competently she handled everything. "They sing your praises all the time. Mom can't believe they waited so long to hire a manager."

She shook her head and blushed sweetly.

"Where are you headed in such a hurry?"

She held up a take-out bag from Renaldo's Italian Kitchen. "Lunch with Jolie."

"Ah, I just saw her. She said she was waiting for a lunch delivery."

"That's me." She thumbed over her shoulder. "I better get over there. Take care, Beam."

"Bye, Jillian." He stuffed his hands into his coat pockets

and headed down Main, his thoughts shifting from the lumberyard purchase to Misty. Mason had called a few days earlier to tell him Misty left a message that she was in Sacramento. His hope that their marriage could be saved was fading.

The nagging feeling of guilt tangoed around his heart. He'd been wrong to insist they get married. He'd forced Misty's hand, and now he regretted his actions. She didn't love him, and was showing no signs of loving Sophia. Love wasn't an emotion he could force, but it was also one he wouldn't live without.

Today, after Owen finished looking over the sales contract, they'd discussed his options for divorce.

He entered the comfort of Rowdy's Bar and Grill and inhaled the enticing scent of beef stew. Acknowledging a few patrons he knew, he skirted around the bartender, and filled a couple of glasses with ice and Coke. Rowdy's office was down a short hall. The door stood open, and his brother sat behind an old wooden desk, shuffling through a stack of receipts. He looked up when Beam set both Cokes down.

"Howdy, bro."

"Howdy, yourself," Rowdy said. "What's up?"

Beam sank onto the sofa facing Rowdy's desk. The over-sized behemoth was the color of butterscotch, and the softest leather Beam had ever felt. "I need an ear."

"Sharing feelings? You know I'm not good at that." Rowdy leaned back and laced his fingers over his flat stomach.

Beam closed his eyes, suddenly exhausted. "Come on, Rowdy. It's about Misty."

Rowdy picked up the glass closest to him and sniffed the contents. "I'm going to need something a lot stronger than this, if you want to discuss my sister-in-law."

Beam opened his eyes and leveled a look at his brother.

Rowdy liked to put on a show of indifference, but he was a good listener and usually offered sound advice. "I talked to Owen today."

"About?"

"I had him read over Mason's partnership contract, which is in order. I wanted you to know, since you don't trust him."

"I told you, it isn't Mason that I don't trust." Rowdy took a swallow from the glass and set it down. "It's your wife."

"I also talked to Owen about a divorce."

Rowdy shifted his bottom jaw to the left, a facial expression familiar to Beam. An uncomfortable subject was on the table, and this was his brother's signal he was debating what to say and what to keep to himself. He stood and came around the desk to join Beam on the sofa.

Beam leaned his head back against the soft leather and stared at a poster of the solar system attached to the ceiling above them. He turned his head toward Rowdy as he pointed up.

Rowdy shrugged. "I like looking at the stars."

"You do know you can walk outside and see the real thing."

"I work nights. Sometimes I don't get out of here until I'm too tired to look up. This is my alternative."

"So you just lay here and look at your ceiling?"

"Are we here to talk about my poster or your wife? Are you filing for divorce?"

Beam ran the fingers of both hands through his hair. "I don't know what to do. Misty found out her mom lives in Sacramento, and left. I'm not sure she'll come back."

"I'm supposed to say something supportive here, right?" Rowdy stretched out his long legs, and blew out a breath. "I'm sorry for you, but I have to add good riddance."

"You don't sound sorry." Beam glanced at his brother. "You don't look sorry either."

Rowdy shrugged and nodded toward the hall. "You knew how I felt about her before you stepped through the door."

"Why do you hate her so much?"

Rowdy slapped his knees as he sat forward. "The question is why don't you? She's been with every guy from here to Seattle. She's rude, self-centered, and arrogant, to name just a few personality flaws. She tried to pass your baby off as someone else's, and then deserted you both. I know you say you love her, but man, I just don't get it."

Beam picked up his glass and took a swallow of Coke. He wasn't sure how to answer, because he wasn't sure he understood himself. He just knew he loved her, and honestly believed if she'd give him—their marriage—a chance, they could be happy. How did he know? Just a faint inkling that made no sense given the circumstances.

"Sorry." Rowdy hung his head. "I really am. I know you're hurting and I wish there was something I could do. I tried to like Misty for your sake, but she makes it near impossible." He patted Beam's knee. "You came for a talk. So talk."

Beam scrubbed both hands over his face. "I just don't know what to do."

"Do you want to hear my opinion, or would you rather I stay quiet and just listen?"

"Haven't I already heard your opinion?"

"Not all of it. I think, if you're seriously contemplating divorce, you should probably file before you sell your plane and house. If I know Misty, she's going to want a huge chunk of whatever you get, and then some."

Beam shook his head. "It won't matter. There was a pre-nup."

Rowdy's eyebrows rose in surprise. "Well, that was one smart thing you did."

"I didn't do it. Misty did."

Rowdy released a barking laugh. "She had you sign a pre-nup, because why?"

"Not sure." Beam rested his elbows on his knees and rolled his tight neck. "Maybe she thought I was marrying her for her money."

Rowdy laughed again. "What money? She cuts people's hair for a living."

⁓

Terrified Arleen would kick her out if she didn't pay her way, Misty got up each morning and drove around Sacramento searching for a job. After five long, frustrating days, she finally found something in a chain hair salon next to a grocery store. She considered it so many steps below where she'd been before getting married, but it was a job. And this salon, unlike every other place she'd applied, was hiring.

Her next stop was a discount clothing store, where she bought the requisite black pants and enough black T-shirts to get through a week. Arleen didn't own a washer or dryer, which meant visiting a laundromat. Misty had never been inside one, and the huge machines that swallowed quarters like she popped Milk Duds intimidated the daylights out of her. The place smelled of overheated clothes, perfumed dryer sheets, and was so full of static electricity, the hair on her arms stood at attention. Still, she managed, and even washed the heap of dirty clothes in her mom's room to prove she was worth keeping around.

Each day, after filling out applications, she stopped in at the twenty-four hour diner where her mom worked. Seating consisted of two U-shaped counters with sticky vinyl stools around each. Booths lined the walls. Through the kitchen window, two hefty men with sweat dripping off their foreheads flipped burgers and assembled sandwiches. The place reeked of grease, burnt toast, and cheap perfume. In an attempt to build a relationship with her mom, she chose to come here, rather than return to the squalid little house she couldn't bring herself to call home. She struggled to belong at the diner, at the house, even at the Laundromat, in the hopes it might please her mom—though all three places disgusted her.

Misty didn't see much of her mom. Arleen worked from six in the evening until two a.m. She was still sound asleep when Misty left in the morning, and already at work when Misty finished her job search for the day. So, to the diner she would go in hopes of a few pathetic scraps of attention.

The reunion with her mom didn't go the way Misty had envisioned. No tears of regret had fallen. They hadn't shared any late night gab sessions, or gossiped over cups of coffee before work. No shopping trips together, or giggling over lunch. They hadn't hugged once, or even touched. No bonding moments could be filed away to pull out and cherish at a later date. Finding her mother was a far cry from the way she'd always dreamed. But she wouldn't complain. She'd found her mom, so she considered herself richer this week than she was a week earlier.

Misty vowed today would be different though. She would make her mom smile when she announced she had a job. She just might get that long awaited hug.

The diner was busy when Misty arrived. She found a seat at the counter her mother was working and Arleen set a Coke in front of her.

"Thanks, Mo…Arleen." She made the same mistake every day. Her mom had been adamant that Misty call her Arleen. She insisted, as friends, they should be on a first name basis. The first day she'd stopped at the diner, Arleen had admitted up front that she didn't want her coworkers to know she had a daughter, especially one as old as Misty. To admit she'd given birth twenty-seven years earlier would mean she'd lied on her application by about ten years. Not that her mom's age would matter in a place like this. Anyone with eyes could see her mother wasn't in her thirties, and that Misty and Arleen resembled each other. Still, the gut punch hurt more each day, rather than a little less. To have a mother she couldn't claim was almost worse than not having a mother at all.

Misty spent the next few minutes wrestling with her hypocrisy. She felt so betrayed and angry that Arleen wouldn't claim her as a daughter. Then her thoughts would turn to Sophia. By not telling Arleen she had a baby, she wasn't claiming Sophia. She felt her reason behind the deception was justified. Arleen would probably kick her out if she discovered Misty had made her a grandma.

While Arleen was at work, Misty searched the house for any pictures of her as a baby. There were none, but Misty didn't have any pictures of Sophia—funny how she'd begun to think of her daughter by that name. In the week she'd been here, she'd gone from defending her mom's every action to questioning not only her actions, but also her motives. Then questioning her own.

Who was she to lay blame? How was she different?

Reality left her scrambling to defend her own deeds while, condemning Arleen's.

"Hello?" Her mother waved a hand in front of her face, bringing her back to the present. "I don't have all night. What's it goin' to be? The special is an open-faced roast beef sandwich."

That sounded good and might be safe from the sweat dripping off the cook's forehead, but after an eon of feeling like a hippo, she decided to go light. "I'll have a salad."

Arleen's mouth turned down in a sharp frown. Her

lipstick had made a home in the crevices around her lips. "Good way to get rid of some of that weight you're carrying around. That's got to be tiring."

Misty should be used to the sharp barbs flung so casually, but they still stung like a bandage being ripped from tender flesh over and over.

Her mom slipped the order pad in her pocket and pulled her hair up off her neck. "What do you think? Should I go short and blonde?"

"No," Misty said.

The skin between her mom's eyebrows puckered. "Why?"

"I forgot to tell you. I have good news," Misty blurted out in an attempt to earn an elusive smile, and to escape telling Arleen she'd look terrible as a blonde. "I got a job today."

"I hope it pays good." Arleen lowered her arms. "Why not short and blonde?"

No congratulations, no yay, or way to go. Just another bandage ripped from the same raw spot. "After I've been at this place for a few days, I'll fix your hair."

"What do you mean fix? And why do I have to wait?"

"I need time to get used to their products. Give me a few days and I'll do your hair. A cut, and color. Not blonde."

The door opened and her mom swiveled a hip—an automatic reflex in anticipation—without missing a beat. "Can you do it for free?" she asked Misty, while winking at the man who'd entered.

Misty glanced over her shoulder. "Do you know him?"

"No, but he's kinda cute, don't you think?"

This time the sting was jealousy, that some stranger could take her mother's attention away so easily. Misty's throat tightened with unshed tears as she searched for something to say that would gain her another minute of her mother's time.

Look at me, Mom. "I'll do your hair for free."

Her mom flashed her tarnished smile. "Really?"

Misty nodded. *Even if I have to use my last dime to pay for the products.*

$\mathcal{A}$ girlish giggle pulled Misty from a foggy dream of Beam. The deep rumble of a man's laughter followed. The numbers on her cheap alarm clock showed it was after three in the morning. More laughter made her sit up. Ice clinked into glasses, then footsteps stumbled down the hall. She heard something hit the wall and a slurred, "Shhh, my roomie's sleeping." The bedroom door next to hers slammed shut.

Even with a pillow held tightly over her head and ear buds blasting music from her phone, her mom, and whomever she was with, kept Misty awake until dawn pushed its way over the horizon.

She woke later than she should have. Even a shower didn't alleviate the grogginess of too little sleep. The first day at her new job would be long. *Thanks, Mom.* She staggered into the kitchen to start the coffee pot she'd invested in, and nearly jumped out of her skin when a man at the table cleared his throat. His shaved head glistened in the morning sun coming through the filthy window. He wore a pair of camouflage cargo pants, and tattoos covered his back, chest, and arms. He reached into the box of cereal she'd purchased with her dwindling funds and popped a handful into his mouth.

"Sorry, darlin', didn't mean to scare ya. You Arleen's new roommate?"

"Yes." *Among other things.*

His dark eyes raked over her. "Where'd you come from?"

She wrapped her cardigan around her body. "Washington."

He raised two bushy eyebrows. "State or D.C.?"

"State." She pulled a mug from the cupboard. "Where'd you come from?"

He chuckled before he took a swig from the carton of orange juice she'd also purchased. "I stay with Arleen when I'm in town."

She raised an eyebrow. "When you're in town?"

"I drive a rig 'cross country."

She hinged her jaw as she scrutinized him. "With a woman at every stop?"

Another gaze raking down her body made her cringe and regret she'd asked the question.

"I don't get any complaints."

She changed her mind about coffee. In fact, she wanted out of the house as quickly as possible. She grabbed her coat off the hook by the back door and slipped it on.

"That's an awful big rock you got on your finger there, darlin'. I see that, and I wonder why you would be living so far from home in a dump like this. You runnin' from some-where...or someone?"

Misty thought about that question as she drove to work, and decided she'd been running *toward* someone. She assumed, when she found her mom, she would also find the love and support she was searching for. She was wrong.

Since childhood, she believed that if her mother ever saw her again, she'd realize her mistake and welcome Misty into her world with loving, outstretched arms. Even though Misty didn't want to admit it yet, the reality of that happening appeared slim. Arleen didn't seem capable of loving anyone but herself. And supporting someone was possibly beyond her realm of understanding.

Still, Misty held a faint hope, like a flickering candle in a windy cavern. She hadn't been here very long. Maybe, over time, her mom would have a change of heart. She would realize what she'd given up, and want it all back.

Sadly, she'd also come to California believing the living conditions would be different. Instead, she would be struggling right along with her mom, making minimum wage, hoping to keep a roof over their heads, and have enough gas in their tanks that they could make it to work. The situation she found herself in was new and appalling. She'd always relied on someone to take care of her needs. But things wouldn't be like this for long. She would figure something out, and soon, because this way of life was unacceptable.

Her thoughts traveled to the man at the kitchen table. How could Arleen be with someone so disgusting? How could she be happy with a man who stopped by when he happened to be in town, and admittedly spent time with other women when he wasn't? Did she just sit around waiting for this guy to show up, or did she also have other men?

As quick as a jolt of electricity, Misty realized she had been wrong about her father all these years. She knew he helped their community, donating money or building materials, when needed. He was honest and humble to a fault. He had provided a comfortable home for his family. But Arleen had left him. She walked away from a husband and daughter who loved her, to live alone in squalor and work in a diner.

Acknowledging Mason had done the best he could, while missing the woman who'd abandoned them, was hard, but true. He'd loved Misty through it all, even though she made life impossible. All these years, she'd treated him horribly, blamed him for every tiny thing that went wrong in her life.

She was as bad as her mother.

Misty pulled into a parking space and lowered her forehead to the steering wheel. Her mom spent six years trying to be a mother, before deciding she couldn't do it. Misty hadn't even spent a day with Sophia. From the moment of Sophia's birth, Misty had turned away, afraid she'd do exactly what Arleen had done—abandon her daughter and husband. She knew before the wedding, before Sophia's birth, that she would be a failure. How could she spend a lifetime looking into Beam's disappointed eyes? She had no maternal instincts, and didn't spend one day trying to develop any.

That made her worse than her own mother.

~

Beam stood and stretched his arms high over his head. After reading over and signing papers for thirty minutes, he was now a full partner of Douglas Hardware and Lumber. Mason stood, and what started out as a handshake ended in a backslapping man hug. "Welcome to the business, Beam. I look forward to working with you."

"Thanks for giving me this opportunity."

"How about a celebratory lunch?" Mason asked as they slipped into their coats.

"I'd love to celebrate, but I'll have to take a rain check. I have one more appointment before I pick up Sophia."

"Not a problem. We'll plan it for another time."

Beam waited on the sidewalk while Mason got in his car and waved when he drove away. After his car disappeared from view, Beam walked in the opposite direction, toward Owen Danielson's office. As happy as he was about becoming a partner, today wasn't a day to celebrate.

An hour later, he picked up his daughter from Aunt Alice.

He entered the house they were renting from Alex, and dumped all the baby paraphernalia on a chair. Alex had done a lot to make the place comfortable and welcoming. Other than emptying the guest room of furniture to set up a nursery, there wasn't much he had to do. He and Sophia had settled in with little effort.

As he unbuckled Sophia from her carrier and removed her coat, he considered how much her birth had changed his life.

Tomorrow morning at eight sharp, he would become a respectable businessman. They would keep the assistant manager Mason had hired. Mason would continue working full time for the first month or two, and then become a part-timer.

Beam stretched out on the sofa with Sophia nestled on his chest. He rubbed his lips against her silky hair, breathing in the sweet lavender scent of her. She was drowsy, and so was he, but he fought sleep, wanting to appreciate this moment. She wouldn't let him hold her like this forever. Soon she'd be crawling, followed by walking, going to school, graduating, and then leaving him for college. His eyes slid shut, committing the weight of her head on his chest to memory.

He blamed filing divorce papers for his unusually nostalgic mood.

CHAPTER 12

Beam came out of the hardware store and locked the door. He stepped back on the sidewalk and looked up at the new sign. Eden Falls Hardware and Lumber had replaced Douglas Hardware and Lumber earlier that day. A silly sense of pride washed over him. He was a business owner.

"Looks good."

Beam turned and noticed Brandt Smith sitting on a bench in front of the fire station. He crossed the street and looked back at the hardware store, nodding in satisfaction. "Thanks."

"I heard you were moving back and buying into Mason's business. Rita Reynolds may be the gossip queen of Eden Falls, but you can't always trust what she tells you."

Beam chuckled. "I guess there's no need to put an announcement in the paper with Rita around."

"No." The firefighter scooted over so Beam could sit. "Have you found a place to live, yet?"

"Yeah, we settled into Alex's rental."

"That's a nice place."

"Yeah, it is." Beam didn't know Brandt well. They played on the same baseball team, but Brandt was fairly new to town. He settled against the back of the bench. "Being back feels surreal. I never thought I'd be living here again."

"Is it a good surreal or bad?"

Beam took a moment to think the question over. "Despite the situation, it's good." He glanced at Brandt. "I assume you know Misty left."

"Everyone in town knows. One thing I had to get used to after moving here from Spokane, small town gossip is fast and vicious."

"Kind of the way everyone thought you and Alex were a couple before Colton came to town?"

"Alex and I were never a couple. We went out a few times. I was new in town, trying to get back into dating, after a bad breakup, and Alex was"—he shrugged—"Alex. She's fun, easy to be around, and safe."

Beam nodded. "That's Alex alright."

Two teens Beam didn't recognize walked past. He wouldn't have paid much attention, except one was almost two feet taller than the other. They would have made an odd pair, except both were dressed in matching Goth black. The taller boy wore a trench coat so long it almost touched the ground. His hair was as black as night, as were his lips. His skin, in sharp contrast, was so pale it appeared to glow. The shorter kid's distinguishing feature was orange hair, too bright to be natural. He held back a chuckle that twitched at his mouth. What were kids thinking these days? If he'd put on a get up like that, his dad would have laughed him right back into his room to change.

The thought hit him between the eyes. *He* was a father. He was now responsible for a tiny being, a miracle. What would he do if Sophia came out of her room one day looking like that? Would they have words? Would he send her back to change? Would the scene end in his anger and her tears?

The notion scared him half to death, and made him feel more alone than ever.

The tall teen glanced their way and nodded. Beam did the same. Brandt held up a hand. The orange-haired kid kept his eyes forward.

He and Brandt watched the boys continue down Main. At one point, their coats fluttered under the streetlight, making them look like a couple of bats about to take flight.

Brandt glanced at him. "Did you ever—?"

"No," Beam laughed. "My dad would have killed me."

"I was thinking the same."

Beam pushed up from the bench. "You pitching for the team this year?"

"Unless someone else wants the job."

"Not me. I never was much good at pitching." Beam zipped his coat as the sun dropped behind the mountain peaks. "I guess practices will start soon."

Brandt thumbed over his shoulder at the fire station. "The guys were just talking about that at dinner."

Beam pulled the collar of his coat up around his neck as the temperatures dropped further. "Hope you all have an uneventful night."

"Me too." Brandt stood. "Hey, we're about to start a game of poker. You want to sit in?"

"My poker days are over for awhile. I have a tiny person who will be ready for a bath, a bottle, and then bed by the time I get her home." Beam turned to cross the street. "Let me and Rowdy know when practices start up," he said over his shoulder.

Brandt waved. "Will do."

∼

One day bled into the next with mind-numbing regularity. Misty woke up, worked all day, ate a salad at the diner, went back to the house, watched television until bedtime, and then did it all over again the next day.

And I thought Eden Falls was boring.

She didn't have extra money to go out, and no friends to go with, if she did. Her only pleasure was a daily walk around a small pond near work. A sign at the beginning of the trail said once around was a mile. That first mile had about killed her, but she'd worked herself up to two miles and felt pretty proud of her accomplishment. She wasn't much of an outdoors person, but found the fresh air stimulating, and appreciated the natural color the sun put in her cheeks. Best of all, her pants no longer cut her in two. *Who knew walking could be beneficial?*

Besides Jillian.

She and her mother didn't have the same days off, so they only saw one another at the diner, where Arleen still referred to her as a friend in trouble, who needed a place to crash.

They didn't talk much, even during the two hours she worked on her mom's hair. Arleen kept her nose buried in a gossip magazine, cackling over the misfortunes of the rich and famous. Out of the blue, she would ask a random question about Eden Falls. "Is Rita Reynolds still the town gossip?" "How many husbands has Patsy Yarberry been through?" "Does Rance still own The Fly Shop?" "Does his wife still run the library?"

After three weeks in Sacramento, Misty missed Eden Falls like a splinter in the bottom of her foot, too deep to dig out, too tender to forget. She missed working at Dahlia's, gabbing with the girls and catching up with clients who, until now, she'd taken for granted. Since she was the new girl at the shop, her regular clients these days were the walk-ins. She actually missed the familiar, overly friendly faces getting in her business.

She even missed her traitor friends. The girls who should have supported her, but took Beam's side instead. Alex, she could understand, since Beam was her cousin, but the others should have been more loyal to her and her situation.

To acknowledge she missed Beam was the worst. They'd only been together a short time, but she'd grown familiar with his ways. She missed breakfast cooking when she got up in the morning, and the way he kissed her brow when he thought she was sleeping. He'd always had his hands on her belly when she was pregnant, his deep laugh rumbling when Sophia kicked. Then, his constant attention had been annoying. Now, it was a fuzzy soft memory. At night, he'd lift her shirt exposing her huge stretch-marked stomach and talked to the baby, promising her a life of wonder and happiness. And love. He promised her ballet lessons and dolls, but added that he'd teach her to fish and catch a baseball. Again, annoying at the time, but now…a sweet memory.

She also thought of Sophia a lot. How much had she changed? Was she a good baby? Was she alert? Did she eat well? Was she sweet natured like Beam or did she take after her mom?

Sometimes late at night when she couldn't sleep, she'd picture how it might have been if she was the domestic, motherly type. She would imagine herself doing things mothers did, things Alex's mom did. Things like fixing dinner, greeting Beam when he came home from a long day, rubbing his shoulders for a few minutes before Sophia's bath time. They'd tuck her into bed together, and then snuggle on the sofa after the dinner dishes were done and the kitchen cleaned.

Those kinds of thoughts always surprised her. She'd shake her head, and wonder why they'd popped there in the first place. That kind of life wasn't what she'd planned before Beam and Sophia. In fact, that kind of life scared her to death. It was a life she knew she couldn't excel at. She would be a complete screw-up as a wife and mother. Not only would she let Beam and Sophia down, she would disappoint everyone remotely important to her.

Beam wasn't into social media, so she couldn't cyber-stalk, but she longed to see a picture of Sophia. She surmised it was normal to be curious—that she might be normal was something she'd started to question. Had her dad sent her mom pictures of her? If she'd received them, there was no evidence anywhere.

Misty walked into the diner after work, same conversation, different day.

"Coke?"

"Diet."

"Another salad?"

"Sure."

"I still think I'd make a great blonde."

"Not blonde, Mo…Arleen."

"The mailman dropped off an envelope for you."

"What?" That was a blip on their instant replay screen. Misty set her drink down. "What kind of an envelope?"

"A brown one." Her mother smirked as if she'd delivered the world's funniest joke.

The door opened and Arleen swiveled her hip. Her eyes grew sultry, and a smile Misty knew wasn't meant for her, crossed her face. "It was a big envelope. I had to sign for it."

"Did you notice who it was from?"

Arleen flapped a hand to let Misty know the conversation was over. A man was taking a seat in her station. "Some attorney. I put it on your bed."

Thirty minutes later, Misty sat on her bed staring down at divorce papers. This is what she had wanted, to be free. She didn't want to be tied down to one man yet, especially not Beam. She wanted to find the man who could make her heart palpitate like in a romance novel. A man who could make her forget everything, including her name, with a kiss. A divorce was exactly what she wanted. She should be jubilant, jumping for joy. Instead, she felt like a fissure had split her chest open, and something vital was seeping out.

Anger slowly filled the crack. Like her father, Beam did everything wrong. This wasn't how it was supposed to end. She should be the one divorcing him. She was the one who wasn't in love. She was the one who left first. Beam had turned everything upside down, again. He had threatened divorce, but she certainly hadn't taken him seriously. He loved her. She saw it in his eyes every time he looked at her.

After reading through the papers a second time, and then a third, she felt too stunned to be angry anymore. Had Beam met someone else, someone who would become Sophia's stepmother? The thought make her sick to her stomach.

Setting the papers aside, she stood and looked out the window into darkness. She hadn't planned to go back to Eden Falls anytime soon, but a divorce took away any reason to go back at all. Maybe Sacramento was where she was supposed to end up. She'd always lived in Eden Falls, except for a few married months in Seattle. This envelope of papers was like a permanent permission slip to separate from a place she'd wanted to escape for years. So, why was she hesitating? Why did it feel like an iron door closing behind her rather, than a field of fresh opportunities opening before her? With a simple signature, she would be free.

She picked up the papers and slid them back into the envelope. She and Beam had no property together. She'd made sure of that. A divorce would be simple, uncontested. Beam would have sole custody of Sophia. Had Arleen given custody of her to Mason? Had she even cared enough to question, as Misty was? She'd read through her dad and mom's divorce papers quickly, only concerned with finding an address, and an explanation for her dad paying her mom money.

Misty set the envelope on the top shelf of her closet, out of sight. If Beam had found another woman, he'd just have to wait to move on. She'd sign the papers when she was ready.

After washing her face, she climbed into bed. As soon as her head hit the pillow, she heard a noise. Wrapped in a sweater, she sneaked down the hall and peeked into the living room. Her mom's *friend* sat in one of the sad looking chairs, pulling off his boots. *Thunk. Thunk.* She didn't like that he'd walked in without knocking. She'd locked the door, so either he had a key, or he'd stopped at the diner for one.

"What're you doing here?"

"Hello to you, too, darlin'." He flashed a smile before he pushed out of the chair and disappeared into the kitchen. She heard the cap of a bottle hit the countertop, and the clink of ice in a glass. When he came back to the living room, he sank onto the sofa and ripped open the bag of pretzels she bought after work.

"Do you always just come in and make yourself at home?"

He took a swallow of whatever he was drinking. "Yep." He picked up the remote, and put his feet on the coffee table, knocking several of the magazines to the floor. "I've been on the road fifteen hours, darlin'. Could you whip up something to eat?"

She scowled. "Whip something up yourself. I'm going to bed."

He raised his eyebrows and leered. "Need some company?"

"You're disgusting," she said, trying to hide the shiver that squirmed down her spine.

"I've been called worse." He took a gulp of his drink and turned on the television.

Misty lay awake listening to the noises coming from the living room and kitchen, terrified the man might try to come into her room. Her door didn't have a lock, and she had nothing to push in front of it to keep him out. She didn't sleep a wink until her mother came home, and then she didn't sleep because of the noise they made until daybreak.

At first light, she took a quick shower, dressed warm, and jumped in her car. She had the day off, but she refused to stay in the house with her mom and that repulsive man. She remembered seeing signs on Highway 50 for Lake Tahoe. Following the map on her cell phone, she drove while questioning her mom's sanity. What on earth did she see in such a despicable human being, who only stopped by on his way through town? Wasn't there anyone in this world Arleen cared about? What about herself? Didn't she have enough pride to care about herself?

All the questions marched through her mind made the two-hour drive fly past as quickly as the miles. She finally pulled over at a scenic view area to take in the breathtakingly beautiful blue lake. She didn't usually take the time to notice nature, but Lake Tahoe and the surrounding area was glorious. She climbed out of her car, and stood in the quiet beauty as a chilly breeze blew her hair across her face. As she twisted it into a knot at the back of her neck, she thought of Beam, a lover of nature. He would have appreciated this view. A smile tugged at the corners of her mouth, as thoughts of her husband swirled around her. If he were here, he would make some sweet comment about the blue of the lake matching her eyes, as he held her hair aside and kissed her neck.

She stopped at a small restaurant that reminded her of Noelle's Café in Eden Falls. The menu was filled with home-made goodness. She had a turkey sandwich on fresh baked bread and a side salad. The waitress was chatty and, for once in her life, Misty sat back and listened. She discovered it didn't hurt one bit to be polite to a talkative stranger.

When she climbed in the car for the long ride back to Sacramento, it was with the hope her mom's friend would be gone by the time she reached the house.

CHAPTER 13

Misty reluctantly shopped secondhand stores, flea markets, and garage sales until she found an affordable bed and an upright dresser for her room. Neither piece was much to look at, but it made her small space feel more like her own. And was more permanent than the inflatable mattress. She hoped it showed her mother she had every intention to stay.

With her dwindling savings, she bought a cheap sofa to replace the sagging one in the living room, and an even cheaper mattress for her bed.

She spent her days off cleaning, because she couldn't stand to live in the filth. Her dad had hired a housekeeper right after her mom left, so all Misty ever had to do was the bare minimum. To her, that translated into picking up her toys and loading the dishwasher occasionally.

After college, she got a place of her own, and hired the same lady that cleaned her dad's house to come in once a week. Housework and buying cleaning products was foreign to her. She read labels, asked questions, and began in the kitchen. She scrubbed from ceiling to floor, exchanging dirty water for clean often. She dumped about thirty-seven hundred bugs from the single light fixture, replaced a few broken hinges on the cabinets, and threw up when she pulled out the fridge. Her *pièce de résistance* garage sale find was a throw rug that covered as much of the scrubbed but still dingy linoleum floor as possible.

Afterwards, she eased into bed, muscles she didn't even know existed screaming in pain. Her definition of clean probably wouldn't satisfy most people, namely Alex, but she didn't care. To her the kitchen sparkled. The only person she was trying to please was her mom, and she'd lived with the grime for so long, just wiping the counter would be an improvement. Misty experienced such a sense of pride at her accomplishments, she decided to tackle the other rooms in the house.

Every day off for two weeks, she worked on another room. In the living room, she ripped down the filthy drapes and stuffed them into the outside garbage can. She washed the dirt off the windows and walls, and hung curtains she found at a garage sale. After adding a few nails and sanding the sad little coffee table, she painted it a happy purple. She replaced the depressing beach scene with a white-framed, flowers-in-a-meadow print she'd found in a clearance bin because the glass was missing.

Other than scrubbing the tub, toilet, and sink until her fingers ached, there wasn't much she could do to spruce up the shabby bathroom. A new shower curtain, held by more than three rings, and a small throw rug found on sale, brightened the space. She bought a clearance reed diffuser for the corner of the vanity. The tiny room smelled like pumpkin spice rather than spring flowers, but anything was better than mildew.

After scrubbing, scraping, scouring, lots of sweat, and blisters, the house finally resembled a place someone, besides her mother, might want to live. Her mom had to notice the work she'd done, had to be able to smell the pine scented cleaner, but not one word of appreciation escaped her.

The slight was just one more stab to Misty's heart. It also conjured thoughts of how many times she had done the same to friends. How hard would it have been to tell Alex her house looked nice the day before Peyton was due back from Iraq, rather than nit-pick tiny details? Why hadn't she told Carolyn she looked gorgeous the night of Alex's wedding, or complimented Stella on her ability to teach—and care for—a room full of second-graders all day? She should have told Jolie her wedding was beautiful—even if she hadn't been included. And she could have encouraged Jillian to ask Brandt out when she noticed her interest. They both loved the outdoors and would probably make as icky sweet a couple as Alex and Colton, despite the fact that Jillian was socially impaired, and Brandt was a Neanderthal in firemen's gear.

Those last thoughts came from unadulterated jealousy. Brandt hired on with the fire department a couple of years earlier. New to town, he sported striking muscles, and a face to match. She approached him one night in Rowdy's Bar and Grill, only to be shot down in front of a whole group of friends. Ever since, she'd badmouthed him every chance she got. Then, she felt he deserved what she said about him. Now, not so much.

As time went on, Misty reluctantly noticed other things about her mom. She never asked how Misty's day was, but was happy to go on and on…and on about her own night at the diner. Their conversations—what little there were—always centered on her day and never Misty's.

Why is it always about you? What makes you so mean spirited? Do you consider what comes out of your mouth before you actually say it? Misty thought the same questions of her mom that Alex and Stella used to ask her. That realization was a real eye-opener. She began seeing herself through her mother's actions, and was ashamed to acknowledge how much she resembled such a callous woman.

Thinking back, there weren't many people in Eden Falls that she hadn't treated awful at one time or another. She considered Alex her best friend, and still she'd tried to seduce her boyfriend by trapping him in a laundry room with her blouse undone, and unashamedly kissing him. At the time, Peyton was the sexiest guy around and, of course, he was Alex's. She had to give Peyton a great deal of credit that day. He hadn't participated in that kiss at all. He high-tailed it out of that room, and never said anything to Alex. But Alex had been just outside the door and had heard everything. Still, she remained Misty's friend.

What did that say about Alex? What did what happened say about her? That she was sadly lacking in the ability to be a true friend, loyalty wasn't high on her list of morals, and she deserved so much worse than she'd ever gotten.

Her mother didn't seem to have any friends. No one but the trucker came to the house, and her mom never went out with anyone. What a sad, lonely life she led. Here Misty sat right in the middle of it, licking her wounds when she should be calling everyone she knew, making amends.

As the days wore on, and Misty discovered more about herself, she felt an overwhelming need to talk to Alex. She wanted to hear her friend's voice, and possibly apologize for that one incident. Several more days passed before she worked up the courage and called Alex's house.

A deep hello shook her memory. Alex was remarried.

Her first instinct was to hang up, but she fought the urge as she sank into one of the two rickety kitchen chairs. "Hi, Colton." She swallowed. "It's Misty."

A long silence followed, and she wondered if he'd disconnected the call. If he had, it would be well deserved. "Hello," he finally said.

She put a hand to her throat, trying to relieve the stranglehold the memories of her previous actions held over her. At the time, she was so sure Colton was the answer. He could get her out of Eden Falls, and provide her with all the things she deserved. She glanced around at her surrounding. All the cleaning in the world couldn't transform the dingy kitchen she sat in. She'd come so close to pulling Colton down into her sinking boat. If it hadn't been for Alex… "How are you and Alex?"

"Happy. We're both very happy."

She could hear the smile in his voice, could imagine it on his face. "I don't think I ever told you congratulations, but I really am glad you and Alex found each other. She was alone for a long time after Peyton was killed."

"Thank you." She knew by the surprise in his voice, her comment was unexpected. "You saying that means a lot…to both of us."

She pulled a plastic apple from the bowl on the table. Even though she'd scrubbed the ugly fake fruit, it still felt sticky. "Is Alex home?"

"She's right here."

"Hi, Misty."

There had been no covering the mouthpiece or wait time before Alex was on the line. She must have been right beside Colton. The idea she might be interrupting the newlyweds would have made her gleeful six weeks earlier. Now she cringed. Tears sprang to her eyes, and she tried to swallow the sob working its way up her throat. While she fought to maintain control of her emotions, Alex's familiar voice enveloped her in a sensation of comfort. "Hi." That was all she could manage at the moment.

"How are you?" was asked softly and full of concern.

Misty pressed her lips together and drew a shaky breath into tight lungs. "I'm okay."

"I heard you found your mom."

She wanted to cry out to the friend who'd always—always—been there for her, *I did, but it's nothing like I envisioned. In fact, it's the complete opposite. It's horrible. She lives in a filthy house, and she works in a diner. I can't believe my mother left me for this!* Alex would understand. Even if no one else did, Alex would. Instead, she said, "She's been here in Sacramento all the time." She meant to laugh, but the noise that escaped sounded more wounded animal than woman. "Just a thirteen hour drive away."

"I'm sorry." Misty knew Alex meant it. She was honest and caring, and knew Misty's heart better than anyone ever had. Misty had taken their friendship for granted since kindergarten. She twisted it to suit herself whenever possible. After all the backbiting and underhanded incidents Misty had pulled, why did Alex remain her friend?

As hard as she struggled, Misty couldn't hold her emotions in check any longer. Her breath came in broken intervals of sound.

"What can I do to help?"

Again, Alex knew. In fact, Alex probably knew Misty better than she knew herself. Misty dropped the plastic apple back into the wooden bowl. "Nothing. I...I'm okay. I just wanted to... I *needed* to tell you I'm sorry."

"Sorry? For what?"

"For what I tried to do with Peyton. I'm really sorry. I just needed you to know that...and well, for everything. You've always—always been a good friend, and I haven't been a very good one back. I'm sorry."

"Misty." The word came out choked. "Everything is forgiven and forgotten."

Just like that, Misty knew she was forgiven. Alex was that

kind of person. Big-hearted. Sympathetic. Nurturing. Caring for people was in her blood. Kindness ran through her like water through a faucet. Misty fell extremely short of all those qualities.

She shut her eyes to gain control. *Show some kindness. What would Alex ask if the tables were turned?* "How's Charlie?"

Alex's laugh floated through the receiver, and Misty wished she were sitting in front of her friend, wished she could see Alex's smile. "Wonderful. Loves school. He just started baseball practice. Brandt is his coach again."

Instant guilt consumed her. She'd never been to one of Charlie's games, though he'd asked her to come many times. Yet, her thoughts didn't dwell on baseball or Charlie long. There was something else she had to know. Her throat tightened uncomfortably, again. "How's Beam?"

The pause was physically painful. "He's okay. He's pretty much taken over the day-to-day stuff at the hardware store. Your dad still works there, but Beam is running things."

"And Sophia?"

"Oh, Misty, she's beyond-words-beautiful. She's growing so fast, and her blue eyes are always alert, taking everything in. When she hears Beam's voice, she turns her head, searching for him." Another weighty pause that Misty knew was to give her a moment to realize all she was missing. Alex was crafty that way. "You don't need to worry about Sophia. She is well taken care of. Beam is so sweet with her. He's an amazing father."

"I'm not. I was never worried." Misty stood from the kitchen chair and looked through the window over the sink. The overgrown backyard was coming to life after the long winter months. Green buds colored the tips of tree branches, and tulips pushed up along the neighbor's fence. The smell of rain wafted through the open window. Instead of brightening her outlook, the sight colored the future gloomier. She was missing spring in Eden Falls. "I knew Beam would take good care of her."

Her own comment reminded her of the morning her mother left her on the steps so long ago. *"Mommy has to go away. Be a good girl for your daddy. He loves you very much."*

"Why don't you come home for a visit?" Alex said, breaking into her thoughts.

Misty couldn't tell her friend how wonderful that actually sounded, not after all the years she'd yammered on about getting out of that town. If she hadn't spent almost every penny she'd earned fixing up this hovel… No, she couldn't go back now. She was too…fragile. She'd never considered herself fragile, even in her most vulnerable moments, but there was no other word to describe how breakable she felt.

"Is Beam seeing anyone?" The question that had been nagging at her ever since she'd received the divorce papers came tumbling out. When Alex didn't answer immediately, Misty's stomach did a pathetic summersault. She had to reminder herself, she was the one who left.

"Not that I know of."

Misty released a breath she didn't realize she'd been holding. Just as she'd done with her friendships, she'd taken Beam's feelings for her for granted. The knowledge that she actually cared surprised her.

She did care for him—and Sophia—more deeply than she ever imagined possible.

"I hope I didn't interrupt you and Colton. I just needed to call, to talk. To apologize."

"I'm glad you called."

Misty battled to draw air into lungs that felt as if they'd shrunk in the wash. Alex knew she was miserable and didn't gloat. She had every reason to take advantage of this moment. Misty would have.

"Consider a visit. I'll call the girls and we'll get together. They'd love to see you."

I doubt that, but I'll hold onto the thought anyway.

"I'm sure Beam would be happy to see you."

I doubt that, too. "I should let you go."

"Call if you need anything."

"I'm fine." *Lie.* "I really am."

"I'm glad you called, Misty. It was good to hear your voice."

All Misty could do was nod before disconnecting the call. She sat down and glanced at the disgusting gray doily still under the bowl of fake fruit. Pushing the bowl aside, she picked the doily up between forefinger and thumb, and pitched it into the trashcan. Then, she stumbled down the hall, climbed into bed with her clothes still on, and cried herself to sleep.

~

*A*fter flying tourists around Washington since graduating college, Beam liked settling into a routine in the hardware and lumber business. At first, he worried that being cooped inside day after day would be hard, but he found he didn't mind when he knew he'd be going home to Sophia.

A new load of fencing was delivered late yesterday, and the fresh smell of cedar still filled the back of the store. He took a moment to look over his new domain and appreciate the way things had fallen into place so nicely.

"Hi, Beam!"

Beam turned toward Charlie as he charged down the aisle. Alex followed a few steps behind.

"Hey, buddy. You on your way to school?"

"Yep." Charlie produced a snaggletoothed grin, proudly displaying a new hole.

Beam squatted down eye-to-eye with the kid. "Hey, you lost another tooth."

"I pulled it out last night all by myself."

Beam ruffled Charlie's black hair before he straightened. "I hope the tooth fairy remembered to stop by."

Alex planted hands on her hips. "Yeah, the tooth fairy that visited our house last night assumed Charlie won the lottery rather than simply losing a tooth."

"I got ten bucks!"

"Ten bucks," Beam said, opening his eyes wide with enough enthusiasm to match Charlie's. "I was lucky to get twenty five cents."

"You and me both," Alex replied. "But we didn't have Colton McCreed living in our house."

Beam laughed. "Gotta love those stepdads."

Charlie glanced around. "Is Sophia here?"

"No, buddy. She generally doesn't come to work with me."

"Aww," Charlie said in true six-year-old disappointment that lasted all of five seconds. "Can I go look at the hammers, Mom?"

"Yes. Just don't do any hammering," she quickly added over her shoulder, because Charlie was already running down the main aisle of the store.

"Okay!" he yelled back.

Beam leaned an elbow on a nearby shelf, smiling after the kid who'd stolen every Garrett heart the minute he was born. "So, Low-rider, what brings you in on this beautiful spring morning?"

"Misty called me last night."

Immediate concern had him straightening. "Is she okay?"

"I don't think so." She raised her eyebrows and a slight smile lifted the corners of her mouth. "Which might actually be a good thing."

"A good thing?"

Her smile grew. "I don't think the reunion with her mother was everything she dreamed it would be."

Beam rubbed the back of his neck when a muscle tensed. "Just about anybody in town could have told her that."

"Right, but she wouldn't have listened. To be honest, neither would you or I, if we were faced with the same circumstances."

He wasn't sure he'd search for his mother if she'd abandoned him, but Alex was probably right. Having never been in that type of situation, he couldn't know how he'd react.

"She asked about you." Alex tipped her head and studied him for a long moment. "She wanted to know if you were seeing anyone."

Her words sent a shot of hope through his system. "What did you tell her?"

"The truth. That I didn't know." She juggled her car keys from one hand to the other, and Beam assumed she was waiting to hear if he was.

"I'm married, Alex, so no, I'm not seeing anyone."

"She also asked about Sophia."

Beam rubbed the back of his neck, again. The tight muscle was telling him it was confession time. "There's something I haven't told anyone, yet. I filed for a divorce. Owen sent the papers to the Sacramento address Mason gave me. I know they were delivered because Misty's mom signed for them."

Alex's eyes grew wide with surprise. "What? Why?"

"Did Misty say she was coming home?"

"No, but that doesn't mean she won't."

Beam held out his hands. "Am I supposed to just sit and wait for her like Mason waited for his wife?"

"I think when Arleen Douglas drove away, Mason knew she wasn't coming back."

"And I don't know if Misty's coming back." He lifted a shoulder. "She hasn't sent the papers back, yet."

"That's good news. Right?" The smile that lit her face one second, faded the next. "Or not, if you're ready to call it quits."

"I don't know what I want anymore. On one hand, it's stupid of me to believe she'd come back. Especially if she found the mother she's longed for her whole life. On the other hand, I keep thinking if she weren't coming back, she would have signed the papers and sent them back by now. I'm torn between wanting her back and not, if she's only going to leave again. I won't put Sophia through her mom coming and going as she pleases." He looked at Alex, hoping she could offer insight. "What do you think?"

"This is Misty we're talking about. I've known her forever, and still wouldn't dare try to guess what she's thinking." She paused a long moment, then she lifted a brow. "She cried."

The news made Beam's heart hurt. "Misty doesn't cry."

Alex smiled. "No, she doesn't, but she did last night."

"At which part?"

"At all the parts. She cried almost the whole time we talked. Before we hung up, I suggested she come home for a visit."

"What'd she say?"

"She didn't say yes,"—her smile grew—"but she didn't say no either."

After Alex and Charlie left, Beam's mind spun wildly. Had he been wrong to file for divorce? Maybe he should have waited, given Misty a little more time.

Or maybe he should have gone after her.

Beam wondered why Misty had called Alex rather than him. Alex said she'd apologized for something that happened years ago, which was another something Misty never did. She'd asked about him, wondered if he was seeing someone. She'd asked about Sophia. That was the biggest shock of all. She'd asked about her daughter for the first time since Sophia's birth. He didn't want to get his hopes up, but how could he not if Misty was asking about them? He just kept turning the information over and over in his mind, with no hope of any answers. Like Alex said, Misty wasn't someone to be second guessed. Perhaps he should call her. Or go to Sacramento.

He pushed that idea to the side. If Misty came back, it had to be her decision. He'd pushed her into marriage. He wouldn't push again.

~

*A*fter work, Misty drove to the post office and mailed the signed divorce papers. Over the course of the day, she convinced herself that what she was doing was right. For once in her life, the decision she made was for the benefit of someone other than herself. Giving Beam an uncontested divorce would be the single most unselfish thing she would ever do. He and Sophia would be better off without her in their lives. So why didn't she feel better inside? Why did it feel as if her chest was caving in, crushing her heart?

Misty had fought tears since her conversation with Alex three days earlier. She hoped by signing and mailing the papers the water works would dry up. They hadn't.

Maybe it was time for answers.

She sat in her car behind the diner and waited until her mom came through the back door for a smoke break. Dusk had fallen, but a light over the door illuminated her mother's sharp features. She pulled her coat tighter around her thin body as Misty approached. "You scared me. Why are you lurking out back? Did you have to work late?"

Misty tightened her own coat and leaned against the diner wall next to her mom. "No. I had to do something after work."

"If you want me to put in an order, you'll have to wait until I finish my break. We've been slammed. This is the first—"

"I'm not hungry," Misty blurted out to stop her mom from chattering on and on about herself. Not once since she'd been here had her mom asked about her husband, or her day, or anything that might involve Misty's feelings.

Her mom pulled her chin back so far it disappeared into a fold of wrinkles. "So, what are you doing in back of the diner?"

"I wanted to talk to you."

"So talk," her mom said, rolling her free hand, a gesture Misty was beginning to hate.

Misty's chest tightened. Confrontation had never been a problem for her, but she felt she was walking a tight rope with her mom. Their—she didn't even know a term for what they shared. Relationship was too strong a word. So was friendship. She'd settle with association—their association was strained, and Misty was afraid it would break if she added more tension.

"When I looked through dad's files trying to find your address, there were some cancelled checks. Checks Dad sent to you, checks you cashed." She glanced at her mom from the corner of her eye. "Were they a bribe?"

"A bribe?" Arleen's laugh turned into a hacking cough, tempting Misty to whack her on the back. She resisted. "Why would Mason be sending me bribe money?" she asked when she could finally suck in enough air to speak again.

So her dad hadn't been sending Arleen money to keep her away from Misty. The truth was what Misty suspected, but didn't want to accept. Arleen had stayed away by choice, because she didn't want to be a wife or mother. "What was the money for?"

Arleen lifted a painted-on brow. "For whatever I need it for. When I'm short, I call. Sometimes he sends a check, sometimes he doesn't."

Misty turned to face Arleen. "Why haven't I ever talked to you? When you call?"

Her mother's eyes darted away. "I call Mason's cell phone."

You didn't want to talk to me. Amazed that every new discovery still stung, Misty swallowed the tears that threatened. Maybe this was why Misty had very few lasting memories of her mom. Arleen had always been like this. She and her dad had learned to cope. *Poor dad. After mom left, he compensated for my behavior since I was six.* Why had Misty made things so much harder for him? "Why would you ask him for money?"

Her mother's mouth dipped into a frown. "Why not? He has plenty."

"But...you divorced him."

"You got that wrong sister. He divorced me." Arleen sucked on her cigarette so deeply, Misty could have fit two golf balls in the hollows of her cheeks. She raised her head to the sky and blew out a stream of smoke. "He had me tracked down and the papers delivered. If I hadn't been promised a nice settlement in writing, I never would have signed those papers."

Suddenly sick to her stomach, Misty had to turn away. She really was her mother's daughter.

"Plus, he promised to keep you, even though you weren't his."

Misty turned her head back so quickly, she almost toppled over. She must have misunderstood her mother because of the blood rushing through her ears. "What did you say?"

Arleen looked at her in confusion. "Which part?"

They were standing so close, Misty could smell the staleness of her mother's breath, see the nicotine stains on her teeth. Her stomach dropped at a sickening speed. She was glad she hadn't eaten much lunch, because she would have lost it all over their shoes. "The part about me not being his."

"You mean he never told you?" Arleen bent over and stubbed her cigarette out in a can at their feet. "Figures. Mason was born without a backbone."

Misty covered her mouth, not yet sure she wouldn't lose her lunch. Her face heated even as her hands grew icy. "Who is my dad?"

Arleen waved a hand as if she'd been asked a trivial question like "What's the special of the day". "I have no idea. I was fifteen and working in a truck stop diner."

Misty stood, propped against the wall, long after her mom went inside. She wasn't aware when dusk turned to darkness, or how low the temperature had dropped. She just knew she didn't trust herself behind the wheel of her car—the car she'd been given by the man she thought was her father.

She didn't remember getting into that car or driving to the little house she couldn't call home. Even showering and scrubbing her skin until it was tender, seemed more like a dream than reality.

She did remember staring at her reflection in the mirror and seeing only resemblances to her mother. There was nothing of her father looking back at her. Why hadn't she ever noticed that before?

She leaned over the toilet and lost her lunch. Not only had

she signed divorce papers today, but she'd also discovered the man she'd called dad for twenty-seven years wasn't even related.

After wiping her mouth, she lifted her hand, and stared at the beautiful ring Beam had given her, along with his hope for their future together. She slipped the ring off and flexed her fingers. They hadn't been married for a year, and yet her hand felt naked without it. She pulled several sheets of toilet paper loose, wrapped her ring up tightly, and carried it into the bedroom. Searching her top drawer, she pulled out a single sock, its mate having disappeared somewhere in the depths of a washer at the laundromat. She stuffed the wad of toilet paper into the toe and slipped the sock into the pocket of a pair of jeans that were finally too big. The jeans went onto the top shelf in the very back of her closet.

She sank onto her bed, and cried herself to sleep, again.

~

*S*pring arrived and, according to the books, the hardware store's sales were up from the year before. With Mason's help, Beam hired two high school boys as summer help. They would work a couple of afternoons and alternating Saturdays until school was out. That gave him five full-time and four part-time employees, not including Mason.

Beam questioned his mom, his aunt, and Alex on what they'd like to see in the store. They'd all voted for more gardening supplies, so he was interviewing a woman this afternoon for their enlarged garden department.

He was with Rita Reynolds, helping her pick out the perfect flashlight when Owen Danielson walked through the door. He wore a grim expression and held a large manila envelope. Beam knew instantly that the envelope carried bad news. The woman he loved had signed the papers that would dissolve their marriage.

Rita held the flashlight over her head as if she might club someone. "How do I look?"

"Menacing." Rita, a tiny woman with bird-like tendencies, wanted to use the flashlight as a weapon rather than emergency lighting. She heard there was a rash of burglaries in Harrisville and was certain the perpetrators would move in on Eden Falls next. "I think that flashlight fits you perfectly, Rita."

Beam rang up Rita's purchase while Owen looked through the how-to books near the register. After he'd seen her out the door, Beam turned to the attorney.

Owen ran a hand over his head, causing his bad comb-over to stand up on one side. "I'm sorry, Beam. I know you hoped for a different outcome."

Beam nodded, not trusting his voice enough to speak, but somehow not embarrassed by the fact.

"I received the papers yesterday. I marked the places where you'll need to sign."

"Thanks, Owen." He cleared his throat and thumbed over his shoulder. "Come back to the office and we'll settle up."

Owen waved the offer away. "Not today, Beam. I'm in no hurry for your money. I'll have Jolie send out a bill at the end of the month."

Beam held out his hand, and Owen shook it.

He followed the attorney to the door and pushed it open as he'd done for Rita. The day was beautiful. People walked the streets, soaking up the warmth, enjoying the sunlight. Spring brought new growth, a renewal of life. The buds on the trees were unfurling their summer greenery. Tulips pushed through dirt that had been frozen little more than a month earlier. Two firefighters were out hosing off one of the trucks.

Business was good, and the town was bustling.

Divorce papers weren't supposed to be delivered on days like today.

Beam turned and wandered the store, answering questions, helping customers. Lily Johnson picked up a can of paint for a corner of the library that needed brightening. She asked after Sophia, which turned his mind to more pleasant things for a few minutes.

He had more blessings than he deserved, and yet he felt as if a hundred-pound weight just landed on his chest. All because, until five minutes earlier, he hoped Misty would come home to him, to them. To the home and life he and Sophia were building.

Misty ran to Sacramento in search of the happily ever after he had hoped to provide.

He shook his head at the thought, which sounded sappy even to him.

CHAPTER 14

Misty walked into the diner and took a seat at her mom's usual station.

A waitress approached, order pad and pencil in hand. "What can I get you?"

"Is Arleen out back?"

"Nope, she was a no-show," the waitress said, popping her gum loudly.

"Is she sick?"

The waitress lifted her shoulder. "Don't know. She didn't call neither."

Misty stood and pulled her phone from her purse on her way out the door. Her mom's number was no longer in service. *Come on, Mom. You didn't pay your bill?*

Minutes later, Misty pulled to a stop at the curb. Her mom's car wasn't in the driveway. *So, she isn't home sick. Where is she?*

As soon as she opened the back door, Misty knew something was wrong. The kitchen cupboards were open and empty. The table and chairs were gone, along with the antiquated refrigerator. Even the microwave Misty had picked up on clearance to replace the grime encrusted one her mother had been using, was gone.

Someone had come in and stolen everything they owned.

Why hadn't her mom called her at work? Why weren't the police here? Where was her mom's car? Had they stolen it, too?

What thief would want an ancient refrigerator?

What if they were still in the house?

She closed the door as quietly as possible, tiptoed through the kitchen, and peeked into the living room—total stupid-girl-in-horror-flick move, but she had to find her mom. The furniture, the new curtains she'd hung, the painted coffee table were gone. Every dog-eared paperback book she'd bought at garage sales, the Kerr jar she'd filled with tulips stolen through the neighbor's chain link fence, had disappeared.

In the bathroom, the vanity door hung open. The thieves had taken the shower curtain and the rings that held it in place. They'd stolen her make-up, curling iron, and hair dryer, even the extra rolls of toilet paper. She picked her toothbrush off the floor and set it on the vanity next to a half bar of used soap, and glanced around for her mom's. *Disgusting. They even took Arleen's toothbrush.*

In her bedroom, they'd stolen everything, including the air mattress she'd stuffed in the closet when she bought her bed. Her clothes were strewn all over the floor.

Stepping back into the hall, she looked at the closed door of her mother's bedroom. Was Arleen in there, lying face-down in a pool of blood? Maybe the thieves had tied and gagged her, so she couldn't call for help. The trucker was the only person Misty could think of who might do this, and she didn't even know the guy's name, or what kind of truck he drove.

Misty put her ear to the rough wood and listened. The

house was eerily quiet. She wrapped her hand around the cold metal knob, turned, and pushed the door open. "Mom?" The room was empty. She walked to the closet, her shoes echoing on the hollow wooden floor. Nothing was left behind.

But…why would anyone take Arleen's clothes and leave hers? Her wardrobe was worth triple—

Realization smashed into her like an icy wave, knocking her breath out with its destructive force, leaving her clawing for air. It wasn't thieves and it wasn't the trucker, or if it was, he hadn't acted alone.

She turned in a slow circle in the middle of the room, sick with certainty that Arleen was involved. They hadn't been robbed at all. Arleen had abandoned her daughter.

For the second time.

Misty's chest tightened to the point of crushing what little was left of her heart. Her knees buckled and she sank to the floor. How could she have been so stupid? How could she have hoped her mom would want to try to build a relationship, when she'd never contacted Misty in all the years since she'd left? Arleen had shown no interest in her, or the life she'd been living. She'd shown no interest in anything but— her ring!

Misty scrambled back to her own room. The jeans she'd hidden in the back of her closet were gone, her closet bare. Dropping to her knees, she threw clothes around until she spotted the single sock, turned inside out, evidence that her mother had found her ring. Still, she continued her fruitless search until she found the length of toilet paper, and knew looking further was futile. Her ring was gone.

She'd tucked the small ballerina jewelry box her mother had given her as a little girl into the top drawer of her dresser. It held several nice pieces her father had given her over the years. Searching through her scattered clothes again would be a waste of time.

Arleen had taken everything, leaving Misty nothing to sleep on but a pile of clothes.

This time her mother hadn't just abandoned her, she'd stripped her bare.

~

*E*aster morning, Beam dolled Sophia up in a dress of yellow ruffles his mom bought for her. They met the rest of the family at church, where his daughter slept peacefully through the hour-long service in her Uncle Rowdy's arms. His mind turned to Misty several times. How would she be spending the day? She'd asked Alex if he was seeing anyone. Now, he wondered the same about her. Was that why she'd sent the divorce papers back after sitting on them a few weeks? Had she met someone in Sacramento and decided to make her life there?

After church, his whole family congregated at his mom and dad's for a huge dinner. Alex confiscated his daughter as soon as he walked into the house, and carried her to the blanket she'd spread out on the lawn in the backyard. She wiggled Sophia's shoes and socks off her feet and kissed her toes, her dimpled knees, and her chunky little thighs.

Colton shook his head as he watched his wife. "She does the same thing to me every night."

"Yeah, I bet she can't wait to get the socks off those big ugly feet," Beam replied.

Charlie dodged around his grandpa to reach their little group, his dog, Barney, by his side. "When is Sophia going to start walking?"

Barney's long tongue slurped up the middle of Sophia's face before anyone could stop him. Her blue eyes grew wide and then her bottom lip poked out in the most adorable way. Everyone watching laughed. Alex gave the dog a kiss on his nose and pushed him away. "Barney, Sophia loves you, but she doesn't want to smell like your slobber. Go play in Aunt Glenda's garden."

"Alex, you keep that dog out of my garden!" Glenda hollered through the open kitchen window.

"Uncle Beam, when is Sophia going to start walking?"

"She has to learn to sit up first, buddy. How about you read to her," Beam said pulling a soft book from the diaper bag. "She likes it when you make the animal sounds."

Charlie plopped down next to Sophia and held the book over their heads. Sophia rolled to her side and cooed at him adoringly. The whole scene made Beam happy, and hurt his heart at the same time.

If Sophia hadn't come along, he would still be here, spending Easter in his parent's backyard. He might have brought a date, but more likely not. He glanced down at his daughter as she cooed at Charlie. She'd changed his life so drastically, yet, he couldn't imagine a day without her. Surrounded by people he loved, he was glad he'd made the decision to move back to Eden Falls for Sophia. She would grow up loving these people, too. She was the center of attention, was fought over, and passed from Uncle Rowdy to cousin JT to Colton easily.

"She's going to be spoiled rotten," Grandpa Dawson fussed, and then took his turn dancing around the backyard with her.

Beam didn't think she'd be spoiled rotten by anything but love, and who didn't want that for their child?

After dinner, JT became Police Chief Garrett and left for duty at the station. It was a school night for Charlie, so the McCreeds made their exit, followed closely by Uncle Denny and Aunt Alice. That left Beam and Rowdy with their parents. They bundled up against the chill that fell once the sun dropped behind the mountains, and went out onto the back deck overlooking the river. Beam snuggled his fed and bathed daughter against his body. The slide of the glider he shared with his mom had lulled her into a peaceful bliss. She looked up into his face for several minutes before the rhythm of movement caused her eyelids to slide shut.

Sophia had celebrated her first Easter.

Beam put his nose to his daughter's dark hair and breathed in her scent. He was sorry Misty was missing memorable milestones, just as Misty's mother had missed hers.

His cell rang. He pulled it from his shirt pocket, surprised to see his wife's name. He connected the call. "Hello?"

Nothing.

"Misty?"

Glenda reached for Sophia when he stood. He handed the baby to her grandma and headed for the sliding glass door, ignoring Rowdy's glare. He waited until he was inside before he said, "Misty? Baby? Are you okay?"

No response.

Desperate to keep her on the line, he started talking. "I wish you were here. We had Easter dinner at Mom and Dad's with the whole family. Sophia was the star of the party. Charlie read books to her, Dad and Uncle Denny danced around the yard with her, and Aunt Alice kissed her until she giggled.

"We're sitting on the deck now, and the sky is full of stars. Can you see the stars from where you are?" He sat down on the sofa in his parent's living room and rested his forearms on his knees. "It's chilly but I have Sophia wrapped up in a cozy quilt. She is so beautiful. She still has a head of black hair and the bluest eyes."

"Alex said she recognizes your voice."

He hadn't expected her to respond. When she did, his breath caught in his throat. Her voice was soft, hesitant, and hearing the unhappiness in it made his chest tight. "She does. I think she already knows she has me wrapped around her tiny finger." Misty didn't respond, so he continued. "She smiles a lot, but she also has a fierce little temper. She lets me know when I'm doing something wrong, or not doing it fast enough to please her."

He leaned back on the sofa with a smile. "Charlie makes her giggle and it's the cutest sound. You can't help but laugh right along with her."

"Is she good?"

Beam tried to tamp down the hope swelling inside him, filling every tiny crevice. Not only had Misty finally called, she was also asking about her daughter. Hope is a small word with vast meaning. He didn't want to hope for something that would never happen, but the fact that Misty was asking about her daughter gave him the courage to hope. "She is so good."

He wasn't sure his next comment would be the right one, but felt it was important for her to know. "I miss you, Misty."

A long silence followed. Then he heard the soft click as the call disconnected. She was gone, and still he wasn't sorry he told her. Even if it ended up being the last time they ever spoke, she would know he missed her.

∼

*M*isty's whole body was trembling when she disconnected the call. She walked through the back door and sat on the crumbling cement stoop, determined not to lose control. Tipping her head back, she looked up at the night sky. The stars weren't as visible here as in Eden Falls, but it was the same sky Beam had been looking at. Without the mountains, her sense of direction was off. Were they even looking at the same side of the hemisphere? Were they both seeing the crescent moon at the same moment?

A sigh turned to a ghostly moan as her gaze dropped to the unkempt backyard. She felt as worthless as the rusted lawnmower covered by vines and weeds that sat in the far corner. She hadn't opened a bank account since moving here, just cashed her checks, and put the money in a jar in her bottom drawer. She'd never dreamed—not in a million years —that her mother would take everything she had, including the very bed she'd been sleeping in. The bed she'd bought with the last of her savings, so she'd feel more at home in this dilapidated little dump.

Where had Arleen run to this time? Not that it really mattered. Misty would not be searching for her again.

She'd actually picked up the phone to alert the police, but, in the end, couldn't bring herself to make the call. Just the thought of telling the cops her mother packed up everything she bought to make this dump a home and moved, leaving her daughter penniless, was too pathetic. To admit her mother had abandoned her a second time was beyond humiliation.

Misty internalized the pain. How did the mother of a brand new baby walk away as she had done? How could she ever judge Arleen when she'd abandoned her own daughter and a husband who loved her? How could she look in the mirror at her own reflection, yet still blame Arleen for anything? She couldn't, because she was worse. Arleen had tried for six years. She hadn't tried for six hours.

She swiped at her falling tears.

She had nowhere to turn. She couldn't go back to Eden Falls and face the people who would judge her for her actions. She couldn't face Beam's parents, Preacher Brenner, or Alice Garrett, couldn't face any of her friends. She had no excuse for turning her back on her husband and newborn, except for the overwhelming urge to find her mother.

Her dream that Arleen would realize her folly and beg forgiveness disintegrated the minute Arleen answered her knock on the door. Misty's desire to be loved and wanted, vanished the moment her mother stole everything she owned. Everything Misty had so foolishly clung to for so many years had vanished in the short hours she'd been at work. Instead of feeling loved, Arleen had accomplished the opposite. She'd never felt more small and insignificant, more unworthy of love in her life. Arleen had decimated her.

She inhaled the sweet smell of something blooming, new growth after a long cold winter. New beginnings. A chance to grow taller and stronger than last year.

Her mind circled around to a word she'd been thinking about a lot since she'd talked to Alex. Forgiveness. Alex said her past actions were forgiven and forgotten. She remembered one of Preacher Brenner's sermons on forgiveness. He said, "Just as love, forgiveness is a gift you can give and receive." Forgiveness wasn't something she gave often or freely, so how could she expect to receive it? If she did go home, would Beam be able to forgive her? And what about trust? Would he ever trust her to stay if she went back?

Could she trust herself?

The list of her victims was a long one. How could she ever begin to atone for all the hurt she'd inflicted over the years?

Misty pushed to her feet, feeling much older than her twenty-seven years. Desolate darkness seeped into her body, until even her skin hurt. She walked through the empty house, flipping on overhead lights as she went. At least Arleen hadn't taken the light bulbs. She could be thankful for that one thing.

Misty didn't even have enough money for a hotel. She'd have to continue sleeping on a bed of her clothes, until she could figure something out.

She'd come to Sacramento because of her mom. Now she had no reason to stay, but where could she go? The only place she wanted to be at this moment was sitting on a deck in Eden Falls with Beam's arm around her.

That realization hit her hard.

She held up her left hand, sad that her ring hadn't meant much to her until it was gone. Now she felt as if she'd lost more than just her ring. She'd lost her way. She'd lost things she hadn't realized she possessed—true friends, family, support, love, and possibly her husband and daughter.

She'd lost everything.

She rubbed her thumb against the inside of her ring finger. It felt naked and exposed. Arleen and, Misty assumed, her trucker boyfriend had probably pawned it first thing. She crossed her ankles, sank down on the pile of clothes in the middle of her bedroom, and cried until she felt she couldn't possibly have any tears left. Then she cried some more.

~

Mason sat in Renaldo's Italian Kitchen, a half-eaten plate of Chicken Milano in front of him. He'd just come from The Fly Shop where he bought a new fishing rod and reel. He'd also signed up for a woodworking class at the community college in Harrisville. Yes, he was going to enjoy semi-retirement. He would be able to visit Sophia more often. Babysitting on Tuesdays, when Alice and Glenda had conflicting schedules, wasn't enough. Tuesdays were his favorite day of the week.

Life was good.

"Hello there, Mason."

He knew the voice before he looked up. Patsy Yarberry was standing near his shoulder holding a drink and a bowl of pasta.

"Mind if I join you? I hate eating alone."

Yes, I mind. But he'd never say that aloud. He stood and pulled out the extra chair at his table. "Please."

She set both her bowl and drink down, then slid into the chair. "Are you sure you don't mind some company? You looked very deep in thought."

He took his chair and tried to keep his eyes on her face, rather than her ample chest with the message *Aged to Perfection* printed across the front of her shirt. "No, I don't mind. I don't care to eat alone either."

She cocked an eyebrow. "But…you eat alone all the time."

He chuckled at her bluntness. "Yes, but that doesn't mean I enjoy it. I usually eat at home, not in public."

"That has to be even lonelier."

"Not really."

"You like your own company?"

Mason lifted a shoulder. "Most introverts don't mind spending time on their own."

She nodded like she knew what he was talking about, which she didn't. Patsy was the complete opposite of an introvert. The most outgoing, comfortable-in-her-own-skin person he knew. He took off his glasses and polished the lens on his napkin, searching for something to fill the quiet that had fallen like a lead balloon. Patsy's presence always flustered him. He slipped his glasses on. "Do you eat here often?"

"I eat here or at Noelle's Café about once a week." She leaned forward, her dark eyes bright with happiness. "I'm not much of a cook."

He stared at her a moment and then chuckled.

She sat back with an infectious smile. "I know you want to say, *'But Patsy, you own a bakery.'*"

"That was on the tip of my tongue."

"Cooking is different from baking."

"How?"

Patsy leaned forward a second time and planted her elbows on the table. Mason found himself watching her animated eyes as they widened.

She told him about the pastry shop and how she got started. And he had no idea where the next hour went, but found he was pleased to have her company after all. She took his mind off Misty, who he hadn't heard from since the week she left. He called her cell phone every Sunday, left a message on her voicemail that always ended with "I love you". He never got a return call. She probably deleted the messages before she listened. But he thought it was important for her to know that, even though he didn't agree with her decision to leave, even though he thought chasing after her mom was a dead end, he loved her and wanted her to come home.

"So, tell me about yourself, Mason. We've lived in the same town for years, and I don't really know much about you, other than the obvious. What do you like to do in your spare time?"

He cleared his throat. Talking about himself wasn't something he enjoyed. He was actually a very boring person. "Until just recently, I didn't have much spare time."

"I heard you partnered up with Beam. How is that going?"

"It seems to be going well. Beam is doing a great job of running the place and I'm enjoying my new part time hours."

"Part time hours," Patsy said in a dreamy voice. "I can only imagine what that would be like."

"Have you ever thought of taking on a partner?"

Patsy pushed her plate back and wiped her mouth. "I can't say I have. I have thought of finding a manager who could help, but reliability seems like a thing of the past."

Mason's mind turned to Beam, his reliable, hardworking son-in-law. "Not if you're very lucky."

~

Three days until rent was due, and the small amount Misty made in the last week wouldn't cover it. The money she gave her mom two weeks ago, and the month before for utilities, had obviously been spent on something else, as evidenced by the shutoff notice tacked to the front door. She had five more days of lights and hot water. *Happy birthday to me.* She got ready for work each morning at the shop because her mom had only left her a half bar of soap. She'd bummed detergent off a college kid at the laundromat with the excuse she'd forgotten hers. She worked as many hours as her employer would allow, and saved every dime. Her diet consisted of bread, peanut butter, and yogurt—ten cartons for ten dollars. The silver lining—she slept on a bed of clothes that were now too big.

She was terrified, and she had nowhere to go.

Misty had always fantasized how different her life would be if she found Arleen. Well, her life was certainly different, just not in any way she'd ever imagined. In her eyes, Arleen executed the ultimate betrayal. She'd left Misty with open wounds that oozed raw pain. Her chest, where dreams of her mother had lived, was now an empty cavern.

After a week of wallowing in sadness, she slowly realized her mother had done her many favors, too.

She'd opened Misty's eyes to the type of selfish existence she'd been living. She'd taken the man she thought was her father, his love and hard work, for granted. He'd done all he could to nurture the little girl who wasn't even his own, and raised her as if she was. He'd made her life comfortable, despite an absent mom. She couldn't remember ever asking for a material item and being turned down by him. She also couldn't remember ever thanking him. Mason wasn't an overly affectionate man, but she supposed that was her fault.

Any time he'd tried, she'd pushed him away. All these years he'd remained alone, because she was too selfish to share him with another woman, and too rebellious to love him back.

She'd taken advantage of her friendships, using and abusing at will. Her mother's cruel remarks had prompted memories of her own mean words and thoughtless deeds. Knowing she'd acted anything like her mom filled her with shame.

The universe nodded its head. *'Atta girl. You're getting it now.*

The idea of going back to Eden Falls was growing stronger. In fact, she thought about it most waking hour. After what she'd done, she couldn't expect Beam to give her another chance. Living up to his expectations, as a wife and mother, would be impossible for someone like her. She hadn't received anything in the mail, so she wasn't sure if Beam was still her husband.

Sophia didn't know her own mother, didn't know she had a mother. Her whole world revolved around her daddy and anyone else who took care of her in Misty's absence. If she moved back and botched it, as she assumed she would, it could hurt Sophia more deeply than if she never showed her face again—couldn't it? And if she did go back, how did one learn to be a mother? Wasn't that supposed to come naturally? What if she never developed that characteristic? Wouldn't that be more damaging to Sophia? After what she'd done, would Beam even allow her to try?

The thought of the initial reception made her sick to her stomach. What would people say of the prodigal daughter who came home with her head hung low? Everyone in town probably despised her. Why wouldn't they? She'd been a hateful person for so long, and for little or no reason other than she was unhappy. To make amends would take forever.

Apologizing would require courage. A quality she always thought she possessed, but now, she wasn't so sure.

All these thoughts pulled her down lower.

She didn't want to go back to Eden Falls, because she had nowhere else to go. She wanted to go home, because it was the right decision. Not just for her, but for Beam and Sophia as well.

Her phone beeped a message. Happy Birthday, Misty. Hope your day is filled with happiness. Alex. They'd celebrated her birthday together since they were six.

A few minutes later a message came through from Beam and Sophia, and then her dad. This continued for Jillian, Stella, and Jolie. Even Dahlia and the girls at the salon, sent a message. Instead of making her happy, the messages brought tears. She'd cried more in the last month than she had her entire life.

~

*A*fter settling Sophia into her crib for the night, Beam pulled his cell phone from his pocket and checked for messages. Again. He'd been checking all afternoon, hoping, but not expecting to hear from Misty.

He wandered into the kitchen, wondering how she'd spent her birthday. Hopefully, she'd done something meaningful with her mom. Maybe they'd gone shopping, or out for a nice lunch. He knew spending time with Arleen would make Misty happy. He hoped she was happy.

Once the dishes were done, the laundry folded, and the house picked up, he climbed into bed with one of Colton McCreed's murder mysteries.

. . .

*S*tartled awake by the ringing house phone, Beam grabbed it before it woke Sophia, silently cursing whoever was calling at two-thirteen in the morning.

"Hello." he grumbled.

"Beam, it's Alex. Colton and I are at the front door. The lumberyard is on fire."

CHAPTER 15

Beam bolted out of bed and grabbed a pair of jeans. Still zipping the fly, he ran down the hall and yanked the front door open. On the other side stood Alex, her husband, and Charlie asleep on Colton's shoulder.

"Colton will drive you over. I'll stay here with Sophia." Alex walked past him, a pillow and blanket in hand, and made a quick bed on the sofa.

While they got Charlie settled and covered, Beam sprinted down the hall and grabbed a shirt and jacket. Alex held his boots out when he reached the front door. "Do what needs to be done, and don't worry about Sophia."

"What happened?"

"JT knew you couldn't leave Sophia so he called us." Alex pointed to the door. "Go. Colton will explain on the way."

He and Colton ran for the SUV parked in the driveway. They both jumped in and Colton backed out with a squeal of tires. "Phoebe Adams was working dispatch when the call came in. Luckily, the fire station is right across the street from the lumberyard. The guys were there in minutes. Harrisville fire department is on their way. So far the fire hasn't reached the hardware store, but they're afraid, with all the wood, it will spread."

Beam could smell smoke and see a haze hanging over the east side of town. "Does anyone know how it started?"

"It's too soon to tell," Colton said pulling to a stop at the barricade the police had set up a block away. Beam jumped from Colton's SUV, and JT opened the barricade to let him through.

A crowd had congregated, obviously roused from sleep by the shrill sound of sirens. Recognizable faces watched flames shoot up from behind the hardware store. Thick black smoke billowed into the night sky, the heat already intense. Beam spotted firefighters on the roof of the hardware store, hoses trained on the stacks and stacks of lumber in back.

A Harrisville fire truck, sirens blaring, came through the barricade. Firefighters leapt off and ran around both sides of the building. They doused the barbershop next door, separated only by a narrow alley, flooding the roof and siding so another blaze wouldn't ignite. Cinders rained down like thousands of tiny stars only to fade to gray ash.

"Beam!" His mom ran toward him. His dad followed close behind. "Are you hurt? Where's Sophia? What happened?" She fired off questions too fast for him to answer while patting his arms and chest, checking for bodily damage.

"Mom, I'm okay. Sophia's at the house with Alex, and I have no idea what happened. I just got here."

He was far from okay, but there was no need to push his mom into hysterics.

Mason and Rowdy joined them before the Eden Falls Fire Chief pushed them back. His mom cried harder when the fire spread to the hardware store. He wanted to join her.

The firefighters fought bravely until driven back by the advancing fire. Those on the roof scrambled down ladders, all but one making it to the ground before the roof collapsed. A collective gasp, and a couple of screams and shouts came from the crowd behind them when the man disappeared. The effort went from fighting a fire to saving a life. Minutes later, a thunderous cheer went up as two firefighters carried the man out. Word spread quickly, the injured firefighter was Brandt Smith. Beam watched, helpless, as Brandt was loaded into an ambulance, and taken to Harrisville Regional Hospital.

As dawn began to lighten the smoke filled sky, Beam stood in numb disbelief as the last wall fell in on the rest of the debris lying in a heap. The lumberyard and hardware store were both a total loss. Everything was gone. Smoke burned his throat and stung his eyes, but he couldn't bring himself to leave the smoldering devastation that lay just yards away.

Life was full of twists and turns, and he'd lived through his share this year. All he could do was pick up the pieces and be thankful for what he did have. One of those things was a great insurance policy Mason reminded him of as they stood watching their business collapse in on itself.

He saw the weariness of the firefighters as they slogged through the mess. They'd worked hard to keep the fire contained to only one business. The barbershop next door received a little charring on one side, but no damage to the roof. The house behind the lumberyard lost two apple trees, and the firefighters had to douse a few hotspots on the side lawn, but they managed to save the house. Luckily, the hardware store sat on a corner, so the firefighters had easy access to the rest of the building. The windless night had also been a tremendous blessing.

His thoughts turned to Brandt Smith. No one knew how

the firefighter was doing, but Beam would make a visit to the hospital before the day was over.

His dad still stood on his right side, his Uncle Denny on the left. His mom left an hour earlier to relieve Alex, so she and Colton could get Charlie ready for school.

Beam raised a hand to his dad's shoulder. "Why don't you go home and get some sleep? You have a business to run." He turned. "You, too, Uncle Denny. I appreciate you coming, but there's nothing more you can do here."

"Jillian Saunders will have everything running smoothly at the gym, but I will go give your mom a hand with Sophia." Sadness tinged his dad's smile. "You take as long as you need to here. Sophia will be fine."

"Thanks, Dad."

Uncle Denny rubbed the spot between Beam's shoulder blades. "I'm sure sorry about this. It's a darn shame."

Beam stared at the charred pile, a dream that had literally gone up in smoke, but that dream could be rebuilt. Meanwhile, he'd have materials delivered directly to building sights, so he could keep his regular contractors supplied. A vacant building at the edge of town might serve as a temporary store. They could use crates and junk lumber for makeshift tables. Just last week, he'd run a few ideas for expansion past Mason. He suggested they include more lawn furniture, grills, and enlarge the gardening section for summer. Mason thought it was a great idea. Sadly, this would give them the perfect opportunity to move things around and make the space more shopper-friendly.

"It *is* a shame, but things happen for a reason. A reason we may never know."

Uncle Denny smiled. "Nice way to put a positive spin on a tragedy."

"A tragedy would be the loss of life, and that didn't

happen. Will you let me know if you hear anything about Brandt?"

"Will do." Uncle Denny patted his back. "You know if you need anything at all, JT and I are always around."

"I do know that." Beam took great comfort in the knowledge he could call any number of people at a moment's notice. Alex stood on his doorstep at two in the morning to watch his daughter, and Colton came to drive him to the lumberyard. He'd watched his and Mason's business burn to the ground while surrounded by supporting family and friends—just one of the advantages of living in a small town.

Life might deliver some hard blows, but anything was possible with loved ones near.

~

*A*fter a miserable, sleepless night, Misty got up, and showered in cold water with a sliver of soap. She'd have to wash her hair at the salon. Peanut butter smeared on her last slice of bread was breakfast. This week's paycheck wouldn't begin to cover rent or utilities. Soon, she'd come to this empty house to find an eviction notice posted across the front door. Then she'd be living in her car. One of the stylists at the salon mentioned looking for a roommate, but did she want to stay in Sacramento? Her loneliness had become an echo resounding through her chest, growing with every heartbeat. She wanted to go home.

Crazy that she was thinking of Eden Falls as home, when she never had before.

Thirty minutes later, Misty pulled into a parking spot at work. She looked at the rundown shop in the rundown shopping center and her despair grew. How had she gotten to this point in her life? She used to be fearless. Indestructible. Now, she was a vulnerable, pathetically hopeless pile of…dung.

Her cell phone beeped just as she opened her car door. She dug around in the bottom of her purse until she found it, grateful she'd paid that bill before her mom left. She read a text message that caused her to gasp for air. She slammed the car door shut, and drove back to Arleen's hovel to pack her few belongings.

~

A groan bolted Beam upright in the hospital chair where he'd obviously dozed off. He glanced at the bed where Brandt was trying to sit, his face white as a sheet, his teeth clenched in pain.

He pushed up from his chair and walked to the side of the bed. "Hey. How you feelin'?"

"I…" Brandt croaked, then tipped his head toward the cup that sat close, yet so very far from a guy with a broken wrist and bruised ribs.

Beam picked up the cup and held the straw to Brandt's mouth. He took a deep pull, and winced as the water hit his smoke parched throat.

Beam lowered the cup. "Small sips." Brandt blinked once, and Beam took it as acknowledgment. He held the straw up, again. Brandt took a tiny sip and closed his bloodshot eyes as he swallowed.

"What…happened?" he rasped.

"There was a fire at the lumberyard. You were on the roof when it collapsed. The fall broke your left leg and wrist, and bruised your ribs."

Brandt released a gruff sigh. "Right. I thought…it was a…dream." He glanced down at the cast on his arm.

"Your leg is too swollen to cast yet."

"I…guess base…ball is…out."

Beam chuckled, and positioned the straw near Brandt's mouth. "For this year, yes. We'll have to get Rowdy to pitch."

"Anyone else…hurt?"

"No. You guys were fantastic at keeping the fire contained. I can never thank you all for your night of hard work."

"Part of…the job. Do they know how?"

Beam shook his head. "Not yet. The state fire marshal is investigating."

Brandt closed his eyes. "Were my mom and dad here…or was I dreaming that, too?"

"They just left. Mason offered them a bedroom at his house, so they wouldn't have the expense of a hotel. You've had a steady stream of visitors—Eden Falls firefighters, Harrisville firefighters, half the town's residents." Beam raised his eyebrows. "Lots of women."

Brandt winced when he chuckled.

A moment later, Beam realized Brandt had drifted into oblivion, again.

*B*eam spent the next morning with his insurance agent, followed by a meeting with the state fire marshal. Then, he joined a salvage team and rummaged through the debris to see if there was anything worth saving. He got home in time to feed, bathe, and tuck Sophia's sweet smelling little body into her crib.

After a long hot shower, he sat down at the kitchen table and tried to make sense of the paperwork his insurance agent had provided.

He jumped at the knock on the front door and realized he'd fallen asleep in the chair, again. He rubbed his stiff neck as he pushed away from the table. According to the clock on the microwave, it was after midnight, and almost time for Sophia's middle of the night bottle.

On his way to the door, he stepped on a plastic giraffe that squeaked loudly, just as a second knock sounded. When he pulled the door open, the person standing on the other side was absolutely the last person he expected to see. He pushed the twanging screen open and blinked to make sure he was seeing right. "Hey."

Misty took a hesitant step forward.

Beam wanted to control the sudden pounding in his chest. Alas, it wasn't a possibility. He pushed the screen door wider. "Come in."

She stepped inside and astonished him by wrapping her arms around his middle. His body reacted immediately. His arms closed around her as he tried to remember the last time they'd held each other. Long before Sophia was born. "What are you doing here?" he whispered into her hair.

"Alex texted me about the fire. I had to come."

She felt so good tucked against him. He fought threatening tears. After all that had happened in the last forty-eight hours, emotions were close to the surface. If tears started, they may never stop. The only thing that kept him hopeful, earlier today, was the assurance the insurance agent had given him, and the knowledge that Brandt Smith was expected to recover completely.

"I was so worried." She tightened her arms around him. "I'm glad you're safe."

He was afraid his voice would squeak like a boy going through puberty, so he didn't respond.

Misty turned her deep blue eyes up to his. "Do they know what happened?"

He couldn't stop his hands from framing her face, drinking in the sight of her. The gesture was so automatic, so natural, he didn't take time to second-guess it. No woman had ever made him feel the way Misty did. She was everything to him, his other half. If only she could believe the same of him. "It's too soon to know."

"Was anyone hurt?"

"Brandt Smith was on the roof when it collapsed. He broke his leg and wrist, but he's going to be okay."

She buried her face against his chest and repeated, "I was so worried. My cell phone died soon after I got Alex's text, so I couldn't call."

Beam nestled his cheek against her hair and breathed in, not courageous enough to ask how long she would stay. He didn't need any more disappointment. He heard their daughter give her first warning squawk and released a huff of air, reluctant to move. "I need to make a bottle. That little sound is going to get a lot louder in a minute."

$\sim$

Beam disappeared into the kitchen leaving her standing at the front door. Misty pushed it closed and turned to survey the small house. She was familiar with the rental, but had never taken the time to notice the details. Beam was a neat person, and everything was tidy except for a couple of toys on the floor, and a baby blanket thrown over the arm of the sofa.

The sounds coming down the hall pulled at her like a vine twisted tightly around her soul, causing her breasts to ache. Crazy since her milk had dried up months ago. Willing her feet to stay put, her heart had different ideas and led her toward the first door down the hall. A nightlight lit the space enough to see little arms and feet flailing. Heart hammering, Misty wiped sweaty palms down her thighs as leaden feet propelled her forward, until she looked down into her daughter's blue eyes. The baby's black hair was matted on one side and stuck up on the other. A gurgle, wet with drool, bubbled from her tiny rosebud mouth. The sound made Misty laugh as a sob worked its way up her throat.

"Hello, Sophia," she whispered.

Sophia's coo constricted Misty's throat uncomfortably. Something deep inside stirred, unfurled like the wings of a bird that had been trapped in the dark for a long time. The wings spread wide and flapped once. The numbness, since her mother's abandonment, was replaced with pain.

Unadulterated, throbbing pain that reminded her she was alive, and she'd given birth to this innocent baby who was staring up at her.

Her daughter was the most pure, beautiful, thing Misty had ever seen.

"Would you like to feed her?" Beam's voice startled her, but Sophia's eyes immediately sought the familiar tone.

Misty shook her head. The very idea terrified her. "No. I've never fed a baby."

Beam took her hand and turned her to a rocking chair in the corner. "There's nothing to it. Sophia does all the work." After she sat down, he set the bottle on the edge of a changing table, and bent over the crib. "Hello, beautiful. Are you ready for a dry diaper?"

The baby released a squawk that made Misty smile as tears stung her eyes. The little gray-haired woman who worked at the post office had a habit of squawking like a bird. If you weren't familiar with it, the sound scared the life out of you. "If I hadn't given birth, I might think she was Rita Reynolds' baby."

Beam grimaced. "Don't even suggest such a thing."

They laughed together. The ease of it made her giddy. He looked her way like he was enjoying it too. That was when she noticed the purple crescents of exhaustion under his mossy green eyes.

After hearing about the fire, she'd been so worried for his safety, she hadn't thought beyond that. She hadn't considered the toll it might take on him physically. She hadn't thought past her own selfish existence. Hadn't taken a minute to wonder how he might react when she showed up at the door. Pushing the selfish Misty aside, she tried to step into his shoes for a moment, tried to consider his feelings. He'd just lost the business he'd been counting on to provide for him and Sophia here in Eden Falls. Her thoughts turned to her dad, or the man she'd always thought to be her dad. He had to be hurting, too.

Beam's movements shifted her attention. He lifted their daughter from her crib to the changing table. His big hands moved adeptly, unsnapping tiny snaps and pulling small tabs.

"You have a special visitor here to see you. Did you know that?" he asked Sophia as she cooed and reached toward his face.

Misty's stomach turned at being referred to as a visitor, but what else could she be to the baby who didn't know her? Her eyes flitted to a picture hanging above the dresser. Her and Beam on their wedding day. She'd been four months pregnant. Beam was standing behind her, his big hands resting on her barely-there belly. He looked so handsome in his tux, so happy and proud at the moment the photo was taken, and she couldn't recall feeling anything. In fact, she couldn't even remember that photo being taken. The shame she experienced so frequently lately, shrouded her in its dark cloak, overriding the giddiness she'd experienced just moments ago. On the dresser, there was another picture of Beam snuggling a just born Sophia close to his face. They both looked so serene—an angel and her keeper.

Beam picked Sophia from the table and turned to Misty. Before she had a chance to protest he set the baby in her arms. She shook her head even as she curled her fingers around the solid weight. "Beam…" she said, aware of the panic in her voice.

"She doesn't bite, Misty. I'll be right here with you the whole time."

She tried to relax as Sophia settled into the crook of her arm. Holding her didn't feel as unnatural as she'd expected. *Did you hold me like this, Mom?* She pushed the thought from her mind. Arleen held no place in her heart anymore, and there certainly wasn't a place for her in this beautiful room Beam had created for their daughter.

"I don't think I can do this," she whispered. "I don't know what to do."

Beam lifted the bottle to Sophia's line of sight, and she reached out. He put the bottle in Misty's free hand and moved it towards Sophia's mouth. Sophia's lips clamped around the nipple, and a birdlike sound came from her throat at the first swallow.

Misty was so tense she worried her arm might shatter if pressure was applied. Beam must have noticed, because he gently pushed her shoulders back into the chair. When he took a step toward the door, terror engulfed her. "Wait! Where are you going?"

"I'm going to get a chair from the kitchen. I'll be right back. I promise."

She relaxed her muscles one by one, as she gently pushed the rocker with a toe. The intense blue eyes watching her were unnerving at first, and then magnetic. She barely noticed when Beam came back and set the chair in front of her. He sat and stretched his long legs out around hers. Sophia's swallows and the tiny satisfied hum from the back of her throat were the only sounds in the room. The quiet was too heavy under the circumstances. Finally, Misty couldn't stand the stillness any longer. "She's so pretty."

"And extremely lucky that she looks like her momma."

Sophia's head swiveled at his voice, her eyes searching.

Misty met his gaze in the dimly lit room. "She has your nose."

"Everything else is yours."

She grew daring enough to run a finger over the cap of downy black hair. "Is she good?"

"An angel." He stood. "She needs to be burped."

All the muscles she'd methodically loosened, instantly tightened. "What?"

"She swallows air when she eats, so she needs to be burped halfway through her bottle."

"I knew I'd do it wrong."

"You didn't do anything wrong." Beam smiled as he set the bottle aside and lifted Sophia to Misty's shoulder. "All babies swallow air. It's perfectly normal."

"What do I do?"

"Pat her back." After a couple of finger taps, Beam added, "A little harder."

"Beam, I don't want to hurt her."

"You have to pat her hard enough to dislodge the air bubbles." He sat on the edge of the chair, and patted Sophia's back until a burp escaped.

Misty pulled her head back and looked at Sophia. "That wasn't very ladylike."

Beam chuckled. "Probably the negative influence of her Uncle Rowdy. Do you want to finish feeding her?"

Did she? Awkwardly, Misty lowered Sophia onto her arm and picked the bottle up. A small feat, but once accomplished, she felt extremely proud of herself. Sophia immediately latched onto the nipple. Misty glanced at Beam who smiled at her. She braved one of her own.

He winked, which caused a silly breathlessness to flutter through her chest.

Sophia was sound asleep minutes later. Beam took her

from Misty, burped her again, and laid her on her back in the crib. Misty stood to watch him spread a light blanket over her. She wasn't sure when Beam left the room—too mesmerized by the rise and fall of Sophia's chest. She watched her daughter's mouth pucker, her eyes twitch under tiny eyelids, unaware of how long she stood over the crib before Beam came back in and led her out. She followed him unquestioningly to the bathroom where he'd set one of his tee shirts and a toothbrush, still in the package, next to the sink. When she stepped in, he shut the door.

She hadn't thought this far ahead. She should probably go to her dad's, but the notion of facing anyone else tonight brought on another round of panic. She wanted to stay, but, for the first time in her adult life, she thought sleeping with a man—even if that man might still be her husband—wasn't a good idea.

She changed and washed her face as her thoughts focused on the spare toothbrush. Why would a man have an extra, unless he'd bought it for someone? Her mind recoiled at the thought there might be a woman here. She hadn't considered that. Was there someone else? A someone who would become Sophia's stepmom, after their divorce?

She tried to control her trembling knees when she left the bathroom. The bedroom door was open, so she took three steps to the threshold. Beam lay on top of the bedding with his hands behind his head. He had a tee shirt covering his chest and a quilt thrown over the lower half of his body. The other side of the bed was empty, the covers turned down invitingly. It had been over two weeks since she'd slept on anything but a pile of clothes. Even while traveling last night, without money for a hotel, she'd slept in her car in a well-lit parking lot.

She looked from the bed to Beam. "I don't think this is—"

"Come to bed, Misty. You look tired."

Bristling slightly, she said, "That's not exactly a compliment."

He took a deep breath and released it slowly. "I didn't mean it as an insult, just an observation. Come to bed. I'll sleep on top of the covers."

She hesitated, but only for a moment. The bed with its soft mattress was just too tempting. She walked over and sat on the edge, feeling any energy she had stored in reserve, dribble into a puddle on the floor. He took her arm and pulled her down, then leaned forward and drew the sheet and a light blanket over her body. Once he was resettled, he nestled her back against his chest, as close as she could be with bedding between them. It took a long moment of fighting emotions before she could say, "Thank you for letting me feed Sophia."

She felt his breath stir the hair at the back of her neck. "You're welcome."

He folded a strong arm around her waist. The weight felt good. A sense of belonging settled over her, and she decided to let it stay—even if only for a short while.

She'd been so close-minded to her marriage. So certain she and Beam would be poor—which would make her miserable—she'd never taken all the other elements of marriage into consideration. Beam offered love and stability, had given her everything she asked for. And she'd taken full advantage, because she was *that* kind of person.

"Why did you let me feed her?"

"You're her mother."

A tear tickled the corner of her eye before rolling over the bridge of her nose and falling onto the pillow. "I haven't been acting like her mother."

"You'll always be her mother, Misty."

"Is that why you let me in?"

~

$\mathcal{W}$as opening up to Misty, and allowing his vulnerability to show, the right thing to do? At this point, he had nothing to lose. Either she understood how he felt about her, or she didn't. If being honest would convince her to stay, then yes, it was the right thing. If the truth caused her to run, then so be it. But this time, if she left, she'd leave with the full knowledge of just how much he loved her.

"I let you in because you are the only woman I have ever loved. Your leaving didn't extinguish that feeling. You and Sophia mean everything to me. We, Sophia and I, need you, Misty. I won't hold you here, and I won't ask you to stay. You have to make that decision on your own."

Her back was to him, her midnight black hair pulled up exposing her delicate neck. Very gently, he ran rough knuckles from her temple to her chin. "But, you can only stay if you love us and want to stay. You have to be sure, because I won't allow you to float in and out of our daughter's life. That wouldn't be fair to her. If you decide to stay in Eden Falls, but not with us, we'll work out visitation with an attorney. There is no middle ground where Sophia is concerned. You might not want to hear this, but in my opinion, that is the one thing your mother did right. She left and didn't come back. Though you believed she would one day, she didn't build false hope or leave you hanging. You had one huge disappointment, not repeated heartaches piling up time after time. Either you're going to be Sophia's mother, or you're not. Take some time to think it through, because I want you to be sure. While you're deciding, you can live at your dad's house and come to visit anytime."

He could tell Misty was crying by her shaking shoulders.

His words might have been harsh, but on this, he wouldn't bend. He was doing what was best for Sophia.

Misty rolled to face him, her cheeks wet, the tears glistening in what little light filtered through the shades. She wasn't a crier, and he was glad to see her doing so now. He believed crying could cleanse a soul, and hoped in this case it was true. Misty needed to rid herself of the belief that her mom could make her life perfect, because that wasn't possible.

Without meeting his eyes she said, "What if I'm too much like my mother?"

He ran the pad of his thumb under her right eye. "Then you'll miss all your daughter's special moments, just as your mom missed yours."

"I'm so scared I'll do it wrong." A small sob escaped, and she covered her mouth with her hand.

"I would imagine most parents are scared, Misty. I was terrified. I remember Alex being scared before Charlie was born. Now, she's just about the best mom I know. I'm sure she made some mistakes along the way." Beam cupped her cheek. "We all make mistakes, because none of us are perfect. If we're smart, we learn from those mistakes. Pretty soon, we're doing a little bit better than we did the day before."

She pulled the sheet up and wiped her face when a fresh flood of tears flowed from her eyes. "Are we divorced?"

He smiled and wondered if she could see it in the dim light. "No, we're still married."

She glanced up. "Why?"

"Because I couldn't bring myself to sign the papers, yet." He ran a hand over the back of her head, tucking her face against his chest. They were both quiet for a long time, each absorbed in their own thoughts. Then he whispered, "Go to sleep, baby. We can talk more tomorrow."

She snuggled in close, and he happily held her all night.

~

*M*isty woke to light filtering across the bed. The reassuring weight of Beam's arm was gone. She tried not to move her body as she glanced over her shoulder, afraid she'd wake him. The bed was empty.

She turned and pulled the pillow he'd slept on to her nose. Their conversation last night ran through her mind. After all she'd done to push him away, she marveled that he still loved her. She felt undeserving, and turned the blame on her mother. A moment later, she realized her folly. Her mother wasn't to blame for her faults. They were all on her.

On her drive from California to Washington, she decided she wanted to change. Maybe there was a pill to relieve self-ishness, a twelve-step program called Self-Centered Anony-mous. She imagined a group of people meeting in the basement of a church, a table at the side of the room offering stale, store-bought cookies, and a carafe filled with weak coffee. When it was her turn, she would stand. "Hi. My name is Misty, and I don't care about anyone but myself. I've treated the man who took me in as his own daughter awful my whole life. I've been despicable to my friends, stole boyfriends, told lies, and demeaned them since childhood. I left the man who loved me enough to marry me, and, even worse, I left my daughter when she was only days old. I'm as selfish and self-centered as my mother."

Everyone would chant, "Hello, Misty."

She got up on an elbow and glanced at the alarm clock on the nightstand, and was startled she'd slept so late. Having gone without for a while, made her appreciate things she'd taken for granted such as beds with decent mattresses.

She climbed from her comfortable cocoon and walked through the quiet rooms of the house. Stopping in each door-way, she imagined herself in that space.

In the kitchen, she found a note propped against the microwave along with a key.

Misty,

I'll be in a meeting for most of the day. Sophia is with Aunt Alice. I'll whip something up for dinner when I get home. I hope you'll join us.

B

He'd brought her suitcase in and set it in the living room.

She enjoyed the luxury of a shower with shampoo and conditioner, applied a little make-up along with a brave face, and left the house.

CHAPTER 16

Her dad opened the back door before Misty reached it, as if he'd been watching for her. Had Beam called to tell him she was in town? His smile was wide and encouraging, but tears still flooded her eyes. She had intended to apologize first for all the awful things she'd ever done. To say she was sorry for the way she'd treated him since her mom left, but the words in her mind conflicted with the words that tumbled out. "Why didn't you tell me?"

A frown creased his brow. "Tell you?"

"That you weren't my real father."

He held out his arms, and she went into them. Somehow, it didn't feel awkward as it always had before. Instead, his hug felt like coming home. His hand cupped the back of her head as she cried on his shoulder. The gesture was simple, but completely comforting. She breathed in his familiar smell of bath soap and cedar, with the light hint of citrus aftershave. And she etched both the moment and his scent into her memory.

"I didn't tell you, because it never mattered to me, Misty.

From the moment I learned your mom was pregnant, I loved you as my own."

He let her cry on his shoulder until she'd run dry. Then he led her to the kitchen table. Like a hive of angry bees, emotions swarmed through her, causing a buzzing energy. Emotions she couldn't quite identify. Gratitude? Humiliation? Regret? Her insides were twisted in a complete turmoil. Before sitting himself, he grabbed a box of tissues and set them near her elbow.

She opened up with her dad as she never had before, told him everything that had happened in Sacramento. He listened quietly and asked very few questions. Over the next thirty minutes, Misty realized her dad already knew what Arleen was capable of. Nothing she told him came as a surprise. When she finished her story, there was no recrimination, or "I told you so". He wore an expression of understanding, rather than pity.

"When I went through your desk to find Arleen's address, I also found copies of checks. You've been sending money to her for years. Why?"

His elbows rested on the table between them. He opened his hands in silent supplication, or perhaps surrender. "Because she asked. Because I knew she was making minimum wage at a diner. I knew she lived in a wreck of a house, and that her paycheck didn't always cover food, rent, and utilities." He lowered his hands to the table and laced his fingers together. "Perhaps it was because I felt guilty for having married her in the first place. When we met, she was sixteen. Of course, I didn't know that, or I never would have looked twice. She appeared so much older. She was beautiful and vivacious, so full of life, just like you said, but she was also very sad deep down. She lived a hard life with alcoholic parents, and escaped the only way she knew how. I thought I could give her a safe place to live. I thought

I could give her what she needed to be happy. But, she hated Eden Falls. This place was too slow and sedate for her. She wanted the bright lights and fast times of the big city. She craved glitz and glamour. She was sure those things would make her happy."

Misty looked down at her own fingers twisted together until her knuckles were white. His words were like a fault line, widening as the earth shook, leaving her and her mother on one side, while all the normal people remained on the other. "Like mother, like daughter."

Mason's smile was sad. "Bright lights and a bigger city didn't bring her happiness. She's still searching for something she'll never find, because it was here. With you. The happiness and love she will never find was right under her nose the whole time, in little Eden Falls, in the daughter she never took the time to get to know."

Mason's comment resonated with her. Deep down Misty knew she'd been chasing the same thing her mother was still searching for and would never find. Oh sure, Arleen might snatch tiny pieces of happiness here and there—the cash she would get for Misty's ring would probably make her real happy, until it ran out. And it would run out.

"Like mother like daughter," Misty repeated.

"But don't you see? You can change the cycle." Mason reached for her hand and squeezed. The worry lines around his eyes softened. "You have the ability to make your life as full and rich *as you choose*. You don't have to live in a big city and wear glamorous clothes, or live in a big house and drive a fancy car to have a life filled with happiness. Open your eyes to all you have right here. If you take the time to notice all the small wonders around you and learn to be grateful for what you have, your life can be filled with joy."

Misty's throat tightened again. She thought finding her mother would solve all her problems. Instead, finding her had created so many more. She was broke. Her self-confidence had been torn to shreds. She might have lost her family. But the experience had taught her something valuable too. There truly was no place like home.

"The most important thing for you to know, nothing you did caused your mother to leave. And there was nothing either one of us could have done to bring her back. She wouldn't have stayed long if we had. Your mother believes there is a pot of gold and will always be searching. Looking for someone or something to make her happy, but happiness comes from within. That's the second most important thing for you to remember from all this."

More tears…but they were good tears. The bad was being washed away, leaving her feeling just a tiny bit buoyant. Her dad had thrown a life preserver out and she finally had the good sense to grab ahold. For years, she'd carried her mother's abandonment like baggage around her heart. Suddenly, that baggage felt a little lighter and she, a bit freer.

"I thought, once she saw me again, she'd want me to stay. Would *want* me. After clinging to that dream for so long, I wasn't sure how to let it go."

"It took me a long time to come to terms with her leaving me, too. I used to hope…"

His sentence faded, and as she did with Beam, Misty put herself in his shoes. Arleen hadn't just left her daughter. She stood, walked behind him, and wrapped her arms around his neck. "I'm sorry, daddy. Can I still call you that?"

He patted her arms. "There is nothing to be sorry for, and I would be hurt beyond belief if you didn't."

"I have a lot to be sorry for." This time the tears didn't hurt. They just dribbled silently down her cheeks. "All the heartache I gave you over the years, all the blame I heaped on your shoulders. You've been such a good dad, and I've always taken everything you've done for granted. I've blamed you for things you had no control over. I've been unfair to you for a long time, and I'm sorry."

He tightened his hold on her arms. "Did she take everything you had when she disappeared?"

"Everything but my clothes and toothbrush." She turned her hand so he could see her naked ring finger. "She even took my wedding and engagement rings."

"Did you report the theft?"

She lowered her forehead to his shoulder. "I couldn't."

"Do you want me to?"

Misty shook her head as sorrow for her mother filled the hollow in her chest. Maybe she had a heart after all. "It's over. Just let it be. Let her keep the money she can get for my things. Maybe it will give her some of the happiness she's searching for. But it's the last she'll get from me."

~

*A*s Mason watched Misty drive away, he smiled with pride. He never thought he would thank Arleen for anything, other than giving him Misty, but he silently thanked her now. She'd shown her selfish underhandedness in full color. Reality had opened Misty's eyes to her own behavior, which made her want to change. She'd been through a lot in a short span of time, but she'd learned from the situation and survived. She had grown in ways he never thought possible. Her apology was proof of that growth. She was going to be okay.

His baby had just crossed the chasm into adulthood.

His baby. As much as it had hurt Misty to learn he wasn't her biological father, her knowing lifted a weight from his shoulders. Since Arleen's disappearance, he'd been afraid to tell Misty the truth, for fear she'd run. Where would she be now if that had happened? He might not have been the best father, but he believed he'd kept her grounded.

Misty was home, and after twenty-seven years, seemed to have found her yellow brick road, which would eventually lead her to the happiness she'd been struggling to find.

He pulled his cell from his back pocket and scrolled to JT's number. He explained what he wanted, and JT said he'd see what he could do. Time for Arleen to realize she couldn't continue on her path of destruction without consequences.

~

*E*ven though a light rain fell, the door of Pretty Posies stood open, so the jangle of the bell didn't announce her arrival. Grandma Garrett built this place and left it to Alex at her death. Because of jealousy, Misty had never taken the time to look around and appreciate what her friend had added. Alex was good to support local artists by displaying their art or pottery. In fact, most of the trinkets and tidbits she sold were made by local artists, which supported the area's economy.

Several flower arrangements lined the shelves of the walk-in cooler. Alex had a rare talent of creating works of art, rather than simple bouquets. Another point of jealousy for Misty. She had tried to master the art of arranging flowers, but never could.

Yet…Alex couldn't cut and color hair the way she could. For the first time, Misty realized they each had their own unique set of talents, something no one could imitate or take away. There was no reason to be jealous of Alex's way with flowers. Instead, she would be proud to know someone who could take a few simple blooms and make something spectacular.

She heard a grunt, and turned to see Alex and Tatum

struggling to move a huge armoire. Alex was dressed casual in jeans and a flowered blouse. She remembered making an ugly comment about that blouse in Rowdy's Bar and Grill about a year ago. She'd tried to make Alex feel bad, when really she'd been envious that Alex looked gorgeous with so little effort.

Tatum was in her usual punk-rocker garb of black with more black. A streak of neon green ran through her orange hair, and she had a bone tied to the crown of her head—Pebbles Flintstone style. For the first time, Misty really looked at her. Under the mascara—so thick it looked like a caterpillar had taken up residence above both eyes—and the hair color, Tatum was pretty. She had enviable cheekbones, beautiful brown eyes, and a slight build, not quite as short as Alex, but rail thin. She also possessed a gentle kindness that drew people close. Like Alex, she cared about people and their problems.

Misty tried to remember one nice thing she'd ever said to Tatum, and couldn't.

"Need any help?"

Tatum and Alex stopped and turned to stare.

Misty waved a hand through the air at chest height, feeling extremely vulnerable.

She needn't have, because Alex came forward with open arms and hugged her tight. "Oh, my gosh, look who's home. When did you get here?"

Alex's use of the word home sounded so good, so right. "Last night." She managed to get those two words out before her throat closed up. Alex released her, and because she had to get this next sentence out, she swallowed hard. "I need a place to stay, Alex. Just for a couple of nights."

"Then you've come to the right person, because I happen to have an empty guestroom."

"Thank you. Brandt's parents are staying at Dad's. Since

he didn't know I was coming, he offered the last two bedrooms to more family members who are visiting Brandt this weekend."

"Not a problem. How long are you here for?"

Misty lifted a shoulder. Her life was so up in the air at the moment, she wasn't sure of her answer. "I don't know."

"Well, the room is yours for as long as you need it." Alex walked back to the armoire. "Come early for dinner?"

Beam's note said he hoped to see her at dinner. Misty set her purse down and followed Alex across the shop. "I have… possible dinner plans."

"Good for you," Alex said, with a glint of happy in her mossy green eyes, the eyes Arleen said were spooky. "Since you offered, we could use help moving this monstrosity."

Misty ducked behind the piece of furniture. Because she couldn't see their faces or perhaps because they couldn't see hers, she said, "By the way, I'm sorry for every rotten thing I've ever said or done to either of you. I know I made fun of the blouse you're wearing, Alex, but I really do think the colors look good on you. And I like your earrings, Tatum."

Misty smiled to herself as she imagined the looks of dismay on their faces. The apology wasn't as hard as she'd imagined, and the burden around her heart lifted, slightly.

Yay, Me!

The universe clapped.

Fifteen minutes later, she stopped in front of the charred rubble left by the fire. The area around the hardware and lumber store was roped off and boarded up. The sight made her stomach sick. She'd never loved the place, but her father had. It had been his livelihood—their livelihood, since she was six years old. Now, it was gone. She climbed out of her car and flipped the hood of her trench coat up against the rain.

Looking over the devastation, she could make out the metal end of some kind of tool. There was also a pile of cans, and another pile of some mesh fabric that looked as if it had melted into a blob of goo.

"Man, the place is demolished."

Misty turned to see a kid with pale skin and orange hair, slicked flat from the rain. He wore a black coat that looked two sizes too big for his small frame. She knew most of the families living in Eden Falls and didn't recognize him. Turning back to the pile of debris, she wondered briefly who his parents were. "Yeah, it is."

"The fire really lit up the sky."

"Did you see it?"

He flashed a crooked smile. "Everyone around here saw it. You could see the glow clear to Harrisville. Anybody know what started it?"

So he wasn't from Eden Falls, but Harrisville.

The rain raised the scent of soot, which made her think of the stale smell of cigarette butts in the can on her mother's front porch. She raised her hand to cover her nose. "I think they're investigating the cause."

When the kid didn't say more, she turned. He was gone.

~

When Beam walked into Brandt's hospital room, he caught the firefighter sitting up in bed, flipping T.V. channels. "Bored?"

"Beyond belief." Brandt turned off the television.

Beam set a pastry box on the table by Brandt's bed. "Patsy sent a treat."

"Thanks." Brandt opened the box and pulled a blueberry muffin free, and then nodded for Beam to help himself.

"Don't mind if I do." Beam shed his coat and shook the rain from his hair. "They haven't put your leg in a cast yet."

"The doctor says it needs a pin. Surgery is scheduled first thing tomorrow."

"Man, I'm sorry."

"Not your fault."

They both turned toward the door when it opened. JT walked in followed by a man Beam met earlier this morning.

"Chet Robertson, this is Brandt Smith. Brandt, Chet is the state fire marshal. He's investigating the fire." He glanced at Chet. "You remember Beam?"

Chet nodded at Beam and shook Brandt's hand, before both men shed their rain slickers and hung them on the back of the door.

"Do you want me to leave?" Beam asked.

"No need," JT said.

Chet pulled a chair to the right side of Brandt's bed and sat. "I hear you have surgery scheduled tomorrow."

"That's what they tell me."

"What's the predicted recovery time?" JT asked.

Brandt winced as he shifted in the bed. "The doc says about six weeks before the casts come off. Want to pitch for the Smoke Eaters?"

JT laughed. "Not even if I wasn't already pitching for the Gunslingers. Sorry you're going to miss the game."

"Yeah," Brandt said on a chuckle. "I bet you are."

JT nodded toward the fire marshal. "Chet is here to ask a few questions. You feel up to it?"

"I feel fine, but I'm not sure how much I can help."

JT walked over to the window where Beam stood, watching rivulets of rain run down the pane.

Chet pulled a small notebook from his shirt pocket and

flipped a few pages. "I've already talked to the men on your shift at the fire station, and Mr."—he glanced at the notebook—"Bennett at the barbershop."

"About?" Brandt asked.

"Since the fire station is directly across the street, I questioned them about seeing anything suspicious the night of the fire. Or anytime before. Same with the barber shop."

Brandt shook his head. "I didn't see anything. The fire alarm woke me. I dressed and followed protocol. I didn't have time to notice if anyone hung around to watch. I thought the fire spread a little too quickly. We were there in minutes of the report." Brandt lifted a shoulder. "But it is a lumberyard."

All things Beam had heard the other firefighters say.

"Did you smell anything unusual?"

"I had my respirator on. We all did."

While Chet made notes in his notebook, JT turned from the window. "Have you seen anyone hanging around town that you didn't recognize? Anyone who made you look-twice?"

"No. Wait…yes. But they weren't hanging around." He glanced at Beam. "Remember that night I was sitting out front of the fire station, and you came over, right after locking up for the day?"

"Yeah."

"Remember those two vampire looking kids?"

Beam chuckled. "Right. I forgot about those kids."

"What kids?" JT asked.

"A couple of boys I didn't recognize walked past." Brandt narrowed his eyes as if trying to recall. "They were dressed in black trench coats, one tall, one short."

Beam nodded. "The short one had orange hair."

"How old were they?" Chet asked.

Brandt lifted a shoulder and looked at Beam. "High school? The shorter kid looked younger than the tall one."

"Can you tell me anything else about them?" Chet asked.

Brandt shook his head.

Chet turned to Beam. "You didn't recognize them?"

"No. I'd never seen them before.

"They don't sound like any kids I know," JT added. "Did they say anything? Do anything?"

"No. They just walked down the sidewalk." Beam leaned a shoulder against the wall and crossed his arms over his chest. "The tall one looked our way and nodded. The little one kept his eyes forward. They didn't stop, and they didn't pay any attention to the hardware store."

"Are you sure you didn't recognize them?" JT asked Beam.

"I haven't lived in town since I graduated high school, JT."

"But you know everyone that lives in Eden Falls. Did these guys look like someone's kids?"

"Don't you think Brandt or I would tell you if we recognized them?"

"Did you see where they went?" Chet asked, impatiently.

Beam remembered their fluttering coats looking like the wings of bats under the distant streetlight. "They never left the sidewalk, just disappeared into the dark."

*B*eam walked through the front door and wondered if he was in the right house. Garlic and oregano infused the air. He set Sophia's carrier on the sofa, unbuckled the straps, and wiggled her from her little pink jacket. Her blue eyes stared up at him as he lifted her and kissed her nose. "Hi, beautiful. It smells like someone cooked for us."

In the kitchen, Misty stood next to the stove stirring

something in a pot. She glanced over her shoulder, raw insecurity written across her face. She pressed her plump lips into a thin line before she smiled hesitantly. "Hi."

He walked over and planted a kiss on the tip of her nose, too. "Hi, yourself. It smells good."

"It does?"

"Yes, it does." Her wide-eyed surprise made him smile. Sophia, sitting on his arm, her back to his chest, squealed. "Sophia agrees, and she doesn't even eat big girl food, yet."

Misty looked from him to their daughter. "She doesn't?"

Beam let his smile drop. He didn't want to spread Misty's insecurity thinner than the sheet of glass it already was. If she decided to stay—and making dinner was a huge step in that direction—she'd learn about babies just as he had, trial and error. "Not yet."

Misty wiped the palms of her hands down the thighs of her jeans. She wore her hair in an easy ponytail and her face was almost void of makeup, just the way he liked it. "Dinner will be ready in a minute." Her eyes were glued to Sophia. "Can I hold her?"

He motioned for her to have a seat, then set Sophia in her lap. He went to the stove to peer down at the bubbling tortellini. "I didn't think you knew how to cook."

Holding Sophia stiffly, Misty leaned forward and buried her nose in the baby's hair. "I hate to disappoint you already, but this isn't cooking. It's opening a jar of spaghetti sauce and a package of frozen tortellini." She looked up at him, her smile tense. "I did melt the butter on the French bread which is probably burning as we speak."

He opened the oven and pulled the bread out from under the broiler. Then drained the tortellini and poured the sauce into a bowl. Misty had even set the table. This was more than she'd ever done for him. "Why don't you set Sophia in her swing right there? She can watch us eat."

Misty awkwardly juggled Sophia. Beam kept a close eye on the struggle, but was careful not to help. In the end, Misty did just fine.

"Buckle her in and push the button on the right to get it started."

Sophia cooed in delight when the swing started its rhythmic back and forth motion. After a moment of watching, Misty glanced at him. "I hope you don't mind that I did this…coming in and cooking without asking you first."

"If I minded I wouldn't have left a key this morning." He pulled her chair out.

She sat and then jumped up. "I forgot napkins. Does Sophia need a bottle before we eat?"

Misty had fixed dinner, set the table, and now, she was thinking of Sophia before herself. He wondered what had happened in Sacramento to change her so drastically. She was a different person. "Aunt Alice fed her before I picked her up."

While Sophia closed her eyes to the rocking of the swing, Beam ate over-cooked pasta, topped with jarred sauce, accompanied by slightly charred French bread. The meal, prepared by his wife, was the best of his life. "Thank you for this. It's really nice to come home and not have to cook."

Her smile was un-Misty-like shy. "I wish I could say I cooked all day." Her eyes brightened. "I did ask Alex for a few of her easier recipes today."

Another step in the I'm-going-to-stay direction. "What else did you do with your day?"

"I saw my dad." She set her fork down and wiped her mouth.

He noticed she wasn't wearing her wedding ring. *What do you expect? You filed for divorce.*

"While I was in Sacramento, I discovered Mason isn't my biological father."

Beam froze with his fork halfway to his mouth. "What?"

Misty carefully arranged the napkin back on her lap without meeting his gaze. "My mom told me Mason isn't my real father. She assumed he'd already told me. Like saying the sky is blue or the grass is green, she just blurted it out in one of our brief conversations."

"Who is your father?"

She looked down at their sleeping daughter. "I don't know. My mom doesn't know. She was already pregnant when she met Mason, and married him without telling him the truth." Her cheeks turned crimson, and Beam knew she was remembering she'd almost done the same thing to Colton. "My dad, Mason—I'm not sure what to call him, when talking about him. He told me I could still call him dad. Anyway, he told me he never cared that I wasn't his. That he loved me anyway."

Beam reached across the table and intertwined their fingers. "I believe him."

Misty's empty smile broke his heart. "So do I."

They cleaned the kitchen in silence, and when a fussy Sophia woke up ready to eat, Beam showed Misty how to make a bottle. "I'm going to stay at Alex's for a couple of nights," she said, when she lifted Sophia to her shoulder for a burp.

Beam hadn't brought up living arrangements, hoping she'd decided to stay. He tried not to show his disappointment, but felt it deeply all the same. "Why aren't you staying with your dad?"

"Brandt's parents are there, and a brother and sister are coming for the weekend, so he has a full house."

He'd forgotten Mason mentioned making room for Brandt's family. "Speaking of Brandt I went to see him today. He's having surgery on his leg tomorrow."

"Surgery?"

"The break requires a pin, but Brandt said it's nothing serious."

"That's good to hear."

Beam spread a blanket on the floor and laid Sophia down. He took Misty's hand and encouraged her to sit with them. Her palm felt good against his. Her being here felt right. He propped Sophia up with pillows and gave her a squishy ring to grasp and gum.

Misty rubbed a hand down her daughter's back. "After I left Pretty Posies, I went to Dahlia's. I was able to get my job back. I start Tuesday."

Her words more than shocked him, but again, he tried to keep his expression neutral. "Is that what you want?"

Her smile was strained, and she blinked frantically as if she were fighting tears, a battle she won. "For now. It makes the most sense. Don't you think?"

"I think you should do what will make you happy."

She raised her eyes to meet his. "Do you really mean that?"

"Yes. I know you want your own salon, and I'll give you the money—no stipulations."

Misty's glance bounced from him to Sophia. "Why would you do that?"

He was probably throwing away any chance they might have at fixing them, but it was the right thing to do. He'd promised. "I pushed you into marriage. I knew you weren't ready, and I held the salon over your head to get you to agree. It was wrong of me, and I'm sorry. You find a place, and I'll finance it."

"What about the lumberyard?"

"I'll figure something out."

He picked Sophia up and snuggled her close, as a countless number of emotions tumbled through him. He'd been parenting alone since her birth, and already filed for divorce.

If Misty left to open a salon, he'd have lost nothing. When Sophia's eyes zeroed in on him, he smiled. "Hello, beautiful. I'll bet its past time for a dry diaper."

"Can I try?"

Beam smiled. "Sure. After the day you've had, changing a diaper will be a piece of cake."

Misty wrinkled her nose, a gesture Sophia was already using. "Unless she pooped."

"Oh, believe me, if she'd pooped, you would know it by now."

CHAPTER 17

Misty could still have her salon. No stipulations. The promise that kept her sane while she was pregnant was within her grasp. Owning her own place had been a dream for so long—since Alex had inherited Pretty Posies— but her quest to best Alex didn't seem important anymore. If she opened a salon, it wouldn't be in Eden Falls. The population couldn't support two salons. Besides, she'd never do that to Dahlia. Especially after she'd rehired Misty. She could possibly find a space in Harrisville, but when would she see Sophia? And Beam? Setting up a salon would take a lot of time in the beginning. Was she willing to give up what she was just beginning to appreciate?

Her mind whirled with the possibilities as Beam walked her through her first diaper change. Sophia was cooperative thanks to daddy keeping her occupied, and she rewarded Misty a gurgle of praise when she finished.

Every time Beam touched her or their eyes connected, her insides quivered like a flight of hummingbirds set free after being confined. Over the course of the evening, she decided she liked the sensation of promise and jitter of anticipation.

After she fed Sophia and tucked her into bed, it was time to head to Alex's. Beam walked her to the door.

"Thank you for dinner, Misty. I appreciated it and enjoyed the company."

Knowing she'd pleased him sent a silly tingle of pleasure through her that grew in her chest, filling her with an emotion that felt suspiciously like love. "It wasn't much, but you're welcome. Thank you for letting me help with Sophia."

"You don't ever have to thank me for that. You're her mother."

She was a little—a lot—disappointed when he didn't try to kiss her goodnight, but understood his hesitation. He had laid it out in the open for her last night. She had a decision to make and she wanted to be very sure that moving in was the right choice for him, for her, and especially for Sophia.

Going into Dahlia's with her tail between her legs had been the hardest part of her day. She'd left months earlier, proclaiming she was meant for bigger and better salons than the dump Dahlia ran.

I sure showed them.

Anna had moved into her station after Misty left, and Dahlia couldn't ask her to move back. Dahlia told Misty she could have Anna's station at the back of the salon. Being fourth station bothered Misty for about five seconds, but she swallowed her pride. She needed a job and second station or fourth, it would be nice to be working, again. She'd missed her job and the people she worked with. Her feelings of superiority were drained dry when her mother left her stripped of anything of value. Her self-importance had been driven humbly to its knees.

She apologized to Dahlia and her co-workers before heading over to Beam's to cook dinner. Now, as she drove the few blocks to Alex's house, she prepared herself for another hard apology to Colton McCreed.

She rang the doorbell, remembering all the times she'd just busted into Alex's house like it was her right. How could anyone be as wrong as she'd been, and still be welcome in this town?

Charlie flung the door open, his usual grin in place. "Hi, Misty! Mom said you're sleeping over. I can carry your suitcase." He pumped up his little arm to show off his muscles. "Look how strong I am."

"You are strong. Thanks for your help, Charlie." She stepped inside, then stopped short. She'd just complimented a six year old and then thanked him. Though it was tiny, she was still going to count it as another step toward becoming a kinder, less-like-her-mother person.

Charlie disappeared down the hall, and Alex came from the kitchen, drying her hands on a dishtowel. "You made it."

Misty felt the shroud of shame and embarrassment descend over her. It was becoming like a second skin. How long would it take to make all the amends hanging like stones around her neck? Months? Years? Though she knew Alex had forgiven her, she couldn't expect Colton to do the same after what she'd done. "Thanks for letting me stay. I hope it's not too much of an impo—"

"Stop right there," Alex said holding up a hand. "Your staying isn't an imposition, just a simple matter of moving some of Colton's things. He's turned the guestroom into his office until we build a house."

Great. Another reason for him to hate me. "I don't want to put him out of his office. I'll sleep on the sofa."

Alex waved the hand she held up. "He's not here. He's in L.A. until tomorrow."

"He is?"

Alex took Misty's arm and guided her into the kitchen. "He's been there most of the week working on rewrites of the book they're making into a movie."

Misty sat in the kitchen chair Alex pulled out for her, glad to have another day to work up her courage. Her apology to Colton would be one of the hardest.

"Are you hungry?"

"No. I ate with Beam."

Alex didn't say a word, but the corners of her mouth turned up slightly.

After Charlie finished his homework and was tucked into bed, Misty and Alex moved into the living room. The last time she was here was the night Alex discovered she was lying about Colton being the father of her baby. She wondered if Alex was thinking the same thing.

"Are you going to tell me what happened in Sacramento?"

Obviously, that's not what she's thinking about. Misty told her story for the second time that day, without any tears. Perhaps she was cried out, depleted of all emotion where Arleen Doug—No. Arleen didn't deserve the distinction of the Douglas name. Misty was finished with Arleen Honeywell.

Alex was sympathetic, and apologetic, and her comforting self, asking all the right questions.

Misty even included the fact that Mason wasn't her biological father.

"What?"

"Seems Mommy dearest was already pregnant when she met my father and didn't tell him." The realization of how much alike she and her mother were hit her again. Hard. "Exactly what I did to Colton. If you hadn't seen through my lie..." She leaned forward and put her head in her hands as tears flooded her eyes. She wasn't as depleted as she'd thought. "I can't believe what I tried to do. I'm just like her."

Alex moved close and wrapped both arms around Misty's shoulders. "Not anymore."

"How can you stand me? After all the crap I've put people through, how can anyone stand me? I can barely stand myself! How will I ever make amends?"

"You'll take one step at a time, one day at a time."

Misty turned to look at Alex. "It will take me forever."

Alex nodded. "A long time, but not forever."

More tears flooded Misty's eyes, but she released a laugh on the next sob. Alex was right. Apologies and trying to make things right would take a long time, but not forever.

Alex's expression grew serious. "I am sorry you had to go through all that with your mom."

"You know what?" Misty took a cleansing breath and wiped her face with both hands. "I'm not. I had to live through it. I had to see what Arleen was for myself. I wouldn't have accepted the truth any other way."

Alex gave her shoulder another squeeze. "You've come a long way, my friend. I'm proud of you."

A short time later, Misty crawled under the cool crisp sheets of the guest bed with the last of her energy. She felt like someone had pulled her stopper out, releasing all the filth that had filled her for so long. She felt cleansed, extremely exhausted, and she welcomed the sweet oblivion of sleep.

~

*M*isty got her chance to apologize to Colton Friday night. He was more gracious and forgiving than she would have been, if the circumstances were reversed. What she'd done was despicable, but Colton waved the incident off with, "Let's forget it ever happened. This town is too small for enemies."

Later, she lay in the guestroom, next to Alex and Colton's bedroom. The newlyweds were discreet, but she still heard the creak of the bed and snatches of whispered words of love.

Their hushed affirmations made her cry over the knowledge of what true love looked like. They had it. Colton's eyes had blazed with love the moment he spotted Alex on the porch when he stopped in the driveway. She witnessed it when Charlie hurled himself off the same porch and into Colton's waiting arms. Love was written on their three faces as they shared a group hug, and evident when Colton gathered Alex close for an I-really-missed-you kiss that would have turned much more intimate if she and Charlie hadn't been standing close by.

Instead of her past feelings of envy, Misty was filled with joy. Joy that Alex had found love again after the devastating loss of her first husband. Joy that Charlie finally had a father figure in his life. Joy that her lie had been found out before it ruined their family's happily ever after.

~

Saturday afternoon, Beam pulled into the parking lot of Eden Falls City Park for the Smoke Eaters first baseball practice. Most of the team was already on the field warming up. He loved this time of year. Green leaves dotted the trees, spring flowers bloomed along walkways, and the promise of summer was just around the corner. Who didn't love summers filled with barbecues, outdoor concerts, and baseball? And Eden Falls had all three.

Practice went well. The team shifted positions around a little. Rowdy took Brandt's place as pitcher and Beam moved to first base. He enjoyed the camaraderie the team shared. They'd played together for several years and were able to anticipate each other's actions and reactions, and respond quickly.

As he was putting his gear away, Rowdy plopped down on the bench next to him. "Hey."

"Hey, yourself. Thanks for stepping up as pitcher."

"Not my forte, but nobody else wanted it."

Beam removed his ball cap and ran his fingers through his hair. "I sure didn't. I never could pitch."

"So, I heard a rumor that Misty's back in town."

"Yeah."

Rowdy punched a fist into his mitt a few times. "And?"

"And nothing. She came back to town when she heard about the fire. She's staying with her dad until she decides what she wants."

"Until she decides what *she* wants?"

"Rowdy, don't do this," Beam said on a sigh. "Misty is staying with her dad until she decides if she wants to stay or not. I won't let her come and go as she pleases with Sophia. If she decides she wants to be married and build our family, she can move in with us. If not, she and I will divorce and work out visitation."

"So you're still married?"

"Yes. I haven't signed the papers, yet." He didn't tell his brother that Misty had signed the papers. She was struggling to fit into a world that was very foreign to her, but he had faith she could do it. What he didn't need were any disparaging remarks from Rowdy.

Rowdy chewed his bottom lip a moment, and Beam could almost see the wheels turning. He finally blew out a breath. "How is the little cricket?"

Beam nodded as he bent to zip his gym bag. "Good."

"Has Misty been over to see her?"

"Not only has she been over to see her, but she's fed her, changed her diaper, rocked her to sleep, and made dinner."

Rowdy snorted. "I didn't know she knew how to cook."

"She doesn't." Beam stood. "My point is she's trying, so give her a break, Rowdy."

Rowdy stood and shook his head. "Sorry, bro, she's going

to have to do more than cook a meal for me to believe she's capable of change."

Beam shrugged in an attempt to relieve some of his irritation, both with his brother and his wife. He was impatient to know what Misty *was* planning to do. She'd come back to town and he'd gotten his hopes up, after he warned himself not to. She cooked dinner and spent time with Sophia, and his hopes rose even higher. But it had been two days and he hadn't seen or heard from her. "Just give her a chance. With a little work, and someone to believe in us, we all have the ability to change."

"Sure," Rowdy said in a tone that told Beam he didn't believe it was possible for Misty. "If you need anything, I'm around."

"I know, man." He patted his brother on the shoulder. "Thanks."

After dinner, Beam sat on the sofa, thinking of his wife, wishing the doorbell would ring, and she'd be on the other side of the screen. He'd been tempted to call Mason all afternoon to see how Misty was doing. He knew after all she'd been through she was fragile. She'd always been a fighter, but Sacramento had changed her. Made her vulnerable in a way she'd never been before. The truth that Mason wasn't her biological father would come out, because they lived in a small town and gossip was how folks entertained themselves. Would Misty be strong enough to realize it didn't matter? Mason had loved her as if she were his own since her birth—that was what mattered. He'd taken care of her when her mother couldn't or wouldn't. After their talk two days ago, he believed Misty realized how lucky she was to have him in her life. If Mason hadn't stepped up, he'd hate to think where Misty would be now.

~

*M*onday morning, Misty stood on her dad's porch, suitcase in hand. As he poured them each a glass of orange juice, she told him she was ready to change, and knew she had to start here. She'd spent the weekend, mostly sitting alone in Alex's backyard, dwelling on the past, and wondering if she possessed the courage to change her future. She decided she did. Her plan was simple and required little money. Mason readily agreed to help.

Next, she called Beam. She hadn't talked to him for a few days, and didn't want him to think she'd skipped town again. His greeting wasn't as warm as she'd hoped.

"Sorry I haven't called. I have some things to do at my dad's, but I'd like to come over and cook dinner for you on Wednesday. Would that be okay?"

"I'll look forward to it."

His agreement made her insides sing like a well-tuned fiddle.

Misty disconnected the call, then she and her dad climbed into his truck and headed to Harrisville. Two hours later, after she and Mason had moved all the furniture from her childhood bedroom to the garage, they began covering the pink walls with a soft gray-blue paint. Misty had never painted a room before, but Mason was a patient teacher. They talked about childhood memories, and Misty grimaced over teenage disasters. She apologized for her rebellious, obstinate, completely selfish ways several times over the course of the afternoon.

Mason finally raised both hands in the air. "Enough Misty. I've made a lot of mistakes, too. We're both only human, so let's just forgive each other and put the past behind us."

Reluctantly she nodded and allowed him to hug her. She

wished forgiving and forgetting was that easy. With her dad, there was nothing to forgive. Mason had done nothing wrong. He'd always been there for her, even if she was too blind to notice. Confusing his gentle ways for weakness was really her weakness. She'd blamed him for everything that went wrong in her life, when all along it had been her own doing.

Her struggle was with forgiving herself.

When Mason went downstairs to get them both a drink, Misty propped her brush over the lid of the paint can and stood back to admire their work. She'd decided last night it was time to erase Arleen, and she couldn't think of a better way than to release this room from its pink and white ruffles, and sour memories. She'd kept it just as it was for the mother she'd imagined Arleen to be. In reality, Misty had conjured an image that had never existed in the first place. It was time to exorcise the belief she or her father were the reasons her mom left. Her only crime had been to hold on to an imaginary dream. Mason's was to love his wife. Time to accept what she thought was true—never was.

Small snatches of memories popped into her mind now, and very few of them included Arleen. Mason had tucked her into bed at night. Mason had dropped her off for her first day of kindergarten. Mason had attended all her parent-teacher conferences. All this time, she'd fantasized about this fabulous mother, whose only flaw was hating small town life. That mother had been a little girl's illusion. All along, Mason had been the fabulous parent.

She also admitted the reason she hadn't bonded with her own baby, both through the pregnancy and after her birth, was so she could leave without a backward glance. Now, all she wanted was to go to Beam and beg his forgiveness. She wanted to hold her baby girl close and whisper how sorry she was. She'd missed so much already, and she didn't want to miss another minute. What she was doing here had to be completed first. She had to let Arleen go from her life for good, and that included erasing the room she'd held onto with the hopes her mother would someday return.

She turned when she heard footsteps coming down the hall. Expecting her dad, she was surprised to see Stella. "Hey," she stammered.

Stella glanced around the room wearing its new color. Gone was the passion pink of yesteryear. "I gotta say this is a huge improvement."

Misty laughed. It felt so good she couldn't stop. Her laughter turned to sobs, and she continued even as Stella walked over and hugged her tight. "I…I'm sorry I…stole your pink pen in…in second grade."

"I knew that was you!" Stella exclaimed with a tinge of a smile.

Misty's sobs grew. "I'm sorr…y I spilled a soda on your new bedspread…and blamed it on…on your little sister."

"That was you, too? Now, I'm going to have to apologize to Oops. I was mad at her for a week."

The reminder of Stella's youngest sister's nickname caused a snort of laughter. Her four sisters had dubbed little Adelaide, who was five years younger than Stella, Oops, and the name had stuck.

Stella wiped her shoulder. "You just snotted on me."

Misty wiped her nose with the back of her hand. "I'm sorry I messed up…your tenth grade dance date with…Scotty Wilkes."

"Oh, well, for that one I forgive you. Have you seen that guy?"

Misty snorted unattractively, again, and then cried harder. "I'm sorry for…every mean thing I've ever said and done… to you."

"Are you sorry for being such a selfish, lousy friend?"

"Yeeesss," Misty wailed.

Stella held her at arms length and started to laugh. "You look absolutely pitiful, and I forgive you."

Misty lifted her paint stained T-shirt and wiped her wet face. "You do?"

"Wow!" Stella said, her eyes wide with surprise. "The old Misty would have been way more concerned with looking pitiful than with being forgiven."

"Oh, shut up," Misty replied, swatting at Stella.

Stella pointed her index finger as if she was holding a gun. "There's the Misty I know."

They both laughed.

Stella glanced around. "So, you got another paintbrush?"

CHAPTER 18

Beam sat in stunned silence. Arson. The state fire marshal had ruled the fire arson.

JT stood up from behind his desk and walked to the line of windows facing town square.

"Does Mason know?" Beam asked

JT nodded. "Chet told him thirty minutes ago."

Chet swiveled his chair to face Beam. "Do you have any enemies?"

Beam shook his head, his mind still reeling. "No. None that I know of."

"Your business was heavily insured."

JT turned, anger flashing in his eyes. "I told you when Mason was here that neither of these men would do something like that."

"And I told you, you're too close to this case, JT. You need to excuse yourself from this meeting," Chet said.

"Why, because Beam's my cousin?" JT jammed his hands on his hips. "Neither Beam nor Mason would burn the lumberyard down to collect insurance money. You've seen—"

Chet stood to faceoff with JT. "I have to ask the questions and you—"

While the two of them shot remarks back and forth, Beam remained dazed. Not only had someone intentionally set the lumberyard on fire, but the fire marshal actually thought the someone might be him. The insinuation made him sick to his stomach. Beam held up his hands to stop the arguing. "If you'll check the records, you'll see the hardware and lumber store have always been heavily insured. My father-in-law is a careful man. He carried the maximum insurance for emergencies."

"Seems he was wise to do so," JT uttered, turning back to the windows.

Beam looked at Chet. "I did not burn down my business."

JT whipped around. "Don't say anymore, Beam. Not without an attorney."

At this Beam stood. "I don't need an attorney. I have over three hundred thousand in the bank from the sale of my house in Seattle. I did not set a fire just to collect the insurance money. I don't gamble. I have no debts, except for the small loan I took out to invest in the lumberyard until my plane sold. The business is…was thriving. We have every intention of rebuilding. You are welcome to my financial records. You'll find everything in order."

Chet sat down again. "I'm sorry Beam, but we have to rule you and Mason out first. I found accelerant in three separate places. There are no surveillance cameras. You were the last to leave, and your only alibi is too young to speak."

"You also said the fire was started around one o'clock in the morning. I wouldn't leave my three-month old daughter at home alone to start a fire. Anyone in this town will vouch for my character. And if there were cameras, there would be nothing left of them or the tapes."

"There has never been a need for cameras in Eden Falls

before, Chet. If you did your homework, you'd know we have one of the lowest crime rates for a small town in the state of Washington."

"I know the state's statistics, JT, but you have to understand, I have a job to do. The first person we always look at is the business owner, and then disgruntled employees." Chet finished the last of his statement by looking at Beam. "Have you had to fire anyone recently?"

Leaning against the wall with his arms crossed over his chest, Beam realized his stance might be taken as confrontational. He had every intention of cooperating, so he relaxed his posture and his attitude. "No. We have the same employees Mason has had for years. I hired a couple of high school kids as summer help, but I've known both them and their parents since the kids were in diapers."

"I'll have to question everyone."

"I'll get you a list of names."

"Are any of the employees disgruntled that you bought into the business?"

"Not to my knowledge."

"Other than insurance fraud and revenge, fires are generally set by pyromaniacs or kids out for a thrill."

"We haven't had a rash of fires, so I don't think we have a pyromaniac in our midst," JT said.

"I tend to agree, but I can't rule it out." Chet slid the notebook into his shirt pocket and stood. "Besides the two kids you and Brandt Smith saw, can you recall seeing anyone else hanging around?"

Beam shook his head. "No, and those two kids weren't hanging around. They were walking down the street."

Chet rubbed two fingers over his forehead as if exasperated by Beam's answer. "How about your estranged wife?"

JT jumped between Beam, who straightened to his six-foot-five height, and the five-foot-eight fire marshal. "Okay, that's enough, Chet. Misty wouldn't do this."

"I have to investigate all avenues."

JT put a hand on Beam's chest, holding him where he stood. "Well, you're wasting your time on this one. Misty didn't set the fire. She was in Sacramento at the time."

"Will she be able to verify that?"

"The place she worked will."

Chet walked to the windows, his back to them. "How soon can you get me the names of your employees?"

When the questioning ended and the fire marshal drove off in his shiny SUV, Beam turned to JT. "Thanks for stepping in."

"Not a problem."

"I mean about Misty."

"We both know Misty is capable of..." JT waved a hand through the air. "...a lot of things, but she's no arsonist."

Beam couldn't deny what was true.

"Alex said she's back in town."

"She is. I'm not sure if she's staying," Beam said before his cousin could ask.

"You okay?"

Between his uncertainty about Misty, and his business being burned down by an arsonist, Beam felt far from okay. He took comfort in knowing Sophia was safe, and his belief that things would work out as they should.

After he left JT's office, he crossed the street to the town square. He usually crossed the square to get from point A to point B. Today he took the time to look around. The deep green of the pines were in sharp contrast to the fresh emerald of the deciduous trees dressed out in their new coat of foliage. Red tulips bloomed in mulched beds, and birds twittered noisily from the branches above. Spring had arrived in all its glory.

And he was suspected of arson.

Beam sank to a bench.

He didn't feel he'd convinced Chet of his innocence. How could he, other than to say he didn't start the fire. In his mind, the idea was too preposterous to comprehend. JT said not to worry, but how could he not? He decided to walk over to Owen's office later. Talking with an attorney might ease his mind.

"Beam? Are you okay?"

He looked up at Misty who stood next to the bench, a look of concern on her face. "Hey. Yeah, I'm fine. What are you doing here?" he asked

She thumbed over her shoulder. "First day at Dahlia's. I wanted to get here early."

He nodded as he continued to stare. She was wrapped in a sweater. He liked that she wasn't wearing so much makeup anymore, or fussing with her hair. It looked soft this morning. So soft, he wanted to run his fingers through it.

"Can I sit down?"

He patted the bench. "Of course."

She sat close enough that he could smell her perfume. She'd changed scents from the harsh one she used to wear to something soft.

"I said your name twice before you heard me. Are you sure you're okay?"

"I just left a meeting with the fire marshal."

"Dad told me they ruled the fire arson. Are you worried about the insurance company?"

He put his arm around her shoulder and pulled her closer. "No. I'm not worried. Everything will work out."

A slight smile touched her pretty lips. "How's Sophia?"

"Good. Mom has her at the gym."

"Is your mom going to have her all day?"

"No, I'll head over in a while to pick her up."

Misty fidgeted with the cuff of her sweater, looking everywhere but at him, and he suddenly had the feeling his day was about to get worse. Mason mentioned this morning that Misty spent yesterday redecorating her childhood bedroom. Actually, Mason said she was erasing all evidence of Arleen. Mason took it as a good sign—an indication that she was moving on. Beam thought more along the lines that she might be creating a room for herself at her dad's.

She finally turned her head to look at him. "I've been thinking a lot about what you said the first night I came back to Eden Falls. I know you have no reason to trust me, but I'd like to come home with you and Sophia. I know I'll be a klutzy wife and mother, but…" Tears sprang into her blue eyes, and she looked down in an effort to hide them.

Beam ran a finger from her temple to her chin and lifted her face so she was looking at him. "But?" he prompted.

"But…" Her voice caught and she swallowed. Tears overflowed and ran down both cheeks. "…if you'll have me, I want to try. I want to come home."

"Your dad said you'd redecorated your room at his house. I thought you'd be staying there for awhile."

She frowned as confusion clouded her face. "No. I just decided it was time for me to grow up, and redecorating my little-girl room seemed like the best place to start."

He pulled her into his arms and let her wipe her tears all over his shirt.

Misty was coming home.

~

*M*isty resigned herself to the hardest task she would face since returning to Eden Falls. She climbed out of her car and entered Get Fit. She'd spent all morning fretting about this apology to the point she felt sick to her stomach. She hadn't told Beam she was coming, afraid he might tell his parents to go easy on her. Easy wasn't what she deserved.

She'd steeled herself to see Glenda at the front desk, but instead Jillian was there, talking to two women. When she glanced over to see who'd entered, she smiled. Misty hadn't expected anything less. Not from Jillian. After the two women headed for the locker room, Jillian stepped around the desk and enveloped Misty in an unexpected hug, which caused the tears she'd finally gotten under control to spill, again. Why would someone Misty had been mean to her whole life hug her?

"I'm so glad you're back." Jillian's smile reached all the way up to her brown eyes, warm and true.

The best Misty could do was nod in agreement.

Jillian reached behind the counter and offered Misty a tissue, which she gratefully accepted. She didn't want to talk to Glenda and Dawson with puffy eyes and a red nose. Jillian didn't say anything, giving Misty time to compose herself. She finally looked up, and knew why she'd been unkind to Jillian all those years. She felt short and dumpy next to the toned, model litheness that was Jillian Saunders. "I'm glad you're here," she choked out.

"I am too. I've wanted to see you ever since I heard you were back in town."

"No, I mean I'm glad you're here today, so I can apologize."

"Apologize?" Jillian actually had the grace to look surprised. "For what?"

"For all the mean things I've said and done over the years."

"You're forgiven."

Just like that. A small laugh escaped on a half-sob.

"You're all making this too easy. It shouldn't be, not after the way I've acted."

Jillian tipped her head, a touch of sympathy in the lift of her brows. "All?"

"Beam, my dad, Alex, Colton, Stella, you…"

"I'll admit you've hurt my feelings more times than I can count, and there have been times when I didn't like you very much, but I'd rather like you. So, if you're being sincere, and you're truly sorry, I'm all for new beginnings."

"I am truly sorry."

"Then let's start over. Beginning today, we have a clean slate. All is forgiven."

"Thank you, Jillian." Misty blew her nose.

Jillian turned when the door to the office behind the reception desk opened. "Jillian, are you…?" Glenda's words trailed away when she saw Misty.

Misty's stomach twisted in a sick spiral, but she mustered a smile. "Hi, Glenda."

"Misty. I heard you were in Eden Falls."

"I wanted…" She paused, but Jillian gave her arm an encouraging squeeze. "I was hoping I could talk to you and Dawson."

Glenda studied her for a long uncomfortable moment, and then nodded. "Dawson is in the office. Come on back."

Misty hadn't expected a sunny reception, but she'd never seen Glenda look so stern. Jillian gave her an encouraging hug before she walked around the desk and entered the office. Dawson was bent over a stack of papers, his reading glasses perched on the tip of his nose. Arleen's words about what a "good-lookin' man" he was came back to her. He glanced up and his gaze ping-ponged between Misty and his wife before he stood and pulled his glasses off. "Misty, honey, how are you?"

Misty stood stiffly, her car keys jingling in her nervous

fingers. "I'm okay." She swallowed once for courage, twice to be able to clear her throat enough to speak. "I wanted to talk to you and Glenda."

His glance bounced to his wife's again. Then the smile she was familiar with, because her husband's was so similar, creased Dawson's face, crinkling the corners of his eyes. "Of course. Have a seat," he said sweeping his hand in the direction of a round table in the corner of their office. He and Glenda sat on one side, Misty on the other.

"Would you like something to drink?" Glenda asked.

She would love a bottle of water, but wouldn't prolong this agony longer than necessary by asking for one. "No, thank you." She looked from Glenda to Dawson. "I got my job at Dahlia's back. I started today."

"So you plan to stay." Glenda's words came out more accusation than question. Dawson reached for her hand, entwining their fingers, an action she'd seen her father-in-law do countless times. This time, for some reason, it touched her heart.

"Yes." When they didn't say anything, she continued. Stronger. "Yes, I'm going to stay. I asked Beam this morning if I could come home. He said yes."

She expected protests from Glenda, whose lips were pressed so tightly together they were devoid of color.

"I came to see you, because…" Here she had to fight back the threatening tears. She did not want to make a blubbering fool of herself in front of her in-laws. She straightened her back and lifted her chin. "I want to apologize for all the hurt I've caused you by leaving. I—"

Glenda opened her mouth, but Dawson stopped her with a look. His eyes moved back to Misty's, an unspoken acknowledgment to continue.

"I acted selfishly, and I know I caused not only Beam, but you"—her eyes moved from one to the other—"both…a lot of grief. I'm not sure how I can make it up to you, but I'd like to try."

"You don't have to make anything up to us, honey," Dawson said. "Sophia needs her mother, and Beam needs his wife. He loves you very much."

His kind voice and his sweet words finally released the waterworks. As tears flowed freely down her cheeks, she admitted aloud, for the first time, that she loved their son. She had never told Beam, but she planned to correct that soon.

As she climbed into her car a short time later, the sudden sense of peace settled over her. The sensation didn't free her of her wrongdoings, but she knew she was on the right track by attempting to make amends.

As Misty drove to her dad's to transport her suitcase yet again, she thought about all she'd accomplished today. She'd watched many of her previous clients in her co-workers chairs. *Get over it. You're the one who left. You can't expect them to come running back to you.* She'd made several apologies, and even if she wasn't forgiven, she felt good about her small achievements. Twice she'd bitten her tongue to keep the old Misty from resurfacing. A couple of snarky remarks had teased the fringes of her mind, but she'd fought them off with the image of her mother's face floating through her mind. She would rather draw her own blood than emulate Arleen Honeywell.

She pulled into her dad's driveway, and saw another apology she would be making. JT's patrol car was parked in the circular drive, along with another unfamiliar SUV. She parked in the back, went through the kitchen door, and followed the voices floating in from the living room. JT stood near the fireplace and turned when she entered. Mason and another man stood from their seats.

"Hello," she said.

"Hey, Misty." JT gestured toward the stranger. "This is Chet Robertson, the state fire marshal. He's investigating the fire and has some questions for you."

"Okay." Misty walked over to join her father on the sofa.

They all sat except for JT who kept his position near the fireplace.

Chet opened a notebook. "Where were you the night of the fire?"

"In Sacramento."

"Can anyone verify that?"

She lifted a shoulder. "The people where I worked. I can give you the number."

"So you did work the day of the fire?"

"Yes, until six o'clock."

Misty glanced at her father, while Chet made notes in his notebook. He flashed a quick smile.

"Can I ask why you were in Sacramento?" Chet said.

"I'd gone to look for my mom."

"And you were living there?"

Yes, I left my husband and my baby daughter. She looked down at her tightly clasped hands. "Yes, since February."

The questions kept coming, until Misty asked if she was a suspect.

"Everyone is until we can determine who set the fire."

"I didn't. My father has owned the lumberyard since I was six. I would never do anything to destroy it."

"One of the employees I questioned said you weren't happy about your husband buying into the business."

"I wasn't at first. If you'll call the number of the salon I worked at, they'll tell you I couldn't have done it."

"But you could have hired someone."

She couldn't help the bitter bubble of laughter that escaped. "My mother stole everything I owned. I don't have enough money to buy a tube of mascara. How could I hire someone to start a fire?"

Chet tapped his pen against the notebook a few times, as if thinking over her answers. She tamped down the hysteria that threatened to surface. She knew he was just doing his job, and understood why she might be a suspect.

"Do you know anyone who holds a grudge against your dad or husband?"

"No."

"Have you seen anyone suspicious hanging around town. Anyone you didn't recognize?"

"I told you I've been in Sacramento since February." An image popped into her mind. "There was this kid…"

"What kid?" JT asked.

She looked at him. "I was at the charred remains of the building last week, and this kid came up to me and started asking questions. I probably would have forgotten all about him, except he had bright orange hair."

JT and the fire marshal exchanged glances. "Did you recognize him?" JT asked.

"No, but he said the glow of the fire could be seen all the way to Harrisville."

Chet flipped pages in his notebook and scribbled furiously before he stood. "Thanks for your time, Mrs. Garrett."

He walked to the door. They all followed him.

After Chet left, JT pulled an envelope from his pocket. He took her hand in his and poured her rings into her palm.

She looked from him to her dad.

"I asked JT to see if he could find them."

"They were pawned in Reno. Your dad paid to get them out."

Misty pressed her lips together to keep them from trembling. Surely, every ounce of moisture in her body would dry up soon. She couldn't believe this much crying was possible.

She took a moment to appreciate the weight of the metal in her palm. Beam had slipped the rings onto her finger as a symbol of his love and commitment. At the time, they hadn't meant much to her. Now, as she slipped them back into place, they meant the love and commitment she planned to show Beam everyday for the rest of her life.

"Thank you." She kissed her dad on the cheek. "Thank you, JT. I appreciate you finding them for me."

"I know where your mom is, if you want to know."

"I don't, but thanks for finding the rings." Mason shook JT's hand and left the room.

JT looked at Misty in question and she nodded.

"After Reno, she and a trucker friend made it to Vegas. That's where he left her. She rented a single wide in a trailer park at the edge of town and found work in a rundown casino as a cocktail waitress."

Way better than living in a nice home in Eden Falls, Mom. At least she knew her mother was safe. That was all that mattered. Now, she would move on. She held up her hand. "Thank you for these."

"All in a day's work, ma'am," he replied using his best John Wayne accent.

She used to think JT was the handsomest man in Eden Falls. Somewhere in the midst of her recent journey, that opinion had changed. "I'm glad you came with the fire marshal. I wanted to talk to you."

He raised a brow.

"I never thanked you for all you did the day I was in labor."

JT chuckled. "You weren't exactly in the happiest of moods that day."

"No, I wasn't, and I'm embarrassed by how awful I acted. You and Alex came right away, and I treated you so badly. I'm sorry. And not just for that day, but for everything." She fought the urge to look away. She would make every one of these apologies eye-to-eye. "The way I treated you when we dated…"

His eyebrows came together in a frown, no doubt wondering if she was being sincere, but then his face relaxed. "Water under the bridge. We weren't meant to be, and we both knew it."

His words rang a bell that echoed through her head. He was right. They weren't meant to be together. For her to recognize and admit the fact was a nice release. Dating him had never felt right. She'd fought the knowledge as much as she'd longed to escape Eden Falls.

For one silly moment, she had the urge to click the heels of her ruby slippers together.

She leaned forward and gave JT a hug. She was sure it took him by surprise, but after a moment, he hugged her back. The tension that had hung like a cloak over them lifted, and she took it as a sign of happier times to come.

After JT left, she went up to get her suitcase. Her dad was standing in the doorway of her bedroom, which still smelled of fresh paint, and probably would for weeks. She liked that fresh scent—new beginnings. "What are you doing?"

Mason looked at her. "Enjoying the view. It's good to see all that faded pink fluff gone."

Misty walked inside and turned in a slow circle, taking in the new quilt on the bed, the curtains, even the new towels in the adjoining bathroom. There wasn't a smidgen of pink anywhere—another release from the past that had kept her tethered to the wrong life. "I always believed that when mom came home, she'd be so excited to see I'd left the room exactly as she'd decorated it for me. I thought *that one thing* would make her realize her mistake in leaving me. When she saw how much it all meant to me, she'd be able to love me."

Mason released a slow breath and shook his head. "I'm sorry, honey."

A slight shudder ran through her. That part of her life was in the past. She was done hanging on to any thread of hope her mother would change. She finally realized setting the past aside left much more room for the new happiness opening up in front of her. "It was time for a change."

"Past time."

She smiled at Mason. Her dad. "I'm going home now. To my husband and daughter."

He returned her smile and opened his arms for a hug. "You have no idea how happy that makes me."

She lovingly returned his hug. "I think I do."

CHAPTER 19

Misty stood on the front porch of Beam's house, suitcase in hand. In a matter of months, she'd gone from wife and mother, to runaway, and back again. Sadly, she could fit everything she owned into one suitcase. As much as she'd wanted to live the rich life, possessions had never meant a lot to her. In fact, she'd always taken them for granted. First, her dad provided them, then Beam. With her mother, she'd actually had to work for things. She'd finally understood the value of the simplest indulgences—such as shampoo and soap—when Arleen took everything.

In a matter of months, she'd rotated a one-eighty. Now, she wanted a house with a comfortable sofa and a quilt to pull over her legs on chilly nights. She wanted a kitchen table where Sophia could do her homework while she watched over her. She wanted to learn how to bake cookies with Sophia and have a hot dinner ready when Beam got home from work. She wanted to make beds and clean bathrooms. Take care of potted plants. And maybe even get a dog.

She looked around the porch with its comfy glider and rattan chairs. She could imagine summer evenings sitting with Beam, watching Sophia chasing butterflies around the yard. The picture was so clear in her mind, clearer than the dreams of glitz and glamour had ever been.

On cue, fresh tears filled her eyes. Still uneasy about being here, she opened the screen and knocked on the front door. A moment later Beam pulled it open.

She felt color heat her cheeks. A new phenomenon for her. "Hi."

He reached down and took the suitcase from her. "You don't have to knock. This is your house, too."

She stepped inside and immediately looked around for Sophia. Beam must have noticed and said, "She's already tucked in for the night."

"Can I go look?"

He released a breath. "Misty, you're her mother. Of course, you can look."

Misty tiptoed into the room and peered over the edge of the crib at the only thing she'd ever done right. Dark eyelashes lay against Sophia's pale cheeks. Her little mouth puckered into a pout, and her brows pulled together. She took two quick breaths, sighed, and her features relaxed into serenity. Misty felt a smile pull at the sides of her mouth. Had her mother ever looked down on her like this? Had she ever felt love swelling in her breast, expanding so immensely she was amazed her chest could contain it? That she could feel so intensely about such a tiny being was overwhelming. Wonderful and terrifying and breathtakingly magnificent all rolled together in this tiny bundle of beauty.

She wasn't sure how long she stood watching her daughter sleep, but when she went into the bedroom she'd share with her husband, her suitcase sat on a chest at the foot of the bed. She opened it and began to put her clothes beside Beam's in the closet and in the dresser drawers that were empty.

When everything was tucked away as it should have been long before now, Misty found Beam on the sofa watching a muted television. He held out his hand to her and she sat beside him, not sure how to proceed. She'd spent her adult life as the pursuer, not shy about going after what she wanted, and almost always getting it. These feelings of apprehension and nervousness were new to her.

Beam pulled her close and settled her under his arm, as if they hadn't spent the last few months away from each other. To be touched and held by him felt so right. He was sturdy and protective, and she felt like she'd come home where she belonged after a very long absence.

"You're beautiful."

Misty felt heat move up her neck at Beam's compliment. His gaze was intent, his mossy green eyes moving over her face. "I won't rush you, Misty. Take your time and settle in. Get used to having a daughter. If you have questions, don't be afraid to ask."

She nodded, emotionally exhausted from her day of work and apologies. She turned her attention to the television when Beam unmuted the sound, but didn't pay any attention to what was happening on the screen. She fought to keep her eyes open for several minutes, but finally gave up. Beam woke her when he scooped her into his arms.

"You've had a long day."

Misty held her breath as Beam carried her down the hall, toward the bedroom. She was terrified for him to see her body. Even though she'd lost most of her baby weight, she had done nothing to tone where that fat had collected.

He set her on the edge of the bed, but she couldn't meet his gaze. Until he picked up his pillow and went to the door. Eyes wide, she turned to look at him. "Where are you going?"

"I think it would be best if I sleep on the sofa until you feel comfortable."

She stood. "Don't leave."

~

*B*eam looked at his wife for a long moment, desire stronger than it had ever been. Yet, he couldn't sleep with her until he knew she loved him. Loved them. And that she planned to stay. He wanted her to choose him and Sophia for love, not because she felt she had no other option. She had to be sure he and Sophia were enough for her. That living in Eden Falls was enough. That his average salary as owner of a hardware and lumber store would be enough.

By sleeping on the sofa tonight, he ran the risk of damaging her already fragile pride even further, but she had to be certain. Her heart wasn't the only one hanging on the line.

He walked to her and wrapped her in his arms, brushed his lips over hers once, twice, and then said close to her ear, "I want you, Misty. I've never wanted a woman as badly as I want you right now, but you've had a crazy few months, and I don't want to rush you."

She stepped back. "You're not rushing me, Beam. I told you I wanted to come home. I wouldn't have said that if I felt rushed. Please, stay."

He pulled her close, again, and looked into her eyes. "Not yet, baby. You've had a long day. You need your sleep."

He left, easing the door closed behind him, hoping he hadn't just made the biggest mistake of his life.

~

*M*isty woke alone the next morning. Falling asleep had taken a long time, imagining Beam, with his long frame, trying to get comfortable on the much too small sofa. She understood—No, she tried to understand his hesitation, but it still hurt.

She heard Beam's deep baritone and an occasional squeal. She slid from the bed and walked down the hall to the kitchen where Beam had Sophia sitting in a seat on the counter, a blue ring around her mouth. She giggled when Beam made the sound of a plane and flew a tiny spoon of something between her lips. She smacked her gums together, and half the mouthful came back out, dribbling down her chin. Beam swiped the spoon under her lip and quickly popped the food back into her mouth. The sight was mesmerizing and pinched Misty's heart. She'd missed so much in her quest for something better. Sophia spotted her and gooed. A sob on a half-laugh escaped making Beam turn in his chair. Her heartache must have been visible because he stood and wrapped an arm around her waist.

"Want to have a go at this messy process?"

Misty swallowed the lump clogging her throat. "Will she eat for me?"

Beam chuckled and Sophia grinned. "She's not picky about who provides the food."

He stood and Misty took the chair he'd vacated. She picked up the spoon and looked from the two bowls to the messy face in front of her. "What is this?"

"Cereal and blueberries."

Sophia patted the tray in front of her impatiently.

"How much?"

Beam leaned close and took the spoon from her fingers. He smelled of soap and toothpaste, which reminded her she hadn't taken the time to brush her teeth. After scooping some cereal onto the spoon, he handed it back to her. She held the spoon toward Sophia, who immediately reached out and knocked it to the floor.

Misty gasped and Beam laughed. He pulled a clean spoon

from a drawer and scooped more cereal up. "You have to hold on tight, darlin'," he said with a grin.

This time Sophia opened her little mouth, and Misty was able to get some of the cereal in. The first few bites were nerve wracking, but Misty caught on, embarrassed that a four month old knew better than her mother. Sophia didn't care if she was spooned cereal or blueberries, as long as the food came quickly. Halfway through, Sophia stuck her fist in her mouth. Misty laughed when she smeared the mess in her hair and down her cheek.

Next was bath time. Misty stood next to Beam at the kitchen sink while he lowered Sophia into the warm water. She giggled and cooed until he lathered her hair, then her bottom lip poked out threateningly. Laughing together with Beam made Misty giddy.

"I told you she looked like her mother."

Misty punched his arm good-naturedly, euphoric to be teasing with her husband. She studied his profile as he rinsed the soap carefully from Sophia's head. His sandy hair was a little on the long side and fell over his brow. Love for his daughter was evident in the light shining from his eyes, and the infectious smile he bestowed on her. He'd loved Sophia enough for both of them, while she was out chasing empty dreams. He'd offered happiness, safety, and stability, and Misty had rejected it all. He'd loved her for a long time. She knew it, and she'd turned her back on him.

Why had she been so blind?

She ran a finger along his forehead pushing that wayward lock of hair to the side and then kissed his clean-shaven cheek. He turned his head, his eyes roaming her face before landing on her lips and staying there. She leaned forward again and kissed the corner of his mouth. His eyelids slid closed, and he stayed very still until she pulled back slightly. They had a baby splashing in the sink and now wasn't the time, but she wanted him to know how she felt inside. She wanted to tell him, but, again, now wasn't the time. She hoped the kiss conveyed the message.

When he opened his eyes, she smiled.

~

Beam and Mason were meeting with the fire marshal before he questioned their employees. Following that meeting, they were going to see their insurance agent. Misty had Wednesday's off so she talked—more like begged—him to leave Sophia with her. He wrote instructions on how to make bottles, got the soft Eeyore Sophia liked to nap with out of the dryer, and secured the car seat in the back of her car, in case they decided to go out. Misty did plan to visit Alice Garrett.

After Beam left, she loaded Sophia up, and they drove over the familiar roads to the Garrett's house. She had trouble unbuckling the carrier from the car seat, but experienced a heady pleasure when she accomplished the task she'd made much more complicated than it needed to be.

Another apology loomed and her stomach flipped to sick once more as she waited on the doorstep. Denny opened the door.

"Misty, honey, come in. Alex told us you were in town." He took the carrier from her and pulled her into a one armed, Garrett bear hug. "How are you?"

"I'm good."

"I see you brought a little visitor with you." He set the carrier on the sofa, unbuckled Sophia, and lifted her as if he'd done it a thousand times. "Hello, pretty girl. How are you this morning?"

Sophia waved her arms and cooed adorably, and Misty wondered how often Denny had held her daughter. Obviously more times than she had. Alice came into the room with the warm, loving smile that had shined on Misty since she was a five year old. A smile she didn't feel worthy to receive. Alice opened her arms, and Misty went into them as if she was still little and hurting. Alice stroked her hair while Misty cried on her shoulder, vaguely aware when Denny left the room with Sophia on his shoulder.

Misty wasn't sure how much time passed, before Alice led her to the sofa. They sat side-by-side, while Misty told her everything that had happened after she left Eden Falls in search of her mother. Alice listened and commented and consoled. Misty had always been able to unload her problems with Alex's mom. She could tell her story and not be judged. Alice said she'd want to search for her mother, if faced with the same situation.

Alice was probably the reason Misty had resented Alex all those years. Her friend had this love in her life everyday. Now that Misty was clearing the dust from her eyes, she realized she'd had it too. Alex had shared her mother freely, never begrudging Misty's interference when she and Alice had plans. She owed Alex many more apologies.

Misty wiped her eyes with the tissues Alice provided. "Thank you for listening to all my blubbering. Crying is all I seem to do anymore."

"Hormones. They wreak havoc on a woman's system, especially after having a baby. You'll be yourself soon."

Misty hesitated. She didn't want to be herself anymore. She wanted to be someone else, a new someone. That was one of the reasons she was here. She wasn't afraid to ask, but she hated showing her vulnerability for all things domestic. "I was wondering if you could help me, Alice."

"You know I'll do anything I can."

"Could you give me a few easy recipes, and maybe watch Sophia while I run to the grocery store. I'd like to be able to make Beam dinner tonight, and I have no idea…" A floundering fish on a dry dock stood more of a chance than she did.

"If you intend to stay and be a wife, you might as well get used to doing these things with a child in tow. Let's get a couple of recipes, and we'll take Sophia grocery shopping with us."

Mason left JT's office after the last of the lumberyard employees had been questioned, and made his way around the square. City workers were hanging a banner announcing the upcoming Memorial Day events. A flag raising, a pancake breakfast, and the Gunslingers-Smoke Eaters baseball game would fill the morning. Alice and Denny Garrett always had a backyard barbecue after the game. The festivities wrapped up with a sunset concert in Town Square, followed by a small fireworks display.

He wasn't sure where he was headed, but felt the need to walk. According to JT, they had no suspects. Whoever set the fire had most likely fit through a small gap in the chain link fence along the back of the property—a gap he should have taken care of before offering Beam a partnership.

The fire was set under a pallet that held a stack of fencing ready for delivery the next day. Someone had actually lit newspaper and kindling, and then shoved it under the pallet where it caught the rest of the wood on fire. Accelerant was also found under a forklift and near the back wall of the hardware store. From there the fire had spread quickly.

"Hello there, Mason."

The familiar voice jolted him back to the present. Patsy stood in the doorway of Patsy's Pastries, hands planted on her hips, her platinum hair pulled up in a clip. She wore jeans and a T-shirt with a saying across the front that he would not look at. "Hi, Patsy."

"I haven't had the chance to tell you how sorry I am about the fire."

"Thank you."

"Do they know anything yet? How it started?"

"They do know how but not who. It's still under investigation, but the fire has been ruled arson."

"I did hear that." She thumbed over her shoulder. "How about an oatmeal raisin cookie or two? I just took them out of the oven."

He couldn't remember the last time he'd been in Patsy's shop, but he hadn't eaten lunch and his stomach growled at the suggestion. "That sounds too tempting to refuse."

He followed her inside and took a moment to enjoy the scents of sugar, butter, and cinnamon hanging heavy in the air. He pulled out his wallet, but Patsy waved it away as she handed him two cookies, still warm, in a paper sleeve. "On the house."

"Thank you, Patsy."

"Maybe you'll enjoy them enough that you'll come in once in a while. You're the only man in town who doesn't seem to enjoy sweets for breakfast."

"I prefer eggs in the morning, but I do like something sweet after dinner."

Patsy raised her eyebrows, and he felt his face heat with embarrassment at his innocent remark. "What I mean—"

"Don't get all flustered, Mason," Patsy said with a laugh. "I know what you meant. You need to lighten up a bit."

He nodded. "Yes, maybe so." He held up the cookies. "I'm sure I'll enjoy these. Thank you."

He walked out of the shop and into the sunshine, feeling muddled. Halfway down the street he turned, and sure enough, Patsy was watching. When their eyes met, she winked.

~

*B*eam came home to wonderful smells for the second time. He could hear voices coming from the kitchen and identified one as his cousin.

Alex sat at the table with Sophia asleep on her chest. Misty stood at the sink washing a head of lettuce. Alex flashed her contagious smile when he entered the room. Misty tried to follow suit, but hers wobbled at the corners. He went to Alex first and kissed the top of his daughter's head. One side of her mouth turned up in a lopsided smile.

"Hey, Low-rider."

"Hey, yourself. How was your day?"

"Crazy. More questions from the fire marshal. Right now they suspect everyone." He walked over to Misty who had turned to watch him. She was dressed in jeans and a long baby blue blouse that enhanced the beautiful blue of her eyes. Even though she'd lost most of her baby weight, her face was still fuller than it had been before pregnancy. In his eyes, she was gorgeous. Always had been.

He put a finger under her chin and lifted her face to his. "Hello."

"Hi." Her voice was soft, unsure, even a bit wary.

His lips met hers in more than a brief peck. He wanted the kiss to say, I believe in you, I'm thankful you're here. I love you. "How was your day?"

She sucked in a deep breath, and glanced at the ceiling. "Interesting. I spent most of it with your Aunt Alice, who showed me how to buy groceries for a family with Sophia along." She lowered her voice. "I feel like I'm in elementary school learning to read and write all over again."

"It's amazing such a tiny being can intimidate an adult so completely." He glanced at Alex and Sophia. "She looks content for the moment. Was she good for you?"

Misty's eye lit for the first time since he'd walked in. "An angel. Alice and Alex are good teachers."

"They sure saved my butt more than once." He hoped his smile to his wife was encouraging. "Whatever you're cooking smells delicious."

"Alice gave me her meatloaf recipe."

Alex stood. "I have to get home and start dinner for my small brood. Do you want me to pass this cutie off or put her in her crib?"

"I'll take her," Beam said. "She needs to wake up or she'll never sleep tonight." *And I want her to sleep tonight.*

❧

As Sophia was transferred from aunt to dad, she opened her eyes and let out an unhappy cry. Beam spent several minutes jiggling and talking to her, but the tears didn't let up until Misty took her from him. She was as shocked as Beam when Sophia settled down.

"Wow." Beam grinned. "You have the magic touch."

Sophia's weight felt good as Misty snuggled her daughter close.

Dinner was another quiet affair. They talked about their day, laughed more than Misty expected, and she finally began to relax in her husband's company. Sitting together at the table reminded her of the many dinners she'd eaten at Alex or Stella's house as a kid. Families around the table discussing their day. She never dreamed of this. Never imagined herself to be where she was at this moment. So why did it feel exactly right?

She let the amazement settle deep inside, and hoped Beam felt the same.

They cleaned the kitchen together as Sophia rocked contentedly in her swing watching their movements around the room. Then she bathed Sophia in lavender baby wash and dressed her in soft pajamas. Beam was never far away, but he let her do the work. She lifted Sophia to her nose and breathed in her soothing sweet scent. She wanted to catalog each moment. She'd missed too much already, and was sad she couldn't get that time back.

They both went into Sophia's room to tuck her in, and then Beam led Misty to the living room by the hand. He didn't touch her often, not like he used to. He seemed afraid she would pull away, and just a few months earlier, she would have. Now, she longed for his hands on her.

They sat next to each other on the sofa. He kept her hand in his, intertwining their fingers and then releasing his hold and rubbing a thumb over her palm.

"You're wearing your wedding ring."

She looked down as his thumb pressed against the back of her platinum band. "Arleen stole my rings. She took everything I owned and pawned it in Reno."

His eyebrows drew together in a frown before he turned her hand over.

"My dad had JT track the rings down, and paid to get them back."

"Why didn't you tell me?"

She lifted a shoulder. "Embarrassment. I didn't want you to know I'd taken my rings off after I signed the divorce papers. I hid them in the back of my closet. Arleen and her trucker boyfriend found them." She realized she thought of her mom more as Arleen than her mom anymore. Kind of sad, but freeing at the same time.

"Why did you sign the divorce papers?"

"Why did you file for divorce?" She hadn't meant her tone to sound so accusatory, but knew the comment came out that way.

Beam rubbed his free hand down his jaw. She could hear the scrape of five-o'clock shadow against his palm. "I felt guilty for pushing you into marriage, and thought it was only fair to give you an out if you wanted to stay in Sacramento."

"I signed because I thought you and Sophia would be better off without me." She curled her palm around his thumb. "I'm glad you didn't sign them when I sent them back."

"Me too."

"You have something on your mind," she said after a long pause. Premonition, a nervous energy had her elbows and knees tingling, anticipation tinged with worry. He looked too serious.

"I do." He intertwined their fingers again. "Have you thought more about building a salon?"

The question surprised her, and so did the realization that she hadn't. Her clients at Dahlia's were walk-ins. A few of her old clients called to book appointments, but most had moved on. She worked four days a week and was finished by five. Once the insurance money came through and Beam started to rebuild the lumberyard, he would have long days and then who would stay with Sophia? Now that she was back and learning so much about her daughter, did she really want her baby girl with relatives or at daycare while they worked? These thoughts made her stomach churn. Because of her selfishness, Sophia had been staying with relatives since Misty had given birth.

"Rebuilding the lumberyard and hardware store is going to take up a lot of your time. I think we should wait until after that is reopened." He began rubbing circles in her palm again. "You are planning to rebuild, aren't you?"

He studied her a moment, his gaze warming her all over. "I bought into the business without consulting you and that was wrong, so I'll ask. What do you think *we* should do?"

Again, he stunned her with his question. As a child, she'd believed both the lumberyard and small Eden Falls had been the cause of her mother leaving. She knew better now. Her dad had been right those many months ago when he said the hardware and lumber store would

provide a good living for Beam and his family. She nodded. "I think you...*we* should rebuild. We'll put off the salon for now."

One of his eyebrows cocked over his mossy green eyes. "I have the money, Misty."

She looked down at their clasped hands, his so large yet so gentle. Beam was honest, and hardworking. He loved her, and she loved him. They could have a very happy life together, if she continued to make changes.

Suddenly, a salon seemed so small and insignificant compared to being a wife and mother. Sometime during her stay in Sacramento, the compelling need to best Alex had left her, along with her desire for success as a business owner. She raised her knee to the sofa and turned to face her husband. "I thought opening my own salon would mean I was successful. Maybe then, my mother would see my worth and love me. My dad was always encouraging, but it wasn't enough. I think I was...the way I was because I felt so unworthy of love—still feel unworthy of love. I want it but have never felt like I deserved it. Maybe that's what I inherited from my mother. Like her dark hair and blue eyes, I inherited her feelings of unworthiness."

Beam cupped her face and ran his thumbs over her cheeks. "Misty, you are worth more to me than you can ever imagine. You are worthy of love just as much as the next person. It's time to stop thinking of yourself as unwanted just because your mother left."

Tears—her new best friends—formed in her eyes. "The hardware and lumber store is more important for our family. The salon can wait. I'll stay at Dahlia's for now."

He searched her face as if looking for a hidden agenda, but he wouldn't find one. She didn't want anything from him, wasn't out to gain a thing. She smiled. "I don't want to get so busy setting up a salon that I can't get to know our daughter."

"Are you certain?"

Misty pondered the question a moment and then smiled as the chasm in her chest began to fill. Her senses were more attuned and her thoughts sharper. "Actually, I've never been more sure of anything in my life."

"If you'd like to stay home with Sophia full time, we have the money. You don't have to work."

She laughed. The thought of telling Dahlia she was leaving, again, was too terrifying to contemplate. Let's keep things the way they are for now."

The moment she'd been waiting for came. His lips claimed hers in a way they hadn't in a very long time. She was his and he was hers. Her chest expanded as the knowledge of what was right and what was wrong became clearer.

He eventually carried her to their bed where they reunited as husband and wife in a sweet blending of bodies and souls.

Right before he slipped off to sleep, she snuggled up as close as possible and whispered, "I love you, Beam."

He smiled.

"*Aww,*" the universe said with a sigh.

CHAPTER 20

Mason made it to the front of the line, paper plate in hand. The smell of bacon and maple syrup hung heavy in the early morning air. The sun was shining down on Eden Falls for this beautiful Memorial Day. Town Square had been the sight of this pancake breakfast for as long as Mason had lived here, and Alex had been a fixture behind the griddles even before she'd won the election for mayor. This morning was no different, except she had her husband by her side.

Tongs in hand, Colton held out three slices of bacon. "How are you this morning, Mason?"

"Hungry. Was it the mayor who put you to work or your wife?"

Colton laughed. "The mayor is a sweetheart. My wife gives the orders."

An arm snaked around Colton's waist. "Actually, it was me who put Colton to work," Patsy said. "Problem is he's eating almost as much as he's serving."

Colton grinned. "I don't see that as a problem."

Patsy looked Mason up and down in a way that made him

feel like he needed an extra layer of clothing. "How about you scoot back here and give Colton a break?"

Mason glanced at the three strips of bacon on his plate as his stomach growled. He'd been in line a very long time, but Colton had been serving longer. He pushed his glasses up his nose with his index finger. "I could do that."

He handed his plate of bacon to Colton with a longing sigh as they traded places.

"Adults get three slices of bacon, the little ones get two," Patsy said, bumping his shoulder with her own.

He worked side by side with her for over an hour. He'd never volunteered to serve breakfast before, preferring to eat, but found he didn't mind meeting and greeting those who came through the line. Beam moved forward with two plates in hand. Misty waited at the Garrett table with Sophia on her lap. The sight of his daughter with his granddaughter made his day all the brighter.

Everything was moving along smoothly, until Patsy asked whom he was taking to the baseball game.

"Uh…well, I usually go alone."

"Me, too, but I hate sitting by myself." Her eyes brightened. "Hey, how about we go together this year?"

The question caught him off guard. Even though he always sat by someone he knew, he'd never taken anyone but Arleen to the game. Going with someone might be kind of nice…but to show up with Patsy would really agitate the gossipmongers in Eden Falls.

Yet, what harm would come from a baseball game in broad daylight? Did he really care if people gossiped about him?

Before he could say yes, she waved a hand through the air. "It took you way too long to answer. Don't worry about it."

"Wait, Patsy," he said, catching her arm as she turned away. "I'd like to go…with you."

She raised a brow. "Are you sure, Mason? People will talk."

He glanced around the square. The whole town was here. They'd be at the game, too. He looked back at her with a shrug. "I've never really had much time for gossips."

~

*M*isty sat in the middle of the Garrett family. It wasn't the first time and, remembering last night in Beam's arms, it wouldn't be the last. Everyone was civil except Rowdy who ignored her completely. She'd hurt his brother. She was smart enough to know it would take more than an "I'm sorry" for him to come around. Hopefully, with time, her actions would prove she was doing her best to change. She would keep Arleen in the back of her mind as motivation.

Her daughter was being passed around, and she adored the attention. Misty loved the smile on her face when she spotted her daddy. The smile on his face was almost as big. As she watched her little family, a feeling of overwhelming love engulfed her, to the point of being almost unbearable. She never dreamed it possible to love so much that it hurt.

With concern etching his features, Beam wrapped his arm around her shoulder and pulled her close. "Are you okay?"

"Your brother hates me."

"Hate is a strong word."

"Strong but true." She glanced around the group of family with a sense of belonging. "Even so, I don't remember ever feeling this happy. That's sad isn't it? To be twenty-eight years old and truly happy for the first time?"

A gentle smile replaced his concern. "We'll just have to

make up for all those lost years then, because I want you to be happy every day from now on."

She swiped a finger under an eye and smiled at her handsome husband. "I'll be happy with you."

He lowered his mouth to hers. "You're doing it right then," he said against her lips.

~

*M*isty's words eased Beam's mind. He'd woke up worried that he'd rushed Misty last night, but their desire for each other had won out. He'd missed running fingers over her soft skin and burying his face in her sweet smelling hair. Nine months had passed since he'd made love to his wife and he'd missed her touch. The look on her face just now had worried him. He'd been afraid she was sorry they'd slept together. Instead, she was happy, which made him think life couldn't get much better.

"Uncle Beam?"

Beam turned and ruffled Charlie's dark hair. The kid had a milk mustache, syrup on his chin and wore a smile the size of a slice of bacon. "Yeah?"

"Can Sophia sit down here on the blanket with me?"

At the moment, she was sitting on Beam's knee, reaching for the superhero on Charlie's tee shirt. "She still hasn't mastered sitting up, but she can roll over for you." Beam plopped her on the blanket and she giggled.

"I have to get over to the ballpark to warm up," Beam said and kissed Misty, again. Something he wouldn't get tired of doing. "I'll see you in a little while." He stood. "By the way, I'm pretty sure your adorable daughter pooped."

Misty laughed. "Oh, and you suddenly have to leave?"

He backed a few steps out of her reach and then winked. Misty said she couldn't remember the last time she was so happy. He couldn't remember the last time he'd seen her smile—not the way she was smiling now—and even when she knew she'd be changing a stinky diaper. It was a beautiful sight. He pulled his cell phone from his back pocket and clicked a quick picture. Today would be the beginning of many family memories.

~

Misty was in the middle of the Garrett clan, again, surprised she didn't feel smothered in their midst. Instead, she felt she was right where she belonged. Her friends were on the field. Sophia was asleep on her shoulder, and the sun was shining. Life had taken a one-eighty in the last year, but it was a solid turn with wonderful results.

She spotted her dad coming up the steps and raised a hand to wave, but he turned to smile at someone beside him. Misty leaned forward to see whom he was with, and her mouth dropped open. Patsy Yarberry? They scooted onto a bench two rows down and across the aisle from Misty. She noticed people around with the same questioning glances as they watched the pair.

Was her dad aware of the stares pointed in his direction? Didn't he care that people would be talking? She certainly did. She didn't want her dad paired with a woman who'd been married—Misty couldn't even remember how many times.

After "The Star-Spangled Banner" JT was first up to bat. Charlie jumped up on his seat a row down. "Come on Uncle JT! Hit it out of the park."

The crowd laughed including Mason and Patsy. Then he leaned toward her and said something. Patsy laughed again and placed her hand on his arm.

This can't be happening. Misty had been wrong to sabotage every date her father had ever gone on, but this couldn't happen. *Of all the single women in the world, he'd picked Patsy!*

She caught snatches of the game. The Gunslingers got two runs and the Smoke Eaters three. Beam hit a double. She cheered with the crowd, but kept her eyes on Patsy and her dad. Patsy leaned into Mason, touched his arm, his hand. Each time, Misty wanted to yell, "Get your hands off my dad!"

Sophia woke during the fifth inning and Misty fed her a bottle. Afterwards, she was passed around so everyone could take a turn loving on her. Sophia was a good trooper and went from person to person happily. Charlie got her to giggle and, as Beam had told her over the phone on Easter, Sophia's laugh was contagious. Everyone around them laughed along with her.

By the eighth inning, Misty couldn't take it any longer. The old Misty would have made a scene, but the new Misty didn't want to disappoint Beam or Glenda who'd cut sideways glances at her throughout the first few innings, so she put Sophia in her carrier and made her way down the bleachers away from Patsy and her wandering hands.

⌇

*M*ason knew when Misty left the stands she was upset, and he would hear an earful from her. He also knew the bleachers were filled with curious eyes and whispers. Surprisingly, he didn't care. He was having a nice time with Patsy. She had a quick wit and dry humor that was lost on him at first. He usually caught the joke after she smiled, a cue that it was okay to laugh.

Obviously, Patsy didn't care what people thought. The

town's opinion of her hadn't hurt business. Patsy's Pastries was one of the most prosperous places on the square.

At the bottom of the bleachers, she left him to congratulate her stepson on the Smoke Eaters win and Misty approached. Beam had taken Sophia from her and she came at him full steam ahead.

"Patsy Yarberry? Have you lost your mind?"

He pulled his glasses from his nose and polished the dust off with the cloth he kept in his pants pocket. "I don't think so."

"You have if you think you're going to date her, which you aren't."

He tipped his head to study his daughter. She really was a lovely woman. Her black tresses fell around her shoulders, her blue eyes snapped with attitude. A little extra weight looked good on her.

He slipped his glasses back into place. "This really wasn't a date, but it would be none of your business if it was, Misty. When you were a child, I took your opinion and concern into consideration, but you are married and have a family of your own. Who I date shouldn't affect you in the least."

"It will be if you're associated with Patsy and her reputation. She's been married more times than anyone in this town can remember, and there has to be a reason for that."

Mason noticed a few interested heads turned their way and lowered his voice. "There was a time you didn't have the shiniest reputation in Eden Falls. You seem to be trying to change that and I'm very proud of you, but that doesn't give you the right to judge Patsy—or anyone else for that matter. I won't have you acting out or treating her badly. Do you understand me? I haven't put my foot down very often with you, but on this, I do."

He turned and walked away. He wouldn't subject Patsy to

Misty's meanness, should she decide to erupt. He'd been alone for over twenty years to please his spoiled daughter. She was now on her own and well taken care of, and he wouldn't bow to her wishes. He knew Misty well enough to know she wouldn't drop the subject so easily. She would try again, because she was used to getting her way. If he chose to date Patsy, Misty's attempt would be in vain—though today hadn't been a date. Unexpectedly, he wasn't opposed to the idea of asking her out. Surprisingly, he'd had a very nice time.

He spotted Patsy standing to the side watching, an amused smile played over her fuchsia colored lips.

"Misty isn't excited about us being seen at the game together."

Mason held up a hand. "Don't worry—"

Patsy threw her head back and laughed. "Oh, Mason, you don't know me at all if you think I can't handle Misty. You're the one who shouldn't worry."

~

In the car ride to the Garrett's backyard party, Beam heard all about the spectacle Mason and Patsy had made of themselves at the game. They'd had such a pleasant morning, he was hesitant to tell Misty he agreed with his father-in-law. It really wasn't any business of hers who her dad dated.

She glanced at him when he turned onto his aunt and uncle's street. "You need to talk to him, Beam. He'll listen to you."

He pulled to a stop at the curb behind Colton's Range Rover and took a deep breath, knowing this wouldn't go well for him. "Misty, your dad is all grown up and able to make these decisions for himself."

She turned in her seat and stared at him. "Not if they involve Patsy Yarberry!"

He looked in the little mirror that reflected Sophia's face in the backseat, afraid Misty's outburst had scared her. She was happily sucking on a fist. "Just because they sat next to each other at the game doesn't mean they're dating. And even if it did, Patsy is a nice woman." He held up his hand to stop her next frenzy of words before he could finish. "Despite her many marriages, she is a successful businesswoman and a great baker. You don't know what caused her marriages to end. Maybe she has bad taste in men."

Misty's jaw tightened. "Are you insinuating there is something wrong—"

"I don't mean your dad. I'm just saying you should give Patsy the benefit of the doubt. Everyone assumes the fault for the divorces must be hers, but no one knows."

She sat back and crossed her arms over her chest. "I can't believe you're on their side."

He reached out and ran a finger down her cheek. "Baby, I'm not on anyone's side. I'm just saying you're jumping to conclusions. You don't know for sure that anything is going on so why get upset?"

She blew out a breath. "He did say they weren't on a date."

"Exactly. Relax. Let's just enjoy the rest of the day."

She opened her car door and he released a sigh of relief. They'd just taken a big step toward fixing themselves, and he wasn't willing to let Patsy and Mason sitting next to each other at a ballgame mess that up.

~

*H*ours later, Beam rolled to his back and groaned. "Woman you're going to kill me."

Misty laughed as she moved against his side. "You're the one who said something about making up for lost time."

He yanked the sheet over them. "I'm not sure that will be physically possible."

"We could try."

His laugh rumbled through his chest.

She couldn't find the words to describe the happiness she felt. It was bigger than anything she'd ever known, more intense than her desire to find her mother had been. Was it possible to hold onto this kind of joy or would it slip away with time?

She tipped her head so she could see Beam's face. "Today was a good day."

"Today was a very good day," he said as his hand slid from her waist to her hip.

"Are you happy?"

"Deliriously."

She reached up and pinched his chin. "I'm serious."

He chuckled, again. "I am, too."

"I almost ruined everything, chasing after an illusion," Misty said, settling an arm across her husband's waist.

"It wasn't an illusion, baby." Beam turned to his side and tucked her against him. "It was a hope, a dream. It was something we all might have done under the same circumstances."

"That's the same thing Alice told me."

"We never know how we'll react to a situation unless we experience it."

Misty had just been so sure her mom would have all the answers…

She sat up as insight struck like a bolt of lightning. How hadn't she seen it before? She'd searched for Arleen, certain her mother would change her life for the better—and she had. After being around her, Misty realized the kind of person Arleen was—sad, lonely, miserable, unappreciative, and mean to name a few of her personality flaws. She'd opened Misty's eyes to see she was turning into the same kind of person, before inspiring her to be different. Arleen did, in fact, hold all the answers. She'd changed Misty's life completely. For the good.

Beam reached for her. "What are you doing?"

A giggle escaped. Then she was laughing.

Beam sat up.

She threw her arms around his neck, tumbling them back into the pillows. "I love you, Beam. I love you, I love you, I love you!"

The universe cheered.

~

If you enjoyed *Beyond Eden*, I hope you'll continue reading! The next book in the Eden Falls Series is *A Taste of Eden*.

To keep up to date on new releases join my newsletter at TinaNewcomb.com.

Following is an excerpt from *A Taste of Eden*.

EXCERPT FROM: A TASTE OF EDEN

CHAPTER 1

February 16

Carolyn West Richmond pushed the pile of clothes down with one hand while yanking the zipper with the other. The new suitcase didn't hold much, but she couldn't risk taking her own.

She hurried to the spare bedroom and reached for a collapsed cardboard box from underneath the bed. Unfolding it, she secured the bottom flaps with duct tape she'd shoved between a stack of sheets in the linen closet. Quickly, she filled the box with new clothes and shoes she'd hidden in garbage bags labeled "give away" in the back of the guest room closet. Leaving her daily wardrobe behind would buy her a few more precious hours.

Running into the master bathroom, she tripped on the edge of the rug and smacked her hip against the corner of the vanity. *That's going to leave a bruise.* The thought almost made her laugh. Almost.

She opened a drawer. Mascara, moisturizer, concealer. These items could be bought on the road. Her goal was to travel light. She started to shut the drawer, changed her mind, and grabbed the concealer. After checking that both tooth-brushes were aligned in the holder, she hung two clean bath towels and straightened the rug. The used towels went into the hamper. She left the room, but returned to run a wet paper towel around the already spotless sinks.

In the bedroom closet, she placed a stepladder under the attic opening, slid the door to the left, raised the insulation, and groped around blindly until her fingers clasped a strap. She lifted a small backpack from its spot, tamped the insula-tion back into place, and positioned the door evenly before climbing down and stowing the ladder. Halfway out of the closet, she hesitated, went back, and ran a hand over the carpet to erase any indentations. Unzipping the backpack, she shifted through the stacks of twenty-dollar bills wrapped with currency straps—her ticket to freedom.

The phone rang and she froze. She glanced around the bedroom, searching for the hidden camera she'd always suspected but could never find. The phone rang again, the harsh sound echoing through the quiet house. She had no choice but to answer. "Hello?"

"Why do you sound breathless?"

"I…ran for the phone." Carolyn put a trembling hand to her forehead. *Stay calm.*

"I called a minute ago. You didn't answer."

Liar. "I was cleaning—running the vacuum. I didn't hear the phone."

"What are you vacuuming?"

Stupid answer. Now I'll have to vacuum, and there's no time.

"Carolyn?"

She glanced at the ruffled carpet in the closet. Her imper-fect camouflage would be covered up with a swipe of the vacuum. "Our bedroom."

"I noticed my bathroom sink looked a little grimy this morning."

Another lie. "Next on my list."

She heard him expel a breath into the receiver and knew what was coming.

"About last night. I didn't expect you to come home early."

Of course, it's my fault that I came home to find my husband with his lover.

"I'm under a lot of stress with the Blanchard account. Taren came over to help me brainstorm."

Carolyn closed her eyes. "Brainstorming wasn't what I walked in on."

"You have no idea the pressure I'm under at work, the stress I endure to provide you with a home and pretty clothes!"

"I work, too, Robert."

"I'm trying to say I'm sorry that things got out of hand," he said, his tone softening.

Again.

"Carolyn, you know it didn't mean anything. You are the only woman in the world for me."

Until your next brainstorming session.

"Look, it wouldn't hurt you to be a little more understanding."

There was so much she wanted to say, and this would be the perfect moment. There would be no repercussions. Thoughts scrambled to the forefront of her mind, but the words would fall on deaf ears. Anything she said would only make him mad, and possibly raise suspicion, since she'd been meticulously taught not to speak out. Besides, they were beyond words, and had been for a long time.

"You know I love you."

You have no idea what love means, and never will.

"Did you hear me?"

"Yes…me, too."

"*You too, what?*"

Carolyn put a hand to her throat to ease the building pressure. Maybe Rob was right. Maybe his making love with Taren meant as nothing as the words he was forcing her to say. "I love you, too."

"How about we go somewhere nice next weekend? We'll take a few days off and just get away."

"That's not necessary, Rob."

"Honey, how many times have I told you to call me Robert?" His voice had taken on the hard edge she was so familiar with. "Shortening my name is unprofessional."

"I don't do it in front of your coworkers." *Even last night when I opened the bedroom door and found you and Taren tangled in our sheets—the sheets you made me sleep on as punishment for coming home early—I called you Robert!*

"Don't do it at all."

A female voice murmured in the background, and Robert cleared this throat. "I have to go. I have a meeting. I'll call you at the restaurant."

He always did. Three o'clock on the dot to make sure she'd arrived. Five o'clock to make sure she was still there. Nine o'clock to check once again before he went to bed. Only tonight someone would be covering for her. "Okay."

"I'll make something special for breakfast, baby."

"Breakfast sounds nice."

"I'll see you in the morning. Oh, and be real quiet when you come home. We didn't get much sleep last night."

He was right. She was berated for coming home early in front of her husband's lover. After Taren left, the berating became violent.

Unfortunately, her compliance to his request for quiet was never reciprocated. Robert making breakfast entailed a gigantic pot-banging mess. After only three hours of sleep, she'd be expected to eat with him, clean the kitchen afterward, and complete a list of chores. Only then would she be able to fall into bed for a quick nap before work.

Except tomorrow morning Robert would wake up to an empty bed. "I'll be very quiet."

"Thanks, doll. See you in the morning."

"Have a nice day, Robert."

As soon as he disconnected the call, she ran for the vacuum. Following through would eat into her valuable time, but not doing the job would raise suspicion before she was far enough away. She vacuumed the bedroom and closet, covering all traces of the ladder.

She lugged the suitcase down the stairs with both hands, careful not to leave scuffmarks on the wooden risers. She wasted precious minutes fumbling with the latch on the car's trunk, wishing she had more time to familiarize herself with the older, nondescript rental. While stowing the suitcase, she raced over her mental checklist, ticking off each item.

Back inside, she ran up the stairs, stumbled, and fell with a *thud*, smacking her shin on the hard wood. *Another bruise.* Backpack over her shoulder and box in her arms, she rushed back down, committing the sound of her heels clacking to a memory entitled *Escape*. She stopped at the door of each room. Everything was mopped, shined, and in its proper place.

No reason for Robert to suspect anything was amiss.

From the kitchen window, her reflection stared back at her. The old glass distorted her features in a weird, Picasso sort of way. The image fit. She pulled her sunglasses from the backpack to cover her black eye and bruised cheek—a gift for coming home early last night—and stepped outside. The fog was thick this morning, which helped conceal her from neighbors' prying eyes. She knew they suspected, yet they never said a word. Better to stay out of others' affairs. She also knew if anyone saw her leaving with a suitcase, they wouldn't say anything to Robert. He'd never win a popularity contest in this neighborhood.

The smell of decaying leaves in the corner of the backyard wafted past. Mold. Rot. More memories filed under *Escape.*

Mist from the fog settled on her face as she looked at the house she'd called home since graduating from culinary school. The roof needed replacing and the old windows allowed cold air to seep in, but the house had been good to her, and she would miss it.

Turning away, she opened the car door, and slid behind the wheel. Inserting the key in the ignition proved almost impossible, her hands were shaking so hard.

Leaving would only provide temporary security. Rob would find her.

She pulled out of the driveway without a backward glance.

ACKNOWLEDGMENTS

I have so many people to thank, people who might be surprised by their influence.

A very long time ago, this novel started differently. Carolyn and her stalker originally made their appearance in Book 1 (*Finding* Eden) with no backstory of an abusive husband. An editor pushed me to dig deeper and the Eden Falls Series was born. Thank you Lynnette Labelle.

Two people advised me to separate the two love stories in this novel. I tried, languished in self-doubt for months, while I rewrote the whole novel. When I finished, the heart of the story was gone. So I rewrote it again. I'm so glad I went with my "gut" on this one.

This time around, I want to thank Romance Writers of America. I've gone to the National Conference every year since 2012. The workshops are amazing and so are the people who attend and present. I've met so many wonderful friends through RWA—Jill Haymaker, Janis Martin, LeAnne Bristow, and Sheila Covey to name just a few.

When I began pitching my books to agents and publishers, I was told sweet romance wouldn't sell. Then I found SweetRomanceReads.com. This group of authors renewed my faith that sweet romance is out there for all to enjoy. I'd found "my people".

I'm grateful to my ever-patient husband, Rick and our eight kids. You have been a huge support over this long road. xoxo!

I can't imagine where I'd be without my beta readers. Chris Almodovar, Holly Hertzke, and Jeanine Hopping, you have supported me and believed in me. Thank you from the bottom of my heart.

Thank you to editors Bev Katz Rosenbaum, Faith Freewoman/Demon for Details, and Jennifer Bray-Weber/The Killion Group, Inc. for your time, talent, and patience. Thank you for allowing my voice to come through while correcting my mistakes.

Dar Albert of Wicked Smart Designs, your talent (and patience with a newbie) amazes me. Thank you for *A Taste of Eden* cover and the banner for my website. I love them both.

I'm grateful to Richard Newcomb of DivDev who worked tirelessly to updated my very outdated website. Hugs.

I would be remiss to not mention the members of my critique group. Dawn Annis, Mary Hagen, C.K. Alber, and Lori Corsentino. Even though you never critiqued *A Taste of Eden*, I couldn't have done it without your support, friendship, and the laughs we share over breakfast. Love you all.

ALSO BY TINA NEWCOMB

The Eden Falls Series

Finding Eden

Beyond Eden

A Taste of Eden

The Angel of Eden Falls

Touches of Eden

Stars Over Eden Falls

Fortunes for Eden

Snow and Mistletoe in Eden Falls

Rumors in Eden Falls

Second Chance Romance Collection

When You Love Someone

Endless Love

Rhythm of Love

Second Chance Romance Collection

ABOUT THE AUTHOR

Tina Newcomb writes clean, contemporary romance. Her heartwarming stories take place in quaint small towns, with quirky townsfolk, and friendships that last a lifetime.

She acquired her love of reading from her librarian mother, who always had a stack of books close at hand, and her father who visited a local bookstore every weekend.

Tina Newcomb lives in colorful Colorado. When not lost in her writing, she can be found in the garden, traveling with her (amateur) chef husband, or spending time with family and friends.

Follow Tina on:

facebook.com/TinaNewcombAuthor

instagram.com/tinanewcombauthor

bookbub.com/authors/tina-newcomb

goodreads.com/tinanewcomb

pinterest.com/tinanewcomb